Praise for

MY PULSE IS AN EARTHQUAKE

"In this wonderfully diverse collection Kristin FitzPatrick demonstrates over and over how well she knows the world and how deeply she understands her fierce and reckless characters. Her vivid plots and immaculate prose carry her readers to the edge of darkness. *My Pulse Is an Earthquake* is a terrific debut."

—Margot Livesey, Iowa Writers' Workshop, and author of
Eva Moves the Furniture and *The New York Times* bestseller
The Flight of Gemma Hardy.

"Kristin FitzPatrick's *My Pulse Is an Earthquake* offers some of the most beautiful prose I've read in a long time, along with some of the most memorable characters. There's magic between these covers. I loved every word, and I'll be reading every word she writes from now on."

—Steve Yarbrough, author of *The Realm of Last Chances*
and professor, Department of Writing, Literature and
Publishing, Emerson College

"With a mesmerizing economy of language, Kristin FitzPatrick fathoms how people either rise to or fail each other in the crucial occasions of their lives. Each finely made story contributes to the book's cumulative emotional power, which is—miraculously—both restrained and shattering."

—Elise Blackwell, author of *Hunger* and *The Lower Quarter*

"Kristin FitzPatrick has a gift for creating wholly formed worlds—simultaneously familiar and unique—that she invites us to enter while she spins out richly layered stories quite unlike any we've heard before. *My Pulse Is an Earthquake* is a truly masterful debut collection to settle into and savor."

—Stephanie G'Schwind, editor of *Colorado Review*

"Bold and refreshingly original, this debut work of fiction is astonishing. FitzPatrick spins out intriguing and richly textured stories, and in doing so reveals the dreams and struggles of children, aspiring artists, and working-class adults. With compassion and insight, these interlinked stories help us fathom the extraordinary vividness of ordinary life."

—Laura Long, author of *Out of Peel Tree*

"Kristin FitzPatrick possesses an extraordinary ability to place fascinating characters into situations that reveal profound mysteries and nuances of the human condition. Long after you've closed the cover on her debut short story collection, you'll find yourself longing to know what happens beyond the small precious glimpse you've been lucky to catch of her characters' vibrant, astonishing worlds."

—Bridget Boland, author of *The Doula*, and owner of
ModernMuse: Energetic Tools for Writers

"FitzPatrick's debut collection is a stunning and intricately woven group of short stories exploring the topic of grief. Grief takes many forms, a concept elegantly articulated in this series of chronologically arranged stories that dips in and out of several characters' lives. With nimble structuring and evocative prose, FitzPatrick's pleasingly cohesive collection offers as many artful callbacks and codas as dazzling explorations of emotional vacancy and rebirth."

—Kirkus Reviews

MY PULSE IS AN EARTHQUAKE

Stories by Kristin FitzPatrick

VANDALIA PRESS

MORGANTOWN 2015

22 21 20 19 18 17 16 15   1 2 3 4 5 6 7 8 9

ISBN:

Paper: 978-1-940425-72-6; EPUB: 978-1-940425-74-0; PDF: 978-1-940425-73-3

Library of Congress Cataloging-in-Publication Data:

FitzPatrick, Kristin. [Short stories. Selections]

My pulse is an earthquake / stories by Kristin FitzPatrick.—First edition.

pages   cm

ISBN 978-1-940425-72-6 (pbk.)—ISBN 978-1-940425-74-0 (epub)

ISBN 978-1-940425-73-3 (pdf)

I. Title.

PS3606.I8833A6 2015

813'.6—dc23

2015007933

Grateful acknowledgment is made to the following publications in which these stories
have appeared, in slightly different form:

"A New Kukla" in *Colorado Review*, 2008; "Center of Population" in *Necessary Fiction*,
2012; "Queen City Playhouse" in *Thomas Wolfe Review* (2011 Thomas Wolfe Fiction Prize),
2012; "The Lost Bureau" in *Epiphany*, 2011; "The Music She Will Never Hear" in *The Best
of Gival Press Short Stories* (2011 Gival Press Short Story Award), 2015; "White Rabbit" in
The Southeast Review, 2011.

Cover design by The Book Designers.

This book is dedicated to the memory of my dad,

Tom FitzPatrick

(1945–2013)

You lift us up.

CONTENTS

QUEEN CITY PLAYHOUSE

It's been three days since Mizz Duesler brought her husband here to die in dressing room 3. He's the reason we're putting on this play in a hurry. It's my job to finish the scenery murals for the Island of Magic. Everybody says that *The Tempest* is an impossible comedy to stage, so why bother, but I painted my way into the place, and now I believe.

Three nights ago, as play practice wrapped up, and I was smoothing on the darkest blue in the night sky, Mizz D came up to me.

"Tess," she said, "you take care of Mr. Duesler until he falls asleep."

I've been here at the Dueslers' place a year: three theater seasons. A year of free paint and canvases, muffins and juice at weekend practices. And the building's warm enough to sleep in.

"Yes, ma'am," I said. I was going to guard the king of the Queen City Playhouse.

Their daughter, Cara Duesler, I know her from school. We're not friends, but she caught me painting in the back of the art room when I should've been in my other classes, and she knew I wasn't about to do murals for the school drama club. She was the star in all her parents' plays, and she told her mom I could help.

Like I say, I'm scenery. There's the audio ladies, Skyboy on lights, and Joe. He's costumes—sometimes he helps me paint, and I help him sew. There's the cast: the king's men, the boat men, Caliban the monster, and then there's Miranda and her father, Prospero the magician, with his invisible spirits and nymphs and reapers. Mizz Duesler directs us all from her headset. I never know how to take her. One way is as lioness on the headset, roaring out stage directions, pawing at my pine forests or my London street scenes, my Emerald Cities. Another way is Sweet Mizz D.

Roy brings the muffins. He's a rich bachelor who plays the hero in most of the shows, burning under the lights while the female lead crosses her arms and schemes and offs with their heads. This play, he's Prospero. Cara plays Miranda, Prospero's daughter, stranded on the island and hypnotized by his tall tales about their royal heritage. But once Prospero takes off his magic robe, ladies and gentlemen, we see right through him. Only Miranda's quick marriage to some gullible prince will make her father a duke again. It takes a lot of tricks to pull it off.

Tonight at practice, we're T-minus two days till opening night. Skyboy rattles along the lighting catwalks. By the time I look up, I see the tail end of his shadow disappear behind a spotlight. Whoowee, would I like that post. Skygirl. How about that? Instead, I'm down on the stage, where I paint and listen to the actors. "Do you swear, in front of God and family?" they say, in their fake preacher's collars. "Do you come in the name of the king?" they shout to intruders. The cast's job is to promise, protect, or poison. Joe and Skyboy and me make it all look convincing.

I'm almost done touching up the sets. This here is where Prospero's slave, Ariel, will lay out bait for the drunken sailors, and over here, when Caliban is plotting to kill Prospero, he will get a little flighty and say this island is all sweet noises. When play practice begins tonight, the actors' voices start as very clear arrangements of words. By the middle of practice, once I am deep into the Island of Magic, the actors are a nest of buzzing bees. Then the only sound I hear is my brushes clinking against paint jars.

Jangling keys yank me out of my painting. I look behind me, where Mizz D holds her keys above her head and barks out one last order before she lets everyone go on break. Since last season, it's like she's been struck by lightning—her hair went from a mop of normal-person brown to a pad of white bristles. "Let. Me. Say. This. Once," she says. "And only once: Please please please put a name sticker on your cubby. At home, please sew your initials into each. Piece. Of. Your. Costume." She sighs, and her whole body deflates. "And be here on time tomorrow for dress rehearsal!"

Then Cara's voice comes through the speakers. She and Roy are backstage already, and she must not have switched off her microphone. "Oh, Father . . . " she says. And then she slips off script. "Ooh, Prospero, may I pluck the magic garment from thee?"

Mizz Duesler's got another daughter, older than Cara. She knows how to shoo away dogs like Roy, but instead of scolding Cara for wandering off with a thirty-five-year-old amateur actor, Mizz D interrupts her own speech to the cast and listens to her daughter's lip smacks.

When rehearsal starts up again, Ferdinand, who is played by a total geezer, tells Miranda he will marry her. Their swift ceremony will make Miranda the next Queen of Naples, and it will pull her father, Prospero, the wronged Duke of Milan, back into royalty. Mizz D stops them and talks about the spectacle this act will need. She touches her headset and asks Skyboy if he's ready to create the invisible spirit effects. I don't hear him answer, but I know he's ready because he's got filters on some lights, cutout shapes on others, all wacked out to crazy angles. He controls the spectacle. Sometimes during practice he sits on the stretch of catwalk above the audio control desk, and I watch his dangling feet. I've never seen his face, but I've heard that he's older.

Mizz D's headset shorts out, and through the auditorium someone yells, "What?" and I realize it's Skyboy. I've never heard his voice before. It's higher than I imagined.

The audio ladies are still on break, so Mizz D says, "Tess! Fix me!"

I wrap some electrical tape around the wire. I play with the buttons. It works a while, and then the battery dies.

"Get it together, Mom!" Cara says.

During the next break, me and Joe go downstairs to check on Mr. D. Joe follows one step behind, babbling about how Shakespeare was a fool for writing such impossible plays and for gathering people into his theaters in the first place.

"All it did was spread the plague," he says.

I want to defend Shakespeare, but I won't fight Joe. I need to show my thanks to him. If he weren't here, I'd have split after the first week.

"I could run this show in my sleep," he says. "Any of us could." I want to pop him for saying this, but he's right. I've seen him stand backstage with sewing pins falling out of one side of his mouth and every character's lines streaming out the other side.

Even a good punch wouldn't change Joe. Once he gets an idea, it imprints itself on him for good, just like the actors' scripts.

When we enter dressing room 3, Mr. D's deck of cards waits on his table. He can't play games anymore, but he likes to touch the cards. He slides a four and an ace next to each other, and then he points to himself.

"Forty-one?" I say. "That's how old you are?"

He blinks. It is when he works this hard to hide the suffering that it shows most.

"No way, Mr. D," Joe says. "You look like Noah."

Mr. D shuffles the cards real slow and smiles. He is a little in love with Joe. We all are.

A stench tells us it's time to change the bedpan. I reach for Mr. D.

"I got it, Tess," Joe says. He lifts Mr. D out of the way. His strength surprises me, and I notice that his shoulders are starting to fill out his jacket. He's nineteen and still waiting for a growth spurt. Maybe it's finally here.

I don't want to embarrass Mr. D, so I look away, up to the photos on the wall that show the work of a bigger man: the old Mr. D. These snapshots of actors remind me that he staged plays nobody else in this part of Cincinnati would dare, like *The Crucible* and *A Raisin in the Sun*, not just *Our Town* and *My Fair Lady*. He helped actors much more talented than Cara rise up, all the way to Chicago theaters, some of them. Cara has no plans for herself. She will take over this playhouse, direct and star in her own productions until someone discovers her. Then she'll sell the place, or dump it onto some cousin, let it go to seed.

Joe's auburn curls bounce as he finishes the cleanup, and Mr. Duesler nods a little to thank him. He says he wants to take a turn giving Mr. D his meds. I okay it and let Joe find the right bottle from the cabinet. He helps the pills down the hatch, and Mr. D's eyelids droop.

Joe waves me outside. He looks at me square, his freckles blazing in the hall light. For the first time, I notice that he is taller than me.

"One of those pills, T," he says, "just one, is instant dynamite." He rubs imaginary money together between his fingers. "Thirty bucks a dose. What do you say? We could make a killing."

I walk away. This is his worst idea yet, and I cannot let it press into him. I want to find Prospero's magic staff and cast the demons out of Joe, but he grabs my arm. "Kids at school already pay thirty to keep a pipe full all night."

I try to shake out of his grip, but he's too strong. I'm no dummy. I've watched them pass it around at the parties I sneak into after Cara and her friends have crashed out, where I fill my pockets with smashed-up potato chips and drink from half-empty cups.

"We wait till he kicks," Joe says. "We sell the leftovers, give a cut to Mizz D. No harm."

"You. Are. Sick," I say.

Joe lets go and skips past me, up the stairs. "A killing!"

I go sit in the director's chair next to Mr. D's bed. He settles into the night's sleep: a snore, a wheeze, a twitching around the eye.

When the door opens, he doesn't wake. Mizz D walks in and kisses his forehead.

"Ice cold," she says. "Shouldn't be long now, Tess."

She usually looks dried up—a new wrinkle each night, like it's her brain swelling and contracting instead of his—but tonight her face is relaxed. She knows she can't control when or how the hero falls.

She takes a few grand strides around the room, her eyes scanning the photos.

"James has always wanted to put on *The Tempest*," she says. "This is our last chance. Do you think we can pull it off?"

"I think he'll know, even from down here, what we're doing up there on stage," I say.

I want to tell her he'll be there with us in spirit, because it might comfort her, but she's stopped listening. Instead, she's fixated on one particular photo, the one where Cara wears a red curly wig and belts out, "Tomorrow!"

"So you'll turn out the lights when you go?" she says.

"Course."

Mizz Duesler leaves. Just as the click of her heels fades down the hall, the volume on them creeps up again.

"Tess?" Her face is in the doorway now.

"Yeah?"

"You said your ride would be here by nine?"

"Yup. Quarter to."

Mizz D checks her watch. "Perfect. Mr. Duesler's usually out for good by eight-fifteen."

Since I started looking after Mr. D, Mizz D stopped jumping on my back about washing and cutting my hair and wearing proper all-black stage shoes, so I stopped stealing money from her purse for haircuts, and I painted black over the orange and yellow splatters on my shoes. But we still keep up this charade, as if I got somewhere else to go and somebody to take me there.

Now, with the hall light behind her, Mizz Duesler's white brush cut glows. If she'd let me, I'd do her portrait as a fresco on the wall right here next to Mr. D. It's been a while since Mizz D gave up asking me to make a small painting, maybe a still life of flowers, and go for a ride with her so I could hand it over to a guard during visiting hours or set it on a gravestone. It's what a good daughter should do, she said.

"You know, Tess," she says now, "once you get your rear end back in school, you could keep going, I mean past high school, and get a job in an old folks' home. That's the wave of the future."

Mr. D isn't old, I want to say, but I shouldn't remind her, so I say, "The future?"

She tries to smile and fails, so she leaves again, without a goodbye. She's too busy to talk to me. She pushed up the date of opening night, and folks all over town swore they'd come. They all know it's the last curtain call for James Duesler.

If I did show up at school again, I'd see Cara sitting in front of where I should be sitting during third period psych class. She'd pass quizzes behind her, over my empty seat and through my ghost to the stoner in the back who used to gnaw at the mats in my hair with his pocket knife. I know she's still going to psych class because her backpack, down in dressing room 4, is loaded with notes about synapses and biofeedback, tuning forks and drooling dogs.

Before I quit school I listened good enough in psych class to know that Cara was having some serious synapse activity every night in dressing room 4, way at the end of the hall, past the trapdoor, where the passage narrows and the ceiling stoops. In there with Roy, her pleasure centers must've lit right up, her primal cortex kicked into overdrive. All that sensory stimuli from Roy, with its positive reinforcement system in place, made her return each night through the maze of backstage prop room and light controls, past the decaying smell of her father in dressing room 3, which would have stimulated a negative response she'd have to suppress. Roy would help her with that. He makes the serotonin flow.

Around ten o'clock, Joe walks into Mr. D's room. He's been upstairs with Prospero's robe. He needs my help stitching up loose threads in the lining and around the collar, so we set to work on a big table out in the hall and listen to Cara argue with Roy in room 4. Something about going home. Once the robe is perfect again, me and Joe carry it to their door.

Roy invites us all the way in. He's just as wrinkled and balding as Mr. D, and even though Mr. D is the one dying faster, in this light Roy is all bone and shadow. I want to grab the makeup at the vanity and brighten him. When Joe slips the robe over Roy's shoulders, Roy stands straight as a show dog. He gives Joe a secret look. Joe's face lights up. Roy is working some kind of magic on him, too.

The robe is fine for now, so Roy keeps it on and returns to the couch. Cara lights a cigarette and hands it to me. Joe doesn't smoke, so she lights two more, carries one to Roy, and sits on his lap. Roy's free hand massages her thigh, so I watch his smoking hand. The nails are pointy and yellowed.

Cara leans away from him and gives me a wide-eyed expression she usually saves for the stage. Does she want protection from the monster?

"My mom's out to prove something," she says, "with all that invisible shit in Shakespeare's script that she's trying to bring to life." She falls back into Roy's arms. "No one can follow that." She runs her foot up Roy's leg, until it disappears under the robe. "Honestly, Tess, do you really think we can make spirits fly?"

Cara wants me to indulge her. She is starting this dumb conversation instead of talking about how her old man's ready to kick it, so I'll tell her what she wants to hear.

"I'm stupid about flying," I say.

Roy laughs. His free hand slides up Cara's leg, and then it touches her chin. "See? Tess agrees with you," he says. His job is to keep the illusion alive.

Cara rests her head on Roy's shoulder.

"You need a bath," he says. "You're burning up. Time to go home." He looks up at me and puts on his Prospero grin. "Our little life is rounded with a sleep."

Joe nudges me. "Yeah, T, our ride's probably here, too."

Everyone says goodnight, and I leave quick so they don't see me slip into room 3.

In the dark, Mr. D's fingertips glow white from bad circulation. He has finished the glass of water it takes him all day to drink. He rocks and sways in his bed. He must be under already, in a real deep sleep. After the treatments and the useless brain surgeries, his gray matter melted down into a dark sea, and now he's ready for the tidal wave.

When the doctors told Mizz D that her husband had two weeks left, she asked Cara to step down into a minor role in the play so she'd have more time to help out at home. But Cara's not the helping type. I will be the daughter Cara isn't. I will guide Mr. D into the night. After all Mr. and Mizz D have done for me—all the blankets and paints, the dinner invitations I turn down and the leftovers they always bring to the theater the next day, all the silence and space they offer me here—I owe it to them.

I take an inventory of the meds in the cabinet. There's the nausea stuff, the blood pressure stuff, and some drugs I had to memorize for the last psych test I took: pills for depression, for seizures, for pain. Mizz D has arranged them into two rows according to their sedation speed: fast, like the instant knockout tabs Joe wants to get his hands on, and slow pills, which don't do much unless you wash them all down at once. I count out what's left: ten days' worth of each one. I think of surrendering all of them to Joe. I wouldn't accept any of the money from him, but at least somebody would benefit from these things. They're not doing much good here. Besides, maybe Mr. D wants to stop taking his meds to make his death more tragic.

No. I stuff the pills into their bottles, shut the cabinet, and curl up on the floor at the foot of the bed.

The next day is final dress rehearsal. My work is done, so I sit in the front row of seats and watch the play fall apart. Cara is out with the flu. Mizz D asks Joe to play the female lead. For a few lines, he has a good time mocking the way Cara plays Miranda, all nose in the air.

It doesn't take long to see that Joe sucks as a girl, so Mizz D yells, "Tess, step in!"

Cara brought me into this place. I'm not dumb enough to think we're friends, but I thought maybe we were something else, like some kind of people that got to put up with each other. Everybody's putting up with her, and she's not doing a thing for us.

"The Miranda costume won't fit me," I say.

"Not my problem," Mizz D says back. "Somebody has to play the part."

Joe flips open Roy's robe to show me the lining we stitched. "No sweat," he says. "There's extra in here." He will add panels to the seams of Cara's costume. He will cover my butt with strips of the magic garment.

I hop up to the stage. I yank the Miranda wig off of Joe's head, and his hair springs free. I pull the wig onto my head and kneel in the same spot Joe gets up from.

Roy sways as he begins Prospero's confession to Miranda: "'Tis time I should inform thee farther. Lend thy hand—"As he takes the robe off, he barfs. It splashes onto my shoes.

The guy who plays the slave spirit, Ariel, stomps his foot. "Oh, perfect. Roy's got the bug, too. Who's gonna play the male lead now?"

Mizz D lifts her clipboard over her head and tells him to shut up. I know what she's thinking: this play is going to the dogs, and Mr. D deserves better.

"This is community theater," Ariel says. "It's not like we have understudies."

"Fine," Mizz D says. "Joe, step in and play Prospero." She holds out a script for him.

Joe doesn't mouth off, doesn't question the order. He takes the script with both hands.

"I feel like shit, too," the spirit Juno says. He touches his forehead. "I'm in no shape to protect anybody from Caliban."

"Yeah," one of the reapers says. "I could hurl any minute."

"I don't care how you feel," Mizz D tells them. "You are all supposed to be invisible!"

Joe balances the robe on his arm like a cartoon waiter with a white towel. With the same arm, he holds out the script, even though he doesn't need it. "Lie there, my art. Wipe thou thine eyes; have comfort," he says.

When he's done buttering me up for the big announcement, I say, "You have often begun to tell me what I am, but stopped and left me to a bootless inquisition."

He puffs up his chest and belts out Prospero's next line, asking me, "Canst thou remember a time before we came unto this cell?"

I tell him yes, I recall my noble life before our exile to the island, "rather like a dream."

"Not bad," Mizz D says. "Keep going. Let's finish this act and then jump to act 3 scene 1 with you two and Ferdinand. The real test."

Joe pulls on Prospero's wig. Then sleeve by sleeve by collar, he dons the magic robe.

We sail through a full scene. Joe comes alive. The sleeves flap when he gestures. The hem spreads around him when he kneels in front of me and says, "Dear Daughter . . . "

Soon it's time for act 3, when Prospero performs his biggest trick. Ferdinand defends Prospero's honor, and then Joe wields Prospero's magic staff and draws the circle where his enemies will stand and fall under his spell. This is where his daughter will secure his future.

Tonight Mr. D really suffers. Hot, cold, hot. Sweating and writhing. I think he has caught the bug. I place another blanket over him, up to the neck, and then I sit up real straight on the director's chair next to the bed. I tilt my head all the way back, like heroes do when they appeal to the gods, or curse them. "Keep going," I say.

I fluff the pillows. I change the channel on the silent TV. Mr. D still grits his teeth and squirms. I cannot comfort him.

When Joe walks in, he's wearing only a thin white T-shirt under his jacket, even though winter is setting in, but I don't question it. He sits in the chair on Mr. D's other side. He hands me my script. We rehearse act 3.

When I step out to go to the bathroom, I hear Joe walk across the room. I tiptoe back to the door and peek in.

I see Joe's shadow first, cast against the wall next to Mr. D. His hair hangs over his eyes, and he hunches over, reaching into his coat like a magician tucking away trick coins or rabbits. He's standing at the cabinet. I storm in, swat his hands down, and yank his jacket off. And there he is in his thin shirt. Now, ladies and gentlemen, is when we see right through the magician to the liar and thief, trickster and monster at once.

I pull the pill bottles out of his jacket pockets and drop the jacket on the floor. "Mr. D's not dead yet," I say. "Some nerve you've got."

"Close enough," Joe says. His face is red, and so is his neck, and his chest, all the way down to his collar. "What good are those to him now?" He places a hand on my shoulder. "Stop pretending, Tess. Just let him go."

After Joe leaves, I stay in the chair a long time, because who can sleep now? I hold Mr. D's hand and recite all my lines—Cara's lines—over him, from the parts of the play when the magic cloak is still in place, the illusions still alive. "Your tale, sir, would cure deafness . . . for a score of kingdoms you should wrangle, and I would call it fair play . . . " His breathing slows and his hand goes limp in mine. I keep going. "How many goodly creatures are there here! How beauteous mankind is! O brave new world that has such people in't!"

When I wake up the next morning, I know what I must do. First I pour all of his slow pills onto a plate and mash them with the bottom of his water glass. I fill the glass at the sink. I spoon up the powder and hold it over his drink, the one it will take him all day to finish. *Just stir it in*, I think. In my hand, the spoonful of magic dust stays suspended above water for a very long time. If I don't do this, Joe will do something worse. If I flush the medicine, Mr. D will suffer more without it. How much more promising and protecting can I do? Now it's a matter of choosing the speed of his departure. *Just stir.*

This is when the damn tears come. I close my eyes to get rid of them, and I imagine those sketchpad-sized paintings I made for my own parents. I stayed up nights getting those crocuses and doves and starry skies just right, and for what?

I open my eyes and look up at the photos of what the Deuslers have done in this place—all that comedy and tragedy they've given to the community instead of each other.

"Get it together, Tess," I say, mocking Cara. "Fix this family."

Mr. D grunts in his sleep, and then his face relaxes, like maybe death isn't so painful at all. But I flip my wrist, and down it goes. *Shhh.* I watch each white granule sink and then, as I stir, the spoon clinks against the glass.

In the moments before the opening night performance begins, the sound from the audience swells. I pick out single voices: a lady explaining the flu that knocked out the star members of the cast, some guy going on about sailing, a kid whining for concessions and bathrooms. But when I skim over the script one last time, the crowd's voices blend together, and it's like I'm holding a seashell up to my ear, and the voices are what's inside, the loud *shhh*, sitting still on a beach before a storm washes over the Island of Magic.

Act 1 begins. In my ears, the men on the troubled ship are just more hush from a seashell until Prospero's brother Antonio says, "Let's all sink with the king." And then boom, I go dizzy and soon I'm under the lights and my tongue goes thick and I think Skyboy's got some kind of hold on me for sure, but Joe must be invoking the invisible spirits to calm me, because one look from him forgives every theft and broken promise, every granule of poison. It rights me. Soon I'm belting out my favorite line—"If the ill spirit have so fair a house, good things will strive to dwell with't . . . "—and I'm ready. Me and Joe deliver every line just as good as we did for Mr. D, from promising Ariel his freedom to dodging Caliban to sweet talking Ferdinand, until Joe's got everyone where he wants them, protected in Prospero's magic circle.

The spotlight swings my way. It heats me up. Alonso, King of Naples, marries me to his son. "Do you promise to love and honor Ferdinand?" he says. "I do," I say, "in the name of the father." And now I'm officially part of the royal family, which makes Joe a right Duke once again, and me a princess. Applause fills the theater. This is when the spirit leaves us.

CANIS MAJOR

Rottweilers get real hungry after they mate. I'm not allowed to watch, so I wait in my room until I hear the gate clang. I open the curtains and see Daddy in the garage, lifting a white rabbit out of the cage. He drops it into Apollo's side of the yard.

I click the stopwatch. The bunny darts this way, that way, but it can't outrun our stud. Apollo stomps and thrashes and snaps its neck. He gobbles the sucker down inside of three minutes. Tufts of fur hang from his chops. Daffodil watches from her side, wagging her stump.

I open the window and hold up the watch. "Whoop whoop, Daddio! A new record!"

Daddy does his victory dance, sliding his thumbs around his overall straps, kicking his feet, then lifting his cap off of his head and churning it around. I do the same in time with him.

Mama marches into my room and grabs my cap. "That's not how a lady acts," she says. "It's a business, not a circus show." She dumps clean laundry on my bed, where Apollo's other dam, Serena, is snoring. Under her paws, today's paper shows President Nixon pointing a finger.

Mama gets wound up tight in mating season, so I show her the stopwatch.

"Well, I'll be," she says. She opens the window screen and

sticks her head out. "Whoop whoop!" She pumps her fists and shimmies. Her bowl cut sways.

Daddy takes his cap off slower this time, holds it to his chest, and blows her a kiss. Even surrounded by dead rabbits and dog shit, he is still a romantic.

Mama smooches at Apollo. "Attaboy!"

He runs toward us, his collar and tags jingling.

"That's Mama's little stallion," Mama says. She reaches down to rub his ears and then she straightens up. "Money, Rosie. Next five, six, maybe eight years. This dog is pure gold."

Mama pulls her newspaper out from under Serena's paws and carries it to the kitchen, where she'll eat up the latest scoop on Nixon calling Charles Manson guilty, then not guilty, in the middle of the trials.

I start folding the laundry, and our new neighbor's voice pipes in from the yard next door.

"Hell of a buster you got there," he says, and the sound of it makes my neck feel hot.

Daddy meets him at the fence. "Nah. You just caught old Apollo on a good day."

Our neighbor twists his crutches into the grass. He offers to train our male puppies to attack more than just rabbits so Daddy can charge three times the usual price for them. "The battle may be three years behind us," he says, meaning the riots, "but the war's not over. Folks are still scared enough to pay through the nose for some peace of mind."

Daffodil growls at Daddy's feet. Daddy tells her to be polite while he kicks dirt over a hole she dug. I reach down and touch Serena's belly. Her own litter will be here in two weeks.

"I'm better off getting rid of the pups young," Daddy says. "They ain't exactly cheap to raise." He pokes a sharp point along the chain link and laughs. "Besides, how am I supposed to take word from a man who don't own a dog himself?"

Our neighbor doesn't laugh. "I used to help the K9 trainers, even patrolled with them a while, but with my leg, Art, I haven't been able to handle large animals."

Daddy freezes up at the sound of a younger man calling him by his first name—a man he calls Officer Ryan—but he lets it slide. Officer Ryan will never patrol again. His knee got shot to pieces on the west side of Detroit, and to most folks, that's as good as losing a leg in the war.

Daddy bows his head. "Sorry. I didn't mean harm by it."

"No harm at all." Officer Ryan stands taller, off the crutches. "Get my prosthetic tomorrow. I'll be ready to train the best four-legged bodyguards money can buy. What do you say?"

We're downriver. The people who buy our pups either live close to Detroit city limits or they've done good enough to move way far north, where folks have a lot more that needs protecting. You never know who might wander out of the shadows and onto your property, they say, and Daddy always nods, but he's not on their team. He doesn't believe in fear, just money.

If he didn't need my help with the dogs, I'd sing in the kids' church choir. So I wait for Thursday nights, when Mama and I listen to my cousin, Vivvi, sing in the adult choir practice.

Tonight the holy water cools my forehead. At the foot of the Virgin along the east wall, we genuflect and light one of the candles in red glasses for my dead aunt, who was Vivvi's mother.

While Mama prays for her sister, I turn toward the choir and spot Vivvi. She's wearing an orange A-frame dress from the church donation box and a green paisley scarf around her neck.

Mama and I move to a back pew when it's time for Vivvi to practice her solo: "On Eagles' Wings." It will be this Sunday's Communion hymn. As the song starts, I wriggle my hand into Mama's. She accepts it and beams at her niece. Vivvi may be a moonfaced towhead who's never had a date, but her voice is like you jumped into Lake Erie on an August Sunday.

While she sings, I close my eyes and recall how she always

whispers a Glory Be over each newborn pup. We adopted her when she was twelve, like I am now. She just turned eighteen, and she's talking about moving out. "Let me take care of me," she has told Mama, but Mama always waves it off as another hippie slogan.

After practice, Vivvi eases her bike into the back of the station wagon, and we all sit in front. She asks Mama to drop her off at her friend Gretchen's house, a house where two girls from Vivvi's graduating class live *away* from their parents.

"All right, but home by nine," Mama says. "Secretarial school starts soon. Gotta rest up."

"I've decided not to go to secretarial school," Vivvi says. "I'm happy as a receptionist."

A year ago, just before Vivvi started her senior year, Mama got her a job answering phones at the auto glass factory, where the foreman is our distant relative.

"But you'll make more money. Just until you get married. Then you don't have to worry about working." Mama hopes that somebody out there will fall in love with Vivvi's voice.

"I like talking to people, and I make enough money." Vivvi chews on her hair. "Enough to live on my own. The girls at the house are looking for another roommate."

Mama stops at a red light and gives Vivvi the same sideways glance she gives me when I say I'm doing fine in math class. Her face scrunches up, but when the red light lifts off of it, the green light pours over her, smoothing and opening the skin. What would her face have done if she'd caught Vivvi and me last week, drawing *x*'s on our foreheads with eyeliner, to mock the Manson supporters, and Vivvi crossing her eyes and saying, "Which way to the bottomless pit?"

In front of Gretchen's house, Mama says, "You can visit here, but you're not moving in."

All I want is for Vivvi to stay with us forever, but she needs somebody on her team right now, so I say, "Why not?"

"Because," Mama says, "Vivvi should pal around with girls from her own church. Not with Lutherans. And why bunk up here when you have a finished basement all to yourself?"

Vivvi still won't reply. I lift my arms and spread them out wide, trying to grab hold of Mama's and Vivvi's headrests. I imagine my body as a hinge: my arms pressing forward to fold the enormous front seat in half, until driver and end passenger meet eye to eye.

"Look on the bright side," I say. "One of the Lutherans is in police school, so Viv's safe."

Vivvi opens the door and steps out. "Someday, Rosie, you'll understand why that worries your mom even more. Besides, Gretchen dropped out of the academy."

She carries her bike up the porch steps. Its reflectors flash, taking me back to a night last winter when she came home with a purse full of glass shards from a windshield somebody dropped at the factory. In the basement, we put down a tarp and spread the shards out. The biggest one was our Dog Star—the brightest point in Canis Major (Orion's larger dog)—and then we filled in the rest of the constellation and watched all the little planets glow.

I lied about Vivvi. She had a date once, if you can call it that. It happened earlier this summer, after the four of us had gone next door to welcome Officer Ryan to the neighborhood. To show his thanks, he said he'd have us all over for supper sometime. Mama said he should just have Vivvi over for her birthday, which meant he'd have me there, too, as her chaperone.

While we waited on the porch for him to open the door, Vivvi said, "A half hour's plenty long to eat supper, isn't it?"

Officer Ryan opened the door then, so I reached into my pocket and hit the start button on my stopwatch.

Inside, an Elvis record was playing "Return to Sender" just loud enough to drown out the ticking of my watch. The house still smelled of mothballs and Pine-Sol. We used to go over there to check on Officer Ryan's grandma before she went into the old folks' home and left her house to him. Her big wine goblets were still collecting dust on the mantel, her rusty candlesticks still mounted to the walls.

Soon as we sat at the table, a young lady entered from the kitchen and served us dinner, so we could all get it over with. She wasn't much older than Vivvi, and despite the blond dye in her hair, she was even uglier.

Officer Ryan picked up his fork and knife. "This is my housekeeper, girls. Grace."

The girl nodded and rushed back into the kitchen.

"Pleased to meet you, Miss Grace," I said.

"Her name ain't Grace," Officer Ryan said. "I meant let's *say* grace."

I laughed, but Vivvi didn't. We bowed while Officer Ryan prayed over the chicken fried steak and the perfectly shaped blobs of mashed potatoes and peas—TV dinners.

We ate in silence while Elvis thanked the rolling sea. Before long, Officer Ryan opened his mouth sideways. He stuck his finger in there and pulled a string of meat free, licked it off of his fingertip.

He pushed his plate forward. "Anyway," he said. "Enough about the help. She only comes over once in a while. I want to know about Vivian." He looked at my cousin like she was an old pickup for sale, and he just might be interested in making a deal.

Vivvi coughed and said, "Not much to say." She kept eating.

So, over "Song of the Shrimp," I told Officer Ryan about me: that I was aces in school, and I trained the dogs to jump yay high, and I could ride Vivvi's ten-speed no-handed all the way around the block. He actually listened to my lies, smiling and nodding, putting his fork down and looking right at me with his gray eyes, until I noticed a golden ring around each pupil.

Vivvi reached into my pocket and we both peeked down at the time. Eleven minutes of her time wasted. *The walls have ears*, Elvis sang. I stopped my watch. Me and Vivvi both sat up straight, hands on armrests, waiting to be set free.

Officer Ryan leaned back and sized up Vivvi's worth again: matted hair, high forehead, long nose, soft chin. What purpose could the homely girl serve?

He pointed to her throat and said, "I hear you got a set of pipes in there. Can you sing to this record?"

But they can't hear a kiss,
Or two arms that hold you tight,
So come on, baby. Don't fight tonight.

Vivvi backed her chair away from the table. "I only sing church songs."

Tonight at 9:16 p.m., I hear Vivvi enter the side door and pad down to the basement. We all leave her alone, and when I wake up on Friday, she's already ridden off to work.

The morning moves fast. After a steady stream of feeding, grooming, and yard cleanup, I chase Apollo around for forty-two minutes, Daffodil for thirty-six. They have to stay strong if they're going to mate two more times in the next three days—this is the prime time of her heat.

At one o'clock, it's naptime: Daffodil and Serena under a shade tree and Apollo on the couch. When I open the back door, Mama kneels in the mudroom and opens her arms. Apollo barrels into her and soaks her with kisses, knocking her off balance. He almost outweighs her.

"Oh, you big bull, you!" she says, laughing. "You big teddy bear."

I watch through the window as Daddy inspects Serena. She is breathing extra heavy and Daffodil is circling her, whimpering.

When the vet came over at the beginning of summer to see

if Serena was really pregnant, he warned us of the risk. We pay top dollar for this vet, so Mama had the right to question him.

"But this was her second heat. You said as long as we didn't mate her during the first—"

"Normally, sure," the vet said, "but she had that first season at almost two months younger than the normal age." He snapped his gloves off and balled them up. I was still holding Serena's head, close enough to smell the vet's sweaty hands. "Gestation and birth can strain them if they aren't done growing." He stood up. "Just be careful, Mrs. O'Neill."

I ask Daddy now if Serena's okay, and he tells me she's an ox.

Apollo picks up his soup bone—part of a cow's knee—and trots into the living room. He hops onto the couch without dropping it. Jaws of steel: another reason his pups will bring in big profits. He faces the fan, sprawls out, and starts gnawing. On the wall above him, President Kennedy's portrait hangs in the spot where Mama tried to put a portrait of Dad in uniform before he left for Korea. Daddy won that battle and set our Catholic president there, in a gilt frame.

Daddy rushes past us toward the shower, where he'll wash the fur and slobber off. I follow in his wake to make a run for the living room, but Mama yanks me back.

"Only thing that turns on that TV is a good report card," she says.

I turn around and trudge into the kitchen. At the table, I slump over my math worksheets and Mama over her *Free Press*. When she gets up to cook, I read the local page, which mentions the anniversary of two missing girls: one for a year, the other six months. The first is from Livonia, west of here. The other's from our church. Her family isn't the kind you want to run away from, so the police are searching dark corners of Detroit, where they always expect to find victims.

For two whole minutes, I suffer through pre-algebra practice. Then I practice signing my name as a married woman who never has to worry about working with roots or variables. *Mrs. M. Rosellen Ryan. Mrs. Oswald Ryan. Officer and Mrs. Ryan.*

I cover my worksheets with the front page of the newspaper, which explains Manson's idea about race wars. Manson says that 144,000 is how many members his family will have when the world takeover happens. Once all those girls have his babies, and those babies have more and on and on, they'll be a great big army, the last white survivors under Death Valley. I put my pencil to work. If he wants to survive the race war, all he needs is about nineteen in his family now. Once he squares that, he'll be near four hundred, and then the challenge is to square it again. But if he gets a guilty verdict, he's back to prime numbers.

Daddy's head appears in the doorway. "Come with me, Rose. Time for a pop quiz."

I fold up the worksheets, stuff them in my pocket, and follow him past the photos that cover the walls of the dining room and hallway: me and Vivvi with each new litter, Mama hugging each tired dam and Daddy each proud sire. Closer to the office, the pictures get bigger and more recent, all featuring Apollo: at one week, one month, two months, eight, nine, a year. When he was little, Vivvi painted the claws on his left paw red to tell him apart from the rest, but we didn't need the marker to spot him in a crowd, standing tall with a halo of light around him.

I stop at the door and watch Daddy settle in at the desk. Behind him, sunlight bounces off of a picture frame in his open suitcase shrine, which he always shuts before buyers walk in.

I kneel in front of it. The frame displays a smaller JFK photo, one where he's standing with Dr. King. There's two speeches on display, too. The first is one of President Kennedy's last warnings about what ought to be possible for all but isn't, and how it better become possible or there will be a rising tide of discontent. One time I asked Daddy what that meant, and he told me I already knew. The other speech is the one Dr. King gave when he got that prize you have to go to Norway to pick up.

He talks about walking down a highway and a runway, and all the people on the ground who helped him fly there, so he could say the prize doesn't even belong to him, that he hasn't made enough peace yet because snarling dogs are still bothering kids in Alabama.

"Too bad those two weren't better at dodging bullets, huh?" Daddy says.

He taps the smaller chair next to him and I sit. His pencil scratches on a notepad, and he mentions Officer Ryan's idea of training our male pups to attack. Daddy's already figured the cost of it—of feeding and caring for the pups all those extra months while Officer Ryan trains them to kill, and then paying Officer Ryan his cut once we sell the killer Rotties—and he presents the numbers to me as a pre-algebra problem I have to solve for profit x.

He hands me the pencil and pad. As I calculate, I hope for a high number, and for a high math grade on my next report card so I can earn the privilege of helping Officer Ryan with the training. I manage to work out a positive x, but it's not as high above zero as Dad needs it to be.

While he checks my work, I face the family tree on the biggest wall. It is Daddy's idea of a multiplication table. He's pinned smaller photos of Apollo, Daffodil, and Serena under their father (an American Kennel Club champion) and the dams of the only two litters their daddy sired before he got hit by a car. His other offspring aren't shown because none had come out as pure as our three, with the butterscotch-colored markings so perfect, the disposition set at such exact angles. Daddy just wants to improve the breed.

Under Apollo and Serena and Daffodil, it's penciled in like this:

Serena's 1st litter - projected Aug 1970.

Daffodil's 1st litter - projected Oct 1970.

There are twelve prongs under each dam and plenty of space at the bottom and on the sides for more generations, more inbreeding with more dams.

Daddy tells me my answer was close to what he expected. I passed. "Who needs summer school anyway?" he says. Another place I'd be if it weren't for the dogs. He straightens a stack of breeding records. "Of course, we can't expect to profit from every pup."

"I know that already, Daddy."

Mama has six sisters: one dead, one in the nunnery, two downriver, and two that stayed in Detroit after the riots, when everyone else was selling their homes at a loss and scampering off, because in an emergency, you can't worry about profits. So to comfort my aunts, Dad gave them free puppies and lied to them about how quick the little ankle biters can scare folks away.

He twirls a pencil and gazes out the window, down the intersecting street and its line of bungalows. "So, what do you think? Should I team up with Ryan?"

I peek over at Officer Ryan's house. It's already been two months since that night when the four of us showed up on his doorstep to welcome him to the neighborhood with a cake and a six-pack.

"What's all this?" he said to us.

Daffodil kept scratching under the fence. Daddy said his welcome to Officer Ryan and we held out the gifts, but the crutches left Officer Ryan with no free hands.

Vivvi said, "Here," and pointed to an empty planter, so we set the beer and cake in it.

"Nice kids," Officer Ryan said. "A lot nicer than I'm used to."

I tell Daddy, "He's probably worth teaming up with, but you don't have to decide yet."

Mama calls out from the kitchen for me and Daddy to come to the table, but Daddy lingers in the office. He is soaking up all the quiet and possibility in this room before lunch, which is the only good part of the day he's got left until he has to go to the barber shop. I've heard him tell Mama he dreads every embarrassing thing about the place—the aftershave stench, the buzzing clippers under all the gossip and boasting and flag waving he has to smile and cut through as he stands behind each chair, raised on its platform—all that arrogance barely stretching across the fear like a bad comb-over. Another time, I heard him say he'd rather trim claws any day than razor the necks of the Knights of Columbus.

As I walk out of the office, I notice Daddy's star chart, which has only the dog constellations on it. Me and Vivvi made it as a Father's Day gift, and that night we all lay on the picnic table, shining the flashlight on Bootes's hounds, Canis Minor, Sirius the Dog Star—all the dogs in the sky and the space between them. As Viv showed us Canis Major, Apollo jumped up and landed on Daddy's belly. We laughed so hard we scared Apollo, and he cowered under us.

Now, under the kitchen table, Apollo rests his chin on my feet to wait for scraps.

As Daddy finishes his meatloaf, Mama says, "You know, the pups'd be worth a mint if we waited and sold them as yearlings, already trained. We'd have a waiting list a mile long."

"It's already half a mile," Daddy says. "Once we buy a third dam, we can crank out a litter every four months. It's gonna get crowded."

"Maybe we can kennel them next door. Cops can probably break the dog ordinance and have as many as they want." Mama clears Daddy's plate and brings it to the sink.

Daddy follows at her heels. He takes the plate from her, sets it down real gentle, and then he holds her hands, looks into her face. Finally, she looks back. Their foreheads tip together.

"Doreen," he whispers, "we have to stick to our plan."

Mama peels away from him and looks at me, wanting to know what I think.

"We got the Superman of the breed on our hands," Daddy says. "His offspring will be"—Mama and I join in—"pure gold." He scrapes his teeth over his lip. "I can't gamble that away."

After Daddy leaves for work, Mama and I finish eating. Out the window, Officer Ryan's Nova appears in his driveway, on the far side of his lawn. He gets out to open the garage door. No crutches hit the ground this time, just his right foot and his new prosthetic left foot. He must have got his hair cut and a shave, too, and a new golf shirt. My stomach churns, and my face gets real hot. *Rosie Ryan.*

"Well, good for him," Mama says. "He deserves a fresh start." She uses her bread to mop up more gravy. "He went down like a real hero in that Woolworth's shooting."

I press my lemonade glass to my neck. "I've never heard him talk about any of that."

Under the table, Apollo lifts his head. I feed him a napkin full of string beans.

Mama stops the bread on its way to her mouth. "Of course not. Big dogs don't bark."

That afternoon, Vivvi doesn't come home at her usual time. Mama and I drive to the factory, where they tell us Vivvi rode off at quitting time like always. We drive to the hippie house. On the porch, a rusted bike that isn't Vivvi's leans against the railing.

A boy about her age answers the door. He is short with dark, wavy hair and olive skin.

"Who the hell are you?" Mama says.

He's shielding his eyes and squinting, like we woke him up. "Gretchen's brother?"

Gretchen is one of the Lutherans: tall and blond. Mama pushes past him until she's in the door.

"Girls? Vivvi?" She hollers up the stairs. "Come on home, honey. It's suppertime."

"The girls ain't here," the guy says. He smiles down at me. "You Viv's kid sister?"

Mama shoots out the door, pulls me down the steps. "Don't you dare," she says to him.

We race home, and then she pulls out the parish directory, starts calling everyone to ask if they've seen Vivvi.

Mama is a light smoker, but tonight while she waits for Vivvi to come home, she burns through a whole pack. She puts me on phone duty for an hour and sits pin straight in front of the TV, where she carries on a debate with Walter Cronkite, challenging and correcting him. I listen from the kitchen and wonder what Mama would have been if she hadn't become a breeder.

When I wake up the next day, Mama is gone. Daddy says Vivvi never came home.

I feed and exercise everybody. I do all of Mama's usual Saturday chores. Daddy mates Apollo and Daffodil again because today is the twelfth day of her heat (the perfect day to mate), but this time I don't watch Apollo chase the reward rabbit. Not at a time like this. Instead, I stay in my room and kneel at the whelping box—my old sandbox—and pray my rosary for Vivvi. Then I take out my colored pencils and doodle on my worksheets. Soon red hearts cover each square root sign. Most hearts have my name and Officer Ryan's name inside. Over the toughest problem, I draw his face. I color in his gray eyes. I use a ruler to draw his teeth and I make his chocolate hair longer, wavier. At the bottom, I sign my future name, *Marybeth Rosellen Ryan*, and slide it under the box.

When Daddy and I sit down to lunch, I ask why we don't tell Officer Ryan about Vivvi.

"Because you don't hang your dirty laundry out for the neighbors to see, understand?"

"Understood."

Daddy leans over his ham and eggs and peers into me, like he's measuring each freckle.

"Your mother hasn't heard from Vivvi for all of thirty-six

hours, and your aunts are already driving around looking." He sweeps his arm toward the street. "Meanwhile, Mom's out there tailing the guy who answered the door at the friend's house." When he sits back and opens his arms to emphasize the point, egg bits fall from his napkin. Apollo licks them off the floor. "Just between us?"

I nod.

"Mom needs to let go. Vivvi is a *teenager*. It's her job to want to disappear."

I lean back, drink my milk, and calculate—I will become a teenager in sixty-three days.

The next day is Sunday, the only day I take off my cap and let Mama groom me. She yanks the brush so hard that my face turns as red as my hair. I start to cry.

"I know," she says, "I'm scared, too."

In church, the usher leads us up to the front pew, which has been reserved for the family of the other lost girl. This is where all the prayers have been directed for the past six months, and where all the hands, on the way out of the Communion line, have reached down to touch the mother's shoulder. Mama stops in front of our usual middle pew, but Daddy motions her further up the aisle. Maybe she regrets calling everyone to tell them Vivvi's been gone all weekend.

"Come on, Dor," Dad whispers, tilting his head and reaching out, "let them comfort you."

She moves toward him, letting her face muscles do what they have to do to get the tears loose. Daddy touches her pinky. I follow them to the front.

Every reading is about shepherds keeping an expert eye on their flock, steering them out into the sunlight, safe from predators that lurk in the shade, like the guy at Gretchen's door. Yesterday Mama followed him to and from work and the store, even noted the type of smokes he bought.

Father's homily is all about giving up the self to save the

other. He recites tired stories about soldiers risking life and limb to rescue strangers, about a nurse that gave her own kidney to save a patient, and then he stops. He takes off his glasses and steps down from the altar. "We shouldn't be here talking about faraway sacrifices," he says. "We should be out there, giving ourselves up to find," and then he names all three lost girls, but all I hear is "Vivian James."

We rush through the kiss of peace and breaking of bread. The choir starts the Communion hymn. Without Vivvi, they sound like they're under water, far below eagles' wings.

After Communion, some guy in a back pew stands up and clears his throat.

"Father, if you'll allow me," he says. This is a small church, but it's still Catholic—you don't speak out of turn. Everybody twists around. It's the owner of the grocery store. He has enough granddaughters to be extra scared. "People," he says, "we can't let the shadows swallow our children."

When the grocer stops talking, he is shaking and scanning our faces. Somebody claps. The whole parish lets out a breath. A few more men stand. They say things like, "We pray for each other's sons off at war, but we gotta look out for each other's daughters." They are circling around the fear of men like Manson, but no one will mention a devil like that in a place like this.

There's no closing blessing, no announcements, no recessional hymn. We just rush outside, and the off-duty officers among us divvy up our town—and rougher parts of Detroit—into search territories. They tell Daddy to take me and Mama home so we can wait by the phone.

A few hours later, Officer Ryan rings the doorbell. He asks Daddy questions off a list.

Daddy is brief. "Sorry," he says. "Our Serena's expecting, and she needs my attention."

Serena hasn't eaten all day, and by bedtime, her temp drops.

These are warning signs of labor. It's too early for that, but we set her down in the whelping box anyway. Apollo doesn't sleep, which means I don't sleep. He keeps lifting his head up, jumping down to the floor, sniffing and licking her. First-time dad. Each time, he jumps back up, buries his head behind my knees, and whimpers. Serena finally growls and bares her teeth at him. I have to laugh, even at a time like this. It's the same way she told him to get lost last year, when he was just her little brother, and not yet her mate.

Apollo groans and fidgets. Finally, his snoring reaches a steady pace.

I face the window, which shows a slice of sky lit up good with an almost full moon. I spot Bootes's hounds and Orion's hunting dogs, and then I close my eyes and see Vivvi up there with the Pleiades, looking down at us. What patterns do we form?

"I'm closer than you think," she says.

I open my eyes and see her pulling her bike up to my window, wearing a white dress.

"I'm okay," she says, just floating out there—Tinker Bell in a green paisley scarf.

Apollo stands and wags his stump. I hold his collar and tags still.

Vivvi cups her hands around her face and peers in at Serena. "Save me the runt?"

She flattens one hand on the screen. Apollo licks her palm.

I bring my hand up to touch Vivvi's. "No, Viv. You'll get the biggest dog."

And now she's riding away, down the street, swerving left and right. She stops under a streetlamp, sets her feet on the blacktop, and turns in all directions, to see if anyone's watching.

I'm watching. When she catches my eye, she smiles, baring too many teeth, and the lamplight casts shadows over her eyes. She's not Tinker Bell this time, more like Captain Hook in a blond wig and nightgown, laughing into all that air between us.

She pedals away, her scarf fluttering. I poke Apollo's fangs so I know it wasn't a dream.

I keep my secret all through Monday morning. Nixon is on Mama's front page again, still backpedaling, but on the local page there's something new: above the list of dead soldiers, my cousin's school portrait glows white on dirty newsprint. "Missing person."

Mama is kneeling in the mudroom, crying over her rosary. It's the only time she asks anybody besides me for help. The fan spins her hair up off of her neck.

In my room, Serena is panting and straining. I flip through the records in the living room until I find a forty-five of the new "Let It Be" single. I play it six times real loud before I gather up my nerve to snap on the gloves and check Serena's temp. Ick. 99.3. It's usually 101.5. Daddy is still busy with the mating and Mama with the prayers, so I call the vet.

"Below ninety-nine, and it's show time," he reminds me, "but don't worry. You've seen false labors before." I tell him it's hard not to worry. "Worst case," he says, "you'll have a premature birth twenty-four hours from when the temp first dropped." He makes a noise with his teeth. "Let's hope it's just blood sugar trouble. Or dehydration. Could just be the weather. Keep her inside." Twenty-four hours is eight o'clock tonight.

By the time Daddy starts getting ready to go to the barber shop, I can't take the silence anymore. I grab Mama's hand and lead her to the front lawn, show her the bike tracks.

I start to tell her about Vivvi, but she claps a hand over my mouth, looks in all directions, and shoves me into the house. She closes all the windows and doors so no neighbors will hear.

"You're just telling us now?" The fan oscillates her way, and her apron billows. "Marybeth Rosellen O'Neill, how dare you keep such a thing from us!"

I haven't been called my full name since I was eight, and

that was for refusing to shovel shit out of the snow. Mama pushed me outside, and the Rotties watched me through the window.

Now she tells me to get the baseball bat from under my bed, and then she hollers up to Daddy, "Call in sick, Art. We're going to the hippie house."

When I hand the bat to Daddy, he lets it hang from his left hand. Finally, he is showing some fear—they've never left me home alone before. "I ran out of time for the rabbit," he says, following Mama out the door. "When Poll wakes up he'll be ready to eat anything in his way."

Serena keeps panting and straining. I take her temp again. 98.6. Apollo won't stop worrying over her, so I put him outside, but he only whines and scratches at the back door.

I call the vet. This time a new receptionist answers. I can tell by the flat handle of her voice that she doesn't like talking to people, especially crying kids. "He's with a patient now," she says, "and it'll take him a while to get to you. You're a long way from Grosse Pointe Shores."

"Tell me something I *don't* know, lady," I say. She hangs up.

I've never done birth work by myself, and Serena is a dam that needs extra help. When I'm deep into side three of the White Album, Apollo's yelping crescendos until I can barely hear the Beatles or my own voice singing every verse and chorus Vivvi taught me—*When I get to the bottom I go back to the top of slide!*—so I rush into the living room to turn up the volume on the record player. *I'm coming down fast but I'm miles above you!* The doorbell rings. I turn off the record, reach into my pocket, and squeeze a rosary bead. Ahh, rescue. The vet is finally here.

I open the door to Officer Ryan. His hair is wet.

"I heard the commotion out back." He looks down at my gloved hands. "Need help?"

"No. I know how to deliver puppies." I clasp my hands behind my back. "No, thanks."

Officer Ryan smiles the way people without kids smile at kids. He tells me he had to deliver babies on his beat. "Human babies, and they all lived. In an emergency, you learn quick."

"Is it the same with dogs?"

"Allow me," he says.

I open the screen door, look up and down the street. "Just until the vet gets here."

I lead him to the whelping box and hand him a pair of gloves. His leg clinks as he settles onto the floor next to Serena. He pets her ears like Daddy does. Serena doesn't have the strength to sniff him out, so she surrenders. Officer Ryan hums something familiar under his breath as he strokes all the way down her body. I realize it's "I Want to Hold Your Hand."

Apollo jingles louder now at the back door. He scratches like hell, ruining his manicure. I check my alarm clock. It's past the dogs' suppertime.

Officer Ryan points to the window box fan. "Turn that on, will ya?"

I set the fan on high. The birthing takes longer than usual. Like always, I stay near the dam's head, comforting her between each delivery. Officer Ryan's face is inches from mine. He grits his teeth as he pulls on the legs of the two breech pups. Over the stench of birthing fluids, I smell his hot breath.

Seven dog babies, all of them alive. We wrap the first few afterbirths in newspaper, check and clean each pup, start setting them down in their feeding spots. Serena tries to keep a close watch on Officer Ryan as he touches her young, but she looks as tired as I feel. Before she has a chance to bite off the last three umbilical cords, Officer Ryan starts cutting them with his pocket knife.

I hold out my hands to halt him. "No, no. My dad doesn't do that."

"Well, he should. The poor bitch needs help." He sits up. "All these girls to look after."

It's only now that I realize Officer Ryan didn't wash or glove his hands. And there is more blood with this litter. The box got pushed and pulled around in the process, and now my math worksheet is poking out from under it, a white burst on the drab carpet. It ripples from the fan's blast. Officer Ryan squints at the repetitions of his name in red ink. I pull my cap down and pretend not to notice. There are more important things going on inside the box, so he looks back into it, forgetting the paper distraction, I hope. *Stupid, stupid Rosie O'Neill.*

"That's a lot of misuses," he says. His hair is half-dry now, and extra wavy.

I lean down and listen until I can hear each pup's steady breathing, and their mother's, and I keep listening as they pile up in the crannies of her body. Ahh, the reward.

"I want to name them after my mom and her sisters," I say.

He stands and walks around my old sandbox, until there is nothing between him and me. His knees are at my eye level. "This was a lesson you couldn't ever learn in school, huh?"

From his back pocket he removes Vivvi's green paisley handkerchief, and wipes more blood off of his hands.

I feel a hot rush over the backs of my legs. Every part of me wakes up.

The dogs need no training, the police no search parties. I have all the evidence I need right here to solve one of the missing person cases and to prevent them from multiplying.

Officer Ryan tries to take my cap off, but I duck and scamper away. When I open the back door, Apollo doesn't wag or whimper or burrow into me. It's his chance to prove that he is the perfection of the breed, to do exactly the type of guarding I need, on instinct—not on command.

He shoots in, his running form perfect, his speed superior, coat sleek except for the hairs standing up along his spine, his lips curled back to reveal his perfect choppers.

"Whoop whoop!" I say.

He is all teeth and growl, knocking Officer Ryan down on the floor at the foot of my bed. Officer Ryan tries to rise up on his elbows and inch backwards, but Apollo pins him.

I dart back outside. Daffodil is snorting and digging under the fence again.

"I should have listened to you before," I say, letting her free.

She sprints into my room, snot and spit flying from her chops.

Daffodil plants all fours on Officer Ryan's torso, snarling and giving him an up-close view of her fangs while Apollo sets to work on his left leg. He chomps down on the prosthetic, thrashing and yanking. Officer Ryan's right leg and arm jerk around like he's trying to make half a snow angel. Keys fall out of his pocket. Within seconds, Apollo has the prosthetic unhinged and Officer Ryan is wailing now, crying out for God and the Virgin and even his own mama, but the fan swallows his plea. Daffodil nips at Officer Ryan's cheek—a warning I don't heed—just as Apollo opens his own jaws and flings the prosthetic out of the way. Its metal parts bang against the back of the whelping box. Then he closes his jaws again, this time on the stump, to hold the body down while Daffodil sinks her teeth into the neck.

I scoop up the keys and soon I'm out the front door, leaving the dogs to watch over each other. Some of them won't survive without human help, but I can't worry about profits now.

I run to the far side of Officer Ryan's house and enter through the side door. The air inside is swampy, like he hasn't opened a window all summer. Every other house on the block has an open stairway to the basement, but he has put a door in front of his. I fumble with his keys until I find the right one, unlock the door, and hold it open while I tiptoe onto the first step.

Downstairs, Elvis is singing "Hound Dog," and somebody else is giggling.

The sweat on my hands makes me lose hold of the doorknob, and the door swings shut behind me, locking me in. I stop breathing a minute and my heart pounds, but then I remember that these basements have big windows you can crawl out of.

My throat gets thick but the words make it out as I step down: "Come have supper, Viv."

The area at the foot of the stairs is painted as a night sky, but the rest of the walls and ceiling are light blue. Thick white curtains. Vivvi's bike hangs upside-down on hooks.

When I find her, Vivvi is dancing around with Officer Ryan's housekeeper and a baby. She is singing, "You ain't no friend of mine."

"Rosie Posie," Vivvi says, handing the baby to his mama. She walks up to me, and she is Tinker Bell again, greeting me in Neverland. Except one eyelid is painted dark, like the phone rang while she was getting ready for something, and then she forgot what it was.

She points to mementos on the wall, Polaroids of all three lost girls with Officer Ryan. The housekeeper is the girl from Livonia: same pointy nose, same jagged teeth. How had I missed that before?

The other photos are large portraits of him in patrol uniform, which my cousin and the Livonia girl stop and kiss as they move about the basement. "Officer of the Peace," it says below each one. He's touching his holsters in some, hugging his K9s in others. They're all shepherds: different build from Rotties, different disposition and disease risks. Different training needs. *No*, I will tell Daddy, *don't team up with Ryan. Don't join the race war.*

The girl from Livonia is singing louder now, over her baby's screams, straight into his face: "You ain't nothin' but a hound dog, cryin' all the time." The baby howls louder.

Besides the pictures, there's a map of the whole metro area, with parts of the fancy northern suburbs shaded in red pencil, including Grosse Pointe. When I lean in and touch the freeway, I notice that the blood on my fingers is hardening. Canine and human blood, which my bare feet must have padded through my house, across the lawn, the driveways, and into this pit.

I step back and turn, adding it all up: red on the walls, white gowns, black eyeliner, and a man in blue, ready for a rising tide of discontent. Helter Skelter.

"Time to go home, Viv. The dogs need us." I point to a window we can crawl out of.

"The windows are painted shut. This is my home now, Rose. I'm needed here, with him."

There's nothing else to do but lift my hand up to hers. I squeeze my eyes closed and wait. If she touches her hand to mine, I will know last night was real.

Instead she laughs, and when I open my eyes, she crosses hers and sticks her tongue out.

"Needed here?" I say. "How did you even get here? You can't stand Officer Ryan."

"He's different than I thought, Rosie. Maybe it's the new leg." She giggles and tosses her hair back. She never does that.

"What did he do so different?"

She smiles into the air behind me. "One day last month, a rainy day, he showed up outside the glass factory right at quitting time, drove me around, showed me his old beat. You wouldn't believe his stories." She sits up real straight now. "He's a true hero, Rose. One that's gonna do even greater things, but only with our help. Just you wait."

I look at a map and imagine his Nova on that side street right there, around the corner from home. Then Vivvi exits through the passenger door, pulls her bike out of the trunk, and rides it home in the rain, like nothing different ever happened.

I knock on her forehead. "Hello, I'm looking for my cousin, Vivvi. She in there?"

She guides my fist down to the table and holds it.

"I couldn't get him off my mind after that day. When you're old enough, you can hear the stories, too. They made me see in him what you saw all along." She winks her painted eye at me and laughs her faraway laugh.

I ignore the teasing. There's no crush for her to tease me about anymore. "What about Gretchen and the others?" I nod toward a closed door. "Are they here, too?"

She looks confused now, and I wonder if Officer Ryan

slipped her some of that forgetting potion they give you when you cross into hell. "Oh, them," she says. "No. They're going nowhere. Your mom was right. I shouldn't have wasted my time with them. Last Thursday, soon as you dropped me off at their house, I rode over here, snuck in the side door."

The girl from Livonia and the baby are spinning around in the center of the room now.

"And her?" I say. "Where is she headed?"

Vivvi lets go of my fist, like she's done with me. "We've already arrived, Rose! Don't you see?" She spreads her arms out wide, as if this locked-up basement is heaven itself. "This is the future."

Then hands are grabbing at her shoulders, pulling her out of her chair—hands that belong to the missing blond girl from church. Her belly sticks out far enough for me to know they are making a whole parish of kids to sing to, and it's only a matter of time before Vivvi contributes.

The pregnant girl lifts my cap up. "When you get older, we'll have you go platinum."

"Oh, no thanks," I say. "Girls all over town have been dyeing their hair dark since you—"

"Since I was set free!" She shoots into the center of the room, lifts her arms, and twirls around until my cap flies out of her hand. "Freeeeee!"

The record stops. Outside, a car door slams. Heels and taps hit cement.

From the closet, the pregnant church girl removes a white dress. "Time to set Rosie free."

The portraits multiply and slide around on the walls, but instead of Officer Ryan's face, they hold the faces of other, more famous men who'd still be out keeping peace on the streets if they hadn't been shot either. *Marybeth Rosellen O'Neill*, they say, *you must dodge this bullet.*

And then the pregnant church girl is coming at me, holding out my new uniform. I grab Vivvi's wrist. We will find a way out.

That's when the door pops open, like a magical suitcase, shooting a beam of light over the stairs. Collar and dog tags jingle. Apollo. Shoes scrape the top step. The vet's voice: "Holy hell." He raises his volume, and his words echo down. "Rosie, are you in here?"

Vivvi faces the sound, and the other girls walk toward it. I look down and realize I'm holding not just the dress but the baby, too. I carry him to the landing, where we all stand in front of the night sky, staring up at the large bloodied dog, the man who's come to set us free, and the halo of light around them.

A NEW KUKLA

It's a bit warmer than usual today, the last day of winter. Richard leaves the house at dawn, but he comes home early to take his wife, Gail, to a nice dinner. One last surprise before the ninth month of her pregnancy.

At three o'clock he trots up the steps and through the door. He has it all planned. In the shower he will sing "Mrs. Brown, You've Got a Lovely Daughter" and then change into a nice shirt, pressed trousers, the tie Gail gave him for Christmas. He won't cover his white collar and tie knot with a scarf. She likes seeing the collar and tie behind the wool lapels of his overcoat. At four o'clock, when he goes to the flower shop to pick her up, he'll wait until she looks away so he can pluck a rose from behind a glass door. A white one, her favorite.

At dinner, he will call her by name. Gail, let's go out tonight. I think my wife would like a table by the window. Isn't that right, Gail? Yes, she will say, a nice view. But he won't say, Gail will have the pasta. When the waiter arrives, Richard will say, Gail, what will you have, dear? He will close the menu and watch and listen and smile while she orders, and then he will ask the waiter to bring him her second choice.

She will like to be called by name. When she asks about Richard's day, he will wave off the question. Work is work, he'll say. That's when he'll place his hand over hers on top of the table and ask, How was *your* day? She'll tell him what the regular customers' kids and grandkids are up to, and she'll say that her sister, Joy, is really keeping the place together. If she is in the mood, if she is not too tired from the anticipation, Richard will ask about the baby. He will tell her that he finally flipped through the name book. Donnelly the dark brave one, Donovan the dark warrior, or maybe Duana the little dark maiden. Tonight they will settle on a name.

But at half past three, after he's taken care of the shower and the singing and the white collar, the doorbell rings. Richard sighs and drops his shoulders. He leaves his tie in a single knot.

A man in uniform stands on the porch, holding a folded flag in both hands. Pins and small ribbons line his breast pocket.

Richard loses his balance. He reaches behind himself, presses his fingertips into the space on the wall just below the framed portrait of Mike: soldier, husband. Joy's husband, who's half a world away, containing Communism.

"I'm afraid Joy doesn't live here right now," Richard says. He has to stop and swallow and loosen his tie to get the words out. "It's her house, but when he was called up, she moved into the flat above the flower shop." He pats his front, his tie. "I'm her sister's husband. I'm family."

The soldier stares at his feet. "Yes, sir."

He must be confused to hear an English accent like Richard's in a neighborhood like this, but then, Richard realizes, this guy has probably heard and seen it all.

He gives Richard a lift to the flower shop. The ride is three blocks: one west, two north. Richard doesn't know whether to direct him to the shop or tell him to keep driving. East, he wants to say, straight into Lake Michigan. His tongue is swollen with the wrong words. It is thick enough to mute him, and he's grateful for this. And then it comes: the jolt in his stomach, the surge up through the chest and into the armpit, down the arm. He coughs and chokes down the burn. His eyes almost pop out of his head. It's happening because he ate his fish and chips too fast at lunchtime. He was excited to get his work day over with so he could get home, and then to the flower shop to see Gail.

The type of heartburn his doctor described doesn't match Richard's symptoms. His pain always sticks around longer, keeps him racing and paranoid, but the doctor gave him nothing for it. "Your blood pressure isn't that high," the doctor said. "You're young. Eat better. Take a walk." He laughed. "Get out of the office."

When Richard and the soldier reach Conlan's Nursery, Richard wants to ring the bell and stand next to the poor guy with his head down, or behind him with a hand on his shoulder, to help him get the words out.

Instead, he walks the soldier in and flips the "Open" sign over. The soldier delivers the message to Joy and holds out the flag. Joy drops her head, brings a hand to her mouth, and retreats to the back room. Gail turns and watches her go.

Richard holds out his hands to the soldier, accepts the flag, and thanks him. The soldier offers his condolences to Gail and lets himself out the door.

The flag feels heavy as Richard carries it to the counter.

Gail stares at it. "Mike was a good man," she says.

Richard rests his hands on either side of the flag. Gail places her fingertips on his nails.

"Be an angel and bring some overnight things from the house?" she says.

He tilts his head, peers into her face. She won't look up.

"Matter of fact, just bring the hospital suitcase by the door. That'll last me a few days." Something's caught in her throat. "Actually, I won't need it till morning. Could you bring it in the morning?" Richard's wife backs away and smiles at him the way she smiles at customers when it's time for them to leave. "Have a good night, honey."

Her face is free of tears. Conlans don't cry in front of guests. She bows her head over the flag again before she turns and walks back toward Joy in the greenhouse.

Richard spends the evening in Mike's chair. He's lost his appetite for anything but scotch and television, so he clicks the dial around until he finds the puppet program. He sings along. That's when he calls Raisa, for the first time in a year.

"You've been married nearly a year," she says. "Surely there is a baby."

"In a month," he tells her.

"A girl," she says. "It has to be." This is all she has to say about it.

He wants to get the tea, or herbs, whatever, at her flat tonight, wants to listen to her kettle whistle, to adjust the antenna and curl under her arm while they watch the puppet program, the same way they used to do.

"Instead," she says, "come to my new job up on the observation floor of the new Hancock building. And be there by closing time." Her husband works first shift now. She has to catch the Howard line home by nine-fifteen.

Richard agrees to meet her on the ninety-fifth floor. She'll have the herbs for his heartburn and a surprise for the baby, too.

At eight o'clock the next night, Richard's ears pop as the lift reaches the twentieth floor of the John Hancock Center. The pressure pushes on his forehead, his temples. He rotates his jaw without opening his mouth. Pop, pop. He doesn't want the other passengers to click their tongues and exchange looks. At the sixtieth floor he grabs the rail behind him. The pressure has landed on his chest. He wants to kneel or lie down.

He hasn't seen the Hancock Center since it opened, not up close. He hasn't strolled down Michigan Avenue since he first left the narrower streets of London to take the university job here in Chicago. The stretch of the avenue near the foot of this tower—the Magnificent Mile—seemed like a romantic place to bring a new girlfriend at Christmastime, so he and Gail took a walk along it. As he led her into the wind, her scarf kept threatening to fly away. He caught it every time. Each time she laughed harder and drew him closer. There is already a taller tower in the works, to be finished next year, but the project may drag on longer, maybe until 1973.

Now, in the lift, it feels like he's already moving down rather than up as the pressure crushes him, forces him to push his shoulders back, pull his head up, and breathe from his gut.

It is ten past eight when he enters the lounge of a place called the Ninety-Fifth, and sees his brother-in-law, Bobby. Richard steps aside to let a waiter by, then stays there, frozen, in the dark space along the wall. It is Bobby's hair that catches his eye. It glows the same orange as the end of the cigarette Bobby holds up next to it. In certain weather, Bobby's hair curls tight as the tobacco shreds when they burn. He flicks ashes onto the floor, spits into a half-empty glass, shouts, curses, and makes a backstroke-like gesture. He is talking to the bartender, who keeps his head down, arranging and rearranging coasters and bowls of mixed nuts and bottles underneath the bar. Even when Bobby leans forward over the bar and asks for affirmation, the bartender does not look up. Bobby has brought the rough and tumble of the Back of the Yards to the Ninety-Fifth.

If Richard could breathe, he would ask Bobby for a smoke. If he could hold down anything beyond the guilt and grief that he feels rising up inside him now as he searches for Raisa, he would take a seat next to Bobby. He would forget his reasons for coming here and kill an evening with Bobby Conlan.

Richard unbuttons his collar until it splays out to the edges of his shoulders. He wants fashion to cycle back to a time when collars weren't big enough to draw attention. The inside of the collar is wet now, as sweat runs from forehead to sideburns and pools above his clavicle. He looks around. The men's room might make a nice place to hide until this Russian woman who isn't his wife finishes her shift, but Bobby might walk in. It's not worth the risk. Richard wants to board the lift again, drop down to street level, and run home.

He figures that Bobby has been working up to this drunken state since noon, after he put the "Back in Ten" sign on the door of Conlan's Nursery, clicked the lock, and marched to the corner store. He probably threw some crisps in the bag to cover the bottle. Lunch. Bobby is probably tired from the day's lifting and change making, from watering the plants, and from staring through the window. This must be his hard day's night out. He is here because he can't blow all his money at the Rusty Harp or the Broken Chord. He can't shoot the breeze with those guys, can't empty his wallet down to driver's license and draft card. Not there, not tonight, in these hours for private grief. Tonight the Conlans—Bobby and the others, but especially Richard's wife, Gail—are preoccupied with their older sister, Joy, the sudden widow. Gail has not left Joy's side since yesterday.

When Richard sits next to Bobby at the bar, neither of them speaks.

Finally Bobby says, "Look at this place. Nice, huh?" He doesn't lift his head.

"Not bad. Come here often?" Richard says.

"I figure I deserve it." Bobby rolls peanuts around in his palm and then pours a few into his mouth.

"You do."

Bobby looks at Richard with one eye closed. He swallows. "You sure you're not spying on me?"

Though it is a joke, the question hits Richard in the gut. Answers lodge in his throat, and the question tells him he needs a drink. He studies the vodkas that line the wall behind the bar. Each brand is too strong, too dangerous for his blood. When he leans forward to order a gin and tonic, he notices the *Southtown Economist* on the other side of Bobby's arm on the bar. The front page features another fallen soldier.

Bobby rattles his glass until all the ice cubes settle. "Commies killed my brother-in-law, Richard. He grew up down the street. Used to look out for me before I learned how to fight." He pulls harder on his whiskey and then cups it in both hands. "I keep picturing it." He looks into Richard's eyes. His pupils are full with more than drink. "I see some red-blooded Viet Cong sneaking up on Mike while he hid under a tree. Maybe Mikey was sleeping under that tree."

Richard watches Bobby's knuckles turn white. The glass shakes. He puts his hand on Bobby's forearm. It feels like a bundle of taut ropes.

"Maybe it was close range," Bobby says. "In the head, so he'd go fast, or maybe in the stomach, and it took hours. The shooter probably stood over him and watched." Bobby's voice cracks. He wipes his thumb under one eye and makes a fist. He draws in air through his nose until he sits up straight.

Richard finishes his drink.

Bobby orders another round. "Mike was smart, like you. You could have been friends."

Bobby is smart, too. He has a full scholarship to the university where Richard is Dr. Sims, assistant professor of history. In the beginning of the school year, Richard saw quite a lot of him, maybe more than he saw of Gail. But lately Bobby hasn't been hanging around Richard's office or bumping into him on the platform, where they wait for the same train.

All of the Conlans are like that: here one minute with arms outstretched, and then off they go without a warning. This morning Richard's hand searched Gail's side of the bed. In that moment between the last dream and the new day, he froze. Panic surged through his middle. He rolled flat on his back, breathed deep, and woke up alone for the first time in nearly a year. He dropped her suitcase off at the flat upstairs from Conlan's Nursery, above the corroding letters of her family name, and then he opened up shop and manned the till so Gail and Joy could lie in bed for another hour. Joy would not want to lose a day's business, would not want the neighbors to wonder. So for an hour, Richard put on a smile and sold a few carnations until Bobby showed up for his shift.

For most of that time, he looked out the window. He felt guilty for enjoying the stillness on his side of the glass as hospital workers trudged home and factory hands rushed out. Guilty for sipping tea before putting some on for his wife, for enjoying small talk with neighbors. And for making plans to see Raisa.

A familiar woman broke his gaze. She walked along the window, right to left, turning to wave at him. She was a cousin on Gail's mother's side, but he couldn't recall her name. She lived on this block: across and a few doors down.

She stomped her feet on the mat before stepping in, but her boots still spread squares of packed snow across the floor. "They got you running the place, now, huh?" she said.

"Just opening up. Gail needs her rest. Joy, too."

"Sisters need to be together." She touched a leaf on a plant Richard couldn't name. She was either a McCormick or a McCarthy. "When do we get our baby?"

"In a month's time. Mid-April, the doctor said."

"That's right. This is the time to rest." She inspected a terrarium. "The ninth month might as well be the seventh day. All you want is a little peace after your creation. You know, before the chaos starts." She approached the door. "Off to the bakery. God bless."

As she left, Richard smiled and held up his hand in the same static wave he had offered to all customers. Soon she would learn that the chaos had already begun. Upstairs, death and disorder would soon wake from a long, silent night, and her family's cries would bellow down Forty-Fifth Street, command black veils and yellow roses into St. Luke's Cathedral, and continue east, bouncing up off of the lake. He wanted to run out and warn her, in a shout that all the neighbors would hear, but this bit of news was not ready to be broadcast.

When the bartender delivers the next round, Richard asks Bobby how he held up at the shop today.

"Business as usual. Mike's picture won't be in the paper until tomorrow," Bobby says.

"How are the girls?"

"Just stayed upstairs. Didn't come down into the nursery at all."

"Gail feeling sick, is she?"

"Didn't complain."

Richard uses all but his last ten dollars to pay the tab and hands the rest to Bobby. "Catch a cab, all right?"

"You're a good man. Jolly good." Bobby's impression of him is getting better. "Gail knows how to pick 'em." Bobby slaps a hand on Richard's shoulder and then turns toward the lift.

Finally, he is leaving. Richard lets out his breath and watches him go, but after a few steps Bobby turns around.

"What are you doing here anyway?" Bobby says.

The weight on Richard's chest jumps, bounces on his lungs and heart. He checks his watch: half past eight. The tick of the second hand pounds in his head. This beat is not drowned out by the low horn of grief. Guilt is not audible either, but he knows Bobby is watching it color his face.

"This is history." Richard clears his throat and forces a smile. "I wanted to be the first Englishman to reach the top of the city."

Bobby looks away, toward the lake. "Always working."

"Say," Richard says. "How's it going in your Western Civ course?"

"Half over."

"And?"

Bobby takes his lighter out of his pocket and thumbs the trigger. "I'm acing calculus."

It has taken twenty minutes and the chain of hints—Bobby's gestures, the dilated pupils, the tear, the sitting on the stool at all, here, in a place like this—for Richard to figure out that

Bobby has failed his history midterm. He wants to yank his words back, shoot them down ninety-five stories. Bobby is good enough at math to understand that he will lose his scholarship, that his draft number will come up. Time to trade in book and pencil for helmet and weapon. Richard is good enough at reading to know what Bobby wants.

He wants Richard to pull a string or two, but he won't ask. None of the Conlans will ask. They'll give Richard that sad face and tell him he's a good man, that Gail and the baby are lucky to be his. Richard will pull. He'll put in a favor to Bobby's professor. To keep Bobby in school, Richard will put in more time. Bobby is his brother now. Time, Richard is learning, is what brothers give.

Raisa is leading a tour from the elevator to the east window when he sees her. From his chair in front of the north window, he turns to watch her gesture or clasp her hands in front of her skirt. The panic and guilt and grief have settled now that Bobby is out of the building; shame and regret—and relief—have taken up residence inside Richard. The relief is one that comes only from seeing Raisa, from recognizing her shape. He imagines she is saying to the tourists, "Look, over there, beyond the reach of the lights, to the site of the city's first shantytown, to the first dock, the old shipping route."

She escorts the group back to the elevator. When they are gone, she walks to the window in front of him. A few unguided clusters and couples wander around.

They look out at the lake.

"They hired me for the German and French groups," Raisa says. "They needed that, as well as English, of course." She sounds happy.

Richard smiles and clears his throat. "And Russian?" he says.

She looks down, shakes her head once right and once left. "I didn't mention that." It is a whisper. She turns around. "Call me Ruth." It sounds like root, or *russe*.

He wants to send his words underground. He does not want to speak German. He chooses French.

"Raisa, I miss you." It is easy to say this in French.

He stands and moves to a spot behind and a few meters to her left. He sticks his neck out, tries not to look down. The lake has thawed into a blue-black sheet. The moon lights up the floating ice patches. It leads his eyes to no opposite shore, no destination. He wipes the sweat from his palms onto his tweed trousers. *Shhhp*. He smoothes his sideburns, slips his hands into his pockets. *Shhhp*.

"Looks like an ocean," she says.

He steps back from the glass, sits down again, lets the gin work. He wants her to give him only one leaf at a time of whatever that stuff is, the herbs he said he needs, so he'll have an excuse to visit her every night. He wants the chest pains to get worse, as bad as they were before his wedding, so he'll need to call her all the time.

When he first saw Raisa, he had been on the train, on his way to the library. At the Roosevelt stop, he stepped out to let people from the middle of the train car make their exit. When he stepped back in, she held the spot on the pole he'd been holding. He looped a finger around it above her hand. He'd just visited Gail at the nursery, where the scents of lilies and lavender wrapped around him. Now he smelled this woman's hair. She looked at him. He let go of the pole, rocked on his heels.

She squinted. "You have irregular breathing pattern." He thought she sounded German.

"I beg your pardon," he said.

Richard heard a rattle. He looked toward it, to where a man with a seat glanced up from his newspaper and frowned. Two foreigners misunderstanding each other.

She lowered her voice. "Your heart. It beats too fast?"

Richard squirmed to get his arm free. He pulled it toward his chest, felt bones and an empty cavity at the sternum. Nothing beating. "Dunno. I suppose it might."

At the next stop, she squeezed through the crowd and out the door, turned around, and made a strange wave of her hand, a beckoning. He followed her to the end of the platform. She produced a paper sack from her pocket.

"Just herbs," she said. "You can drink it like tea. Free, for you."

"I don't think so." He walked away.

"If you want it, be on same train same time tomorrow."

A week later he could smell her across the car. It was October and still humid. He followed her home, drank her herbal cures. The tightness in his chest eased up.

"Stay," she said. "I'm making supper."

Her husband worked nights. She had no children. Her apartment was cold. He brought her small gifts: nothing much really, just candles or daisies or oils from the hippies outside the market. She did not thank him—she could buy her own flowers and perfumes—but she did not throw his gifts away. Once when he walked out of her washroom, he caught her smelling the flowers, eyes closed, lips curved. She turned toward him and drew in a sharp breath.

He waited.

"Tea?"

While she cooked he drank whatever she made and watched television. He wasn't sure he was being cured of anything, but she had what Gail didn't: experience. She knew how to boil a man's tea, to judge by the slump of the shoulders how much to ask about his day, to use leaves and oils for making it all better. He clicked the dial past news and sports and variety shows until the puppets from *Kukla, Fran and Ollie* came on.

On the last night he stayed later, until the hour before her husband returned. She stroked his neck and pulled his head under her chin. "You deserve this every night. Everyone does."

"I'm getting married soon," he said. "Hopefully I'll get what I deserve." He sprang out of her hold, held himself up by his arms and leaned over her, with one hand on each side of her waist. The sheets felt warm under his palms, warm with her body heat.

"And what is it called in English, the erasing of the first marriage?" she said.

He swallowed the word down, but then it rose up, sliced his throat. "Annulment." He dropped back to his side of the bed. "No, I won't have to do that. She knows, but we're not telling her family or the church about my past. They'd never have it."

Raisa pulled the covers up higher, over her shoulders. "Lucky man."

He climbed onto her again. "Don't ask, don't tell. That's the best way, isn't it now?"

"It is the only way."

"Especially if I'm going to become a Catholic tomorrow, for God's sake." He shook his head. "So after tonight, I won't deserve anything."

She laughed and pulled him closer.

Tonight he studies her profile as the lights touch it through the window. She is so close to the glass. The year has been good to Raisa. She wears her hair down and curly, but it is pinned back in a way that conceals the gray that creeps into blond, and in a way that reveals her face. Her lips are painted pink. If she were to smile and he were allowed to touch her, he could thumb a line all the way from the corners of her mouth up the sharp angle of her cheekbones and stop next to eyes that burn a blue flame. He could hold her face in his hands with his fingertips in the hair behind her ears. Her new hairstyle and her year without him have erased ten years, maybe fifteen. That would bring her down to thirty, so young that they may be mistaken for siblings. Richard and Ruth. A grown-up Hansel and Gretel carrying on in some foreign language.

A tear slides down her face, draws a line from eye to cheek before she wipes it away. She looks across the water. Richard watches her shoulders rise and her head bow.

"Excuse me," she says in English. She walks to the ladies' room.

Groups and couples shuffle toward the elevator. Soon, Richard and Raisa will be alone.

Maybe Raisa isn't crying because of him. Maybe she has had a hard day. Richard won't ask, and she won't complain. He won't either. He won't tell her that his day began at the nursery, because she might ask why. She doesn't want to hear that later, at work, he began the painful transition to a new project—pulling out of the British fur-trade era and throwing himself into a civil-war biography. He won't tell her he spent the morning boxing up a year's work and the afternoon gathering an overview for the next year: north, south, battles, death, and then migration, desertion, rebirth.

While Raisa cries in the restroom, he watches taillights and headlights move up and down Lake Shore Drive. Northbound on the right. Eventually he will have to learn to drive on the right. He and Gail will move to the suburbs, buy a car, a house with a garage. She will want more children and a bigger house farther away from the city. Away from campus and public transit and the Hancock Center.

Raisa's voice sneaks up behind him. "Richard," she says.

He turns. Her face glows.

"The view from in there is the best. Ladies stay a long time. You should see."

She sits two chairs away from him while they watch a couple steal their last looks and saunter away. She gives him a smile that means, *Come here, you.* It is the kind of expression Gail hasn't learned yet. Shame and regret vanish, and whatever's happening in his chest is not crushing. He stands. She leads him by the arm toward the restroom. He laughs and resists, but she pulls him closer, wraps her arm tighter around his.

The south wall of the ladies' room is glass all the way down to the floor. From here, the lake hugs the left side of the city. His eyes jump from white lights of office buildings to museums to the river. The green-black spot, he figures, must be Grant Park, the launch pad for the protests. Farther south is the bottom of the lake: industry, Indiana, colored lights.

He wishes it were earlier, so they could watch the sun dance a finale on the lake, on Buckingham Fountain, on windows and rooftops. Though he wants to know, he doesn't ask her what time the tiny bulbs flicked on over the marina. He squints until each boat's and car's and train's chain of lights blends together. She slips her hand over his on the railing. His eyes shift focus, and he watches their reflection in the window. Her face is still blurry. Only glass stands between them and all that light. He touches it with one finger. It is cold enough to burn him.

He steps back from the window, close to the corner stall. He keeps glancing toward the door, keeps listening.

From under the sink Raisa produces a bundle, wrapped in a homemade blanket. "Open it," she says. "It's for the baby." It is a nice gesture.

He unwraps the blanket. Inside is a puppet of Kukla, from the program they used to watch. On their first night together she had shown him a blond doll she was sewing for a neighbor. "My first *kukla*," she said. "You know, a doll." He asked if she had seen the Kukla puppet on *Kukla, Fran and Ollie*. And so their ritual began.

And this is how it ends? By unveiling the product of what they once had? She has reduced those warm nights in the dead of his first foreign winter, to Kukla, a little balding man with black eyebrows pointing directly up. Grief shoots guilt out now, out of the ninety-fifth floor with a brassy blast of anger.

He knows now that she kept watching the show without him, because the doll is spot on for the original, and oddly, Kukla looks a lot like Mike, like that soldier portrait on the wall that Richard sees when he looks at anything today. He throws the blanket back over it. Maybe Raisa has become a feminist, and giving a male puppet to a baby girl is making a statement. America can do that to women.

"He looks like the real thing," Richard says. "She'll love it."

"You don't like it. Forgive me. I just thought . . . "

"It's okay, really. It was kind of you."

"What will you name your new daughter?"

He starts to breathe clearly now. Raisa, he wants to say. "Fran," he says.

She laughs. "Really?"

He loosens his grip on the bundle. "Why not? She's got the second most comforting voice in America."

She smiles and lowers her head. She is flattered. He takes both of her hands. Together they hold the bundle. It brushes against the railing and the glass.

"She'll learn to sing straight away," he says.

"Instead of crying?"

"Yes," he whispers.

She steps away and reaches under the sink again, behind a pipe. He notices a run starting in the ankle of her stockings. He watches the rip spread upward and begin to trace a mile of leg. He turns back to the window and his eyes travel down South Lake Shore, to the point where the Eisenhower cuts in.

"Your pain is back?" she says.

"Come again?"

She stands up and holds out a plastic bag with large capsules inside. "The herbs got expensive. These are better. The bartender here sells them. You'll forget your pain in no time."

He opens his hand. She shakes out two blue pills.

It is past nine when she tells him she's glad he called, glad he came to see her. She needs to talk. She's had trouble keeping it all together, but she's been making more time for her husband. They're not getting any younger, she says. She thumbs behind them, to indicate the north side of the city. "He is home, cooking supper for me. I teach him. He's getting better."

He wants her to say this in French, wants her smile to look foreign if it's got to be for someone other than him. He studies her hand, follows the bending and bulging green veins until they disappear at the knuckles. The skin is folding, settling in irreversible patterns of lines.

"I'll walk you to the train," he says.

They descend to the street without a word. She is in a rush, and he is inching along. He motions for her to go underground ahead of him. The temperature has plummeted, and now he misses his scarf.

"Thanks again," he says, and holds up the blanketed bundle.

She squeezes his hand, turns, and hurries down the stairs.

When Richard's train approaches the platform, it does not slow down or speed up but slides south out of the black tunnel for a moment before entering another. It rolls under the fluorescent lights until its shadow on the ceiling grows larger, curves and expands forward, and reaches the platform ahead of the train. Bodies step off. Bodies step on. The conductor's voice is under water, as if the snow has drained into the tunnels and turned the subway into a submarine. This is a southbound Englewood-Jackson Park train, the voice says. Southbound toward the Dan Ryan Expressway.

The light inside the train does not cast shadows and does not dim for pockmarked skin or wrinkled trousers or mismatched socks under crossed legs. In the tunnels, the inside light is less merciful to the preachers who move from car to car. Often Richard has imagined a northbound commute home on the Ravenswood line or even out west on the suburban train, any route that stays above ground. But tonight he knows he will stay in the Back of the Yards. He will wait on the Dan Ryan platforms with street preachers and dice throwers and pill pushers and girls who slip phone numbers into the pockets of his overcoat. Richard presses his hand to the glass. If it is cold or hot he doesn't notice.

The subway shoots like a torpedo from Chicago Avenue to Grand, under the skyscrapers and aboveground to Roosevelt. Once the train surfaces, on this first night of spring, snow blankets the tar-paper roofs of buildings that huddle close to the tracks. Farther out it covers the tops of letters on signs above the Lucky Dragon restaurant and above Comiskey Park so that each letter in "White Sox" is covered appropriately. Everything special stays hidden until spring comes, when doors and windows open to draw the sun in.

Groundhog Day is one of the stranger American phenomena. The man next to Richard elbows him each time he turns a page and snaps his evening news. "That little shit didn't have a shadow this year. So what's this?" The man slaps the weather report and sweeps an arm into the aisle toward the snow outside.

Richard laughs through his nose and shakes his head. The pills have loosened him up. In his best impression of Bobby he says, "No kiddin'."

"Out Like a Lion" is the second-page headline on the man's newspaper. Lions, lambs, groundhogs. A rodent in his hole decides when winter ends. The lowest of creatures casts shadows or doesn't, dictates the next two months in the future of the most intelligent species on Earth.

Richard comes home to a cold house. Before he turns up the furnace or the lights, he sees it as he did on his first night alone there, after he'd rented it from Joy and Mike. It is furnished in dark woods. Chairs and hutches are networks of cylinders and rectangles. There are few curves or carvings, but they are strong woods, heirloom pieces, the kind that yield surprising worth if you bother to appraise them. The hutches hold crystal, china with green flourishes, teapots, and trinkets. A shaft of moonlight reveals a pattern in the tablecloth. It paints the white lace blue, the oak and maple black.

In the basement, Richard digs through a box marked "History Books." He pulls out a picture frame, takes a handkerchief from his pocket, and uses it to dust the glass. "Iris," he says. His daughter, the secret child from the secret failed marriage, stands with her favorite gift at her second birthday party: the dragon puppet Richard's mother made. It was a likeness of a character from *Kukla, Fran and Ollie*. Once she had opened it, his father slipped his hand in the dragon's back, opened the mouth, and they all sang, "Ollie Ollie Ollie." Before Richard snapped the photo, Iris had giggled so much he had to ask her to stop and smile for the picture. "Daddy, look!" she said, and held out the gift. She laughed so hard her eyes folded into her face, her mouth stayed open, and her hair bounced below her newspaper hat. Her mother—Richard's first wife—had left it curly and down so that it seemed to grow sideways out of her head like a mess of golden yarn, like his hair. It made him giggle too, so much that the camera shook. She stood off-kilter in the frame, at once offering the gift to him and sliding away, tumbling over.

Only a few months until he sees her again. Every summer, he goes to England to visit Iris. That's the deal he made with her mother. There's the option for Iris to visit him in Chicago, but as soon as he met Gail, he knew there was no way. He can't risk the Conlans and everyone at St. Luke's seeing proof that he'd already ruined one marriage. Last summer when he took Gail to London with him, they told everyone they were going to visit his parents. Richard hopes the new baby won't keep him and Gail homebound this summer, because he doesn't want to miss a chance to see Iris.

Richard packs her picture back into the box. He phones Gail in the flat above the shop. He waits. Too many rings for such light sleepers. He walks the one block west, two north, and up the stairs. Halfway there, he realizes that he grabbed the Kukla doll on the way out, and he tucks it under his arm. Without a sound he slips the key in. The lock turns too easily. The light is on in the kitchen, a single bulb on a chain. He tiptoes the six steps to the bedroom. The bed is empty. Gail's suitcase sits in a corner, forgotten.

A fist pounds on the door. He peers through the hole and sees the cousin. McCormick, McCarthy. He gulps, catches his breath. In. Out. Another pound. He turns the knob and pulls.

A white cloud rises from her mouth. "I looked out my window and I saw you run up the stairs and I says, 'It's another break-in.'" Her shoulders and chest heave. "But then, 'No, it's him,' I says. 'The Englishman.'" She huffs, and another cloud carries the question. "They're all at the hospital, so why are you here?"

"Sorry, just popping by. Are they—?" He points behind himself, to the suitcase. "It's time then, is it?"

"Soon as the water broke, *shhhp*." She sweeps an arm out. "Off they went. Hours ago."

He darts to the cupboard and grabs cash from a hidden coffee can.

She steps inside. "I'll turn out the lights and lock up." She hands him the suitcase and the doll. "No time like the present, Daddy."

He runs down the steps, along Forty-Fifth to Racine. He can feel the cold in his fingertips now. He pumps his arms, full with doll and suitcase, as he runs south toward Forty-Seventh. There will be a cab. There has to be. His lungs burn and he wheezes. The suitcase wobbles and yanks at his wrist, slaps his knee.

He doubles over in front of the church, his church. In a few days, Father Duggan, who is Mike's uncle, will say all the right things in there. Michael didn't deserve this. No one does, Father will say, especially not this husband, son, brother, friend, soldier. They will not have much of a wake without a body. They'll just have a flag and a picture surrounded by flowers, but by the end of it all, in Mike's parents' house or in the back of the Rusty Harp, the older men will all sing their Irish mourning song about meeting the soldier again in sunshine or shadow. They will teach Richard the words.

In case Richard had trouble finding the words to direct the cab driver, he and Gail had mapped out the route to the hospital. She had scribbled phone numbers of cab hire companies at the top. Hell if he remembers now where they left the map.

He walks into the wind, finds a steady pace, and consults the maps in his mind. Political, topographical, pre-Columbian, ancient Greek and Latin. He hangs each one in front of him on the wall of snow. He counts the lines on the time zone map between Greenwich Mean and Central Standard. This is difficult because he hasn't called home in a while. He tries to recall whether it's daylight saving season yet, and the difference makes him feel even farther away.

It helps a bit to know that in an hour, his father will wake up, slump over his eggs, open his stationers' shop, and sell a few papers, as he says. His mother will send more stationery to Richard and Gail, emblazoned with *S*. Write more letters, she will say. It is what she always says. Richard will fill the pages and send them back to London with pictures of the baby. His mother will clip them to the fridge, next to the photos of Iris, and then his mother will bring her hand to her mouth. "Sisters," she will say in a whisper.

At Forty-Seventh and Halsted, Richard spots a cab. It's late on a Wednesday, and it's snowing. He is lucky. He does not deserve this rescue. The car grows as it cuts through diagonal sheets of snow. The headlights come into focus. Now that Richard is still, he feels the wetness. The snow has drenched the space where his scarf should be, pasted his trousers against his shins, and seeped into his stockings. He feels it at the ankles, but the toes are numb.

The hospital is a bit outside the driver's range, but it's on his way home. His skin is the color of Gail's eyes, the color of rich soil under patches of snow.

His voice is gravel. "This your first kid?" he says.

It is a simple question: yes or no? It tells Richard to just choose one, because this is just small talk with a stranger. His memory calls up the right answer, and then the acceptable answer grabs it on the way out, strangles it. While he coughs, he watches snow curl around a traffic light, a telephone pole, but all he can see is Iris's photo in the basement box.

Finally he gets the word out. "Yes. Pardon me, but I'm a bit nervous. Thank you for picking me up. It's kind of you."

"This is America. Got to make a dollar."

The voice on the radio introduces King Oliver's Band, and the driver turns up the volume. "Canal Street Blues" helps Richard relax. He is ashamed of this calm he feels during Gail's pain. He is ashamed to be late. Research, he will tell her. *I had to conduct historical research at the top of the city.*

King Oliver helps Richard steady his breathing. Out the window, vans and trucks and economy cars race by Richard and the driver and King Oliver.

"Say, man, would you call this jazz or blues?" Richard says.

The driver pauses. He corrects the wheel over the metal grates on the bridge. Richard cringes and shrinks down out of his rearview. He wants the driver to reverse and drive over his words, back and forth a few times, then pull over and help him kick them into the river.

"Well, I always thought it's jazz," the driver says. He shrugs. "But old Oliver went and called it blues, didn't he? Maybe it's both, or maybe it's just the blues." He tries to catch Richard's eye in the mirror. "So, you hoping for a son?"

"Any kind'll do." Richard swallows, clutches the doll. The blanket is soaked through.

"You think your kid will look like his pop?"

"Hope not, for his sake."

They laugh.

"Have you got a son?" Richard says.

"Two boys. A girl, too. People say the first boy's my double. Don't know if that's true, but I like hearing it." He looks straight ahead and smiles.

"Your kids watch television?"

"Sure. All the time."

The driver drops him off at emergency. Richard is a few dollars short. He tucks what he has into the bundled doll and holds it over the front seat. "My best to your family," he says.

The driver turns toward Richard's offering, swiveling his shoulders and neck farther than he has to. "Yours, too."

His legs and lungs are heavy, but Richard passes the elevator by. He takes the stairs two at a time. He stops and heaves on the landing between three and four west. It is a considerable effort to breathe deep and stand tall.

When Richard enters the lobby, Gail's father is leaning against the nurses' desk, smiling at a girl in uniform. He looks up at Richard. It's been a hard day, and Richard isn't making it any easier.

"Richard," he says. It sounds like a question. "You made it. You just missed the calls Bobby put in to your office."

Richard looks at Bobby, who hovers over a paper coffee cup. Bobby meets Richard's eyes for an instant and shrugs. He is giving Richard time to explain.

Gail's grandmother is concentrating on a ball of white yarn she holds in both hands. She holds it just loose enough to feed into the blanket Gail's mother knits. There is very little slack on the line. Gail's mother, Mrs. Conlan, is forty-five. Raisa is forty-five. Gail has urged him to call her mother Mum, or at least Marian. Marian and Robert. Mum and Dad.

"I had some field research up north," Richard says. Mrs. Conlan stops knitting. The grandmother does not look up. "I should have left a phone number with Gail. I'm sorry. I'm really sorry, for everything." He bows his head, and then it comes: the tears, the shaking across the back of his shoulders, the tightness in the sternum like a cough that lasts all winter. He looks up but does not lift his head. "I'm sorry, Mum."

Mrs. Conlan stands up, crying as she walks toward him. Gail looks the most like her: white skin, black hair, eyes like dark wood, full lips, small frame, all in soft curves. Mostly dominant traits. She hugs him for the first time since his wedding day. In that final squeeze before releasing him, her knitting needles dig into the space between his shoulder blade and spine.

Mr. Conlan clears his throat, and his wife pulls away from Richard. "Get in there, son," he says. "You're about to be a father."

Joy is standing in Gail's room. She doesn't occupy her hands with needles or newsprint. She is letting Gail crush them. "It won't be much longer," she says.

Richard does not want to disturb the sisters. He stands in front of the door and back a bit, outside of Joy's view. In the throes of labor, Gail looks just as calm as she had on the day they met.

It was the day he moved into Joy and Mike's house. Gail had shown up at the front door with oatmeal cookies.

"My grandmother says I shouldn't have made these," she'd told him. "She says English people don't like the same kinds of cookies we like, but it's all I know how to make."

"Well, you're in luck," he said. "I'm a misfit." He let her in.

She looked around and kept saying what a nice house it must be to live in. "Joy and Mikey will have a nice family here, when he gets home from his tour," she said. "When they move back in, maybe you can rent the apartment above our flower shop."

A nurse walks to the door of Gail's room and opens it. "Mr. Sims?" she says.

Joy sees Richard now and nods for him to come in.

Gail doesn't seem to notice the call of Richard's name, but when she opens her eyes and gasps for air, she sees him. He rushes toward a sloppy embrace. They shake.

"We missed you," she says.

They let him stay. He stays through Gail's pushing, thrashing, and sweating. A doctor's voice announces each step forward: a dilation, a head, a shoulder emerging. Birth, and severance, before cries of relief.

A boy. Bald, pink, screaming.

They let Richard stay through the morning. He waits for each time the baby returns, and each time he whispers an apology for wishing this boy, his boy, had been a girl. He searches the face for his mother's pointed nose, his father's cleft chin. He inspects the head for a strand of black hair among the white fuzz. My son has blond hair, he will say in his next letter home, and eventually, My son has learned to walk, to speak, to read. He thought his first mother-in-law had said some babies start out with blue eyes, like his. Like Iris's. My son looks just like my daughter. He had never held her like this, in these moments between asleep and awake, not on the day she was born.

He extends the baby out and up. Every muscle in Richard's body relaxes, and the baby dips in his hold, but Richard has the back of the child's head in his hand. Tears pour down his cheeks, trickle out and soak into his sideburns when he smiles. "Ollie Ollie Ollie," he sings.

WHITE RABBIT

In the main floor lobby of the ad agency where Uncle Bobby is a top seller, he gives Ollie a quick noogie and then plants a hand on the back of Ollie's head. Uncle Bobby's hair is the color of McDonald's orange drink here in the bright lights and in the sun that filters through the tall windows. Ollie wonders if, when Uncle Bobby wakes, the curls are as puffed up and unruly as the white-blond mess of his own hair every morning.

"You know, Richard, he'd learn a hell of a lot more if he dropped out of that school," his uncle says to his father.

"Watch it, Bob," Ollie's dad says. "You're the only one he listens to."

Uncle Bobby tightens his grip and says to Ollie, "We'll have fun today, huh?" On the last word, he rocks Ollie back and forth, to rattle the bones, to snap the neck.

"Your mother won't know you were here," Ollie's dad says. "Do we have an understanding?"

Ollie nods more than necessary. His mother thinks he is spending the day at his dad's work.

"Don't touch *anything*. Just get all your homework done."

Uncle and nephew wave goodbye to Dad, and then they have the elevator car to themselves. Uncle Bobby presses the close-door button, but not any of the number buttons.

"Look," he says. "I don't care what you did this morning, and I'm not mad at what you done at school yesterday. Shit, I'd keep Miranda away from St. Luke's every day if your aunt would let me. You, too. It's a regular prison."

"I'm free from that place for two days," Ollie says, "but I'm so dead."

On the thirtieth floor, they pass through two rows of ringing phones and polite voices asking who's calling. The lighting is soft. Yellow ribbons hug pencil jars. Plants spill over the sides of desks, where stars and stripes bandanas choke teddy bears.

Ollie knows why everyone tied them on today. He heard all about it on the radio yesterday while his mom drove him to school:

As we mark the 150th day of the Iran Hostage Crisis, we have news that President Carter sent a secret rescue fleet of Marine pilots to save the American captives inside the US embassy. We regret to report, however, that two of the aircraft collided en route to Tehran, resulting in eight men down. The surviving personnel had to abort the mission. Saving the hostages now looks like an even steeper climb for the president on his difficult path to reelection.

The radio announcer didn't even say a prayer. A moment of silence, he said. And in that break in the noise, Ollie heard the echo of the announcer's last words in the whir of passing cars along the Eisenhower Expressway: No way to reach the center of all that sand, so choppers had to turn around and that's when the crash happened, when the heroes killed each other.

Along with the yellow ribbons, miniature flags stand at attention everywhere on the thirtieth floor, plus one flag that is too big for a desktop. The pole is not thick enough for the opening of the vase, so its flag dips and folds. A lady with a side ponytail pops up from behind it.

"Why isn't he in school?" she says.

Uncle Bobby doesn't slow down as he answers. "Holy day. They celebrate all the saints down there. Ones you never heard of." He jerks on the brakes and points toward the inside of a room. He pulls out a chair not at the big desk but at a round table, an island in the middle of navy blue carpet.

"Just sit right here. You got your candy dish, your magazines, and a Rubik's Cube I need some help with. I been moving the stickers around." Uncle Bobby peels Ollie's book bag and coat off his shoulders, sets them on another chair. "I was hoping you could make me look like a regular genius instead of a cheating pansy."

"Easy cheese," Ollie says, but he won't touch the cube. He knows Bobby had the thing done in six hundred Mississippi, and they both know it would take Ollie all week.

"Easy for you, Einstein." Bobby turns to leave, but then he stops and turns back. "After my meeting we'll do lunch." He walks to the center island and offers his fists. "Pick a hand."

Ollie makes his choice. Bobby's right wrist bones roll. Nothing. The left wrist: nothing. Ollie knows this trick. He reaches into Bobby's sleeve, under the cuff link and starched cotton.

"Nah!" Bobby says. He reaches into Ollie's back pocket, and shows the find: a matchbox with the name of Ollie's favorite restaurant, The Oasis. "You play your cards right, maybe we can go there tomorrow, too."

"But I'm on punishment both days."

"Not when you're with me." Bobby picks up his papers and his fancy pen and makes for the door. "Don't think of it as suspension. It's a two-day vacation." He rushes out.

Ollie touches things in Uncle Bobby's office. He reads *Gentleman's Quarterly*. He runs his thumb along a signed picture of blond ladies in rabbit costumes. They wear fishnet tights.

He tries to feel relaxed and vacationy, but he can't. At the window, instead of looking out toward the other buildings, Ollie looks straight down. He counts cars on the street. A foot hangs out of a passenger window, a police flasher winks. Red, blue, red. It's the tail end of April, the first tease of summer. Everyone wants to break free, but everyone knows freedom is something far away, because in Chicago there is no spring.

Ollie steps backward, toward the center of the room. It isn't the office in *Bewitched* where the man in the tie tilts back in his leather chair and kicks his wingtips onto the big desk, but it is a space bigger than Ollie's bedroom, and it does have a swively chair and paperweights and a black phone with twenty-two buttons. On the walls, posters hang in frames. They advertise chewing gum, headache medicine, bottles of pop.

In Bobby's chair, Ollie swivels left, right, back to center. His feet sway. He'll feel better once he thinks of a new direction for his report on human miracles, the Houdini report he'll present when he's allowed to go back to school. He'll start by announcing that the Great Mystifier, the King of Handcuffs, was so hungry as a young amateur that he had to eat rabbits for dinner. Ollie hopes the class won't say, Big deal, everybody did that in the old days.

He writes that down, but then he remembers what Sister Mary Smelly Pits has said. "*New miracles*, Oliver. The report has to be a current events story. Don't waste our time with old tales." The name of their religion book, after all, is *New Life*. In it, Ollie does the commandment crosswords and searches for letters that spell out sins. V-a-n-i-t-y, t-h-e-f-t. Problems that God needs us to fix ourselves, when He's tired of saving us.

Among Uncle Bobby's family photos, Ollie sees himself. He and Bobby last summer in an open-book frame: on the left page, they hold up a huge fish, and on the right they're buried in sand.

Ollie sits on the floor with his homework and ponders the miracle: Harry Houdini could hold his breath for three minutes. Chained, wrapped, or boxed up, he always escaped. Before that, others bound themselves, too. Steve Brodie had himself tied up and jumped off a bridge. He surfaced, sure, but he wasn't under for long. And not even Mark Spitz can make it through one hundred Mississippi. Houdini was the only genius at trapping himself.

He considers the variables. What if Houdini had a chemistry set like the one Uncle Bobby gave Ollie? Would he blow stuff up under water to keep himself busy during those three long minutes?

If Sister Mary Smelly Pits opens her big mouth and mentions the great magician's final, failed attempt, if she points out that he drowned trying to show off, Ollie will remind her that Harry Houdini deceived even God by magically changing who he was. This is one trick Ollie can explain. He writes it down: *Poof! The Rabbi Weisz becomes Weiss and soon, his son Erik, or really Ehrie, turns into Harry Houdini, a big white rabbit.*

At school, Ollie loves hearing biblical stories of escape and rescue, loves the way Sister tells them with all the roaring and gnashing, all the knee-slapping humor you could ask for in a tragedy, but they're not the same. Just last week, she belted out the tale of Daniel and the lion during the language arts period, while the class wrote letters to the hostages in Iran. Even though the story didn't have a lot of cool tricks, it was exciting enough to distract Ollie from his imagining of one particular hostage, who looked like his sister would look if she'd been born alive instead of dead and then grown into a real person and worn white silky blindfolds and cuffs. Pale skin, midnight hair. It was a very pretty girl he pictured, even though his dad had told him that all the girls had been let out of the embassy. Women, the hostage takers said, can't possibly be spies, so they can go back to the land of the free. What his dad didn't tell him was where his sister went, and if she was finally free, too.

Ollie colored in the flag and filled in the blanks on the Hostage Letter Worksheet:

April 20, 1980

Dear Hostage,

How are you? My name is _____. I am in the fourth
grade at St. Luke's School in Chicago, Illinois. I am ___ years old
and I like to play _____. Every night I pray for your safety.
When I found out about your capture, I felt very _____.

Sister let them close with either "God loves you" or "Never
give up," but Ollie wanted to be different. "Can you see through
the blindfold?" he wrote. "Are you still alive?"

Hallway sounds distract him now: fancy shoes clap at their
own arrival, slacks swish and *vip*. There are voices, too. "What's
new with the Stroh's account?" "Looking good, Joe." "Any messages, Pam?" "New perfume? Mmm. New indeed." It sounds
like the man is talking down the woman's neck.

Ollie opens the book. The average human can stop breathing
under water for ninety seconds. A pack of East German Olympic
swimmers have set more recent records, but those new revelations
won't count to Sister, because this is an assignment about human miracles, and Communists are not human. Therefore, no human can measure up. Except. Guys who try out to become Navy
SEALs get eliminated if they pop their heads up for air before a
million minutes go by. They are what Ollie refers to in his report
as true escape artists. During their underwater missions, no one
will ever see their bodies or know the might of their lungs.

An old lady sticks her head into the office. Yellow makeup
on her eyes, block-shaped earrings. "Why are you sitting on the
floor? Didn't you find anything interesting to play with in your
Uncle Bob's desk?"

"Haven't looked," Ollie says.

She crosses her arms and scans the room, like Bobby's office is a haunted house. "Come with me," she says. Scratchy gray polyester pants stretch across her bottom.

She shows him her workspace—that's what she calls it—and lifts up big pictures of her dog, her fat husband, fat son at his graduation. He holds a rolled-up paper wand. Big deal.

The theme of her workspace is Snow White. A family of plush figures flanks the dark-haired girl in the big dress: birds and rabbits and all her dwarf boyfriends. Because Ollie is on his best behavior, he doesn't ask why an old lady would collect dolls and bunnies and miniature men.

At the dwarves' feet is a stack of flag bandanas.

"Tell me about these bandanas," Ollie says.

"Oh, those handkerchiefs? I hand 'em out to the other girls." She smiles, and there's metal between her teeth.

He picks up the secretary's front page section of the *Chicago Sun-Times*. The headline is not as large or as bold as it was yesterday, but it still spells out trouble in Tehran.

She grabs the newspaper, slams it into a drawer. "Don't you worry about a thing. Inside the embassy anything can happen, sure. It is not such a safe island. A bomb in a mailbox, a spy in the bathroom. Who knows?" She taps a finger hard on the desk and bounces it up, shakes it. "But if our hockey team can beat the Russians on the ice, we can get our guys out of the sand."

Next she shows him how she processes and files the new business. Yawn. When she's not looking, Ollie stands with his back to the dwarves and slides bandanas into his jeans pockets.

"Happy days, you bet," she says. "Your Uncle Bob's handshake closes every deal." She has a faraway grin, like his mom's when she gushes about Ollie's good grades, good conduct.

The phone cuts her off, and her voice rises into hello and yessir and how can I help you?

Ollie slips two fingers into the drawer and picks out the newspaper. He stuffs that treasure up the back of his shirt. Only

Snow White witnesses his crime. And the seven little pansies. And their snickering animal friends.

It's rude of the secretary to make Ollie wait while she's on the phone. He has work to do, too. He slips yellow ribbons off of drawer handles and ties one in Snow White's hair. Then he pulls her wrists together. He loops and loops.

Yesterday afternoon at school it was parachute day for his cousin Miranda's kindergarten gym class, which meant the teacher would make each kid run under it while the rest of the class fanned it up. What if Miranda tripped, fell, got the wind knocked out of her in the darkness under that parachute, and the stampede of other kids padded her down, into the wood floor? He had to save Miranda from the parachute, so he'd scooped her up on the playground at lunchtime and led her into the janitor's closet.

"Look," he told her. "When I was your age, I had to do the same shit. Don't let the gym teacher fool you."

From a shelf he pulled down silk scarves, which were really handkerchiefs, for juggling or other tricks. On the shelves was not just the magic stuff the nuns had taken from Ollie so many times, but other kids' yo-yos and Rubik's Cubes. Puzzles, too. The lost with no hope of rescue or the stuff that nuns held ransom from troublemakers. Frozen assets of criminals.

He tied one of the longer scarves around Miranda's head. With smelly wool blankets, he tucked her into the laundry cart, or whatever it was. Some kind of bin. Because this was different from the parachute. This was a different type of rescue.

Ollie climbed in and wrapped the chain of scarves around him and Miranda, around their backs, at the waist. And then came the silence, like the quiet under the parachute, except this was a trick he knew how to undo. He wanted to teach her how to disappear. He leaned back, tied the last scarf around his own eyes. Everything disappeared. Then, a bright flash through eyelids and silk. He pulled the blindfold up. First a yellow wedge of light appeared against the wall, and then it opened into an arc, letting light flood into all the corners.

Scene: a boy and his girl cousin in the janitor's closet, skipping school. Frowning nuns in the hall and a "What-do-you-think-you're-doing-young-man?" Frantic teacher, principal, mother. Two days suspension. Silent ride home. Dark television. Plunk of ceramic bowl onto wooden dinner table, ping of silver scrapes. Loud chewing.

With the chains and straitjackets, Houdini vanished. Poof, gone. Sometimes you can find him on the news, in the face of a prisoner who broke out or died trying. Same light in the eyes, a hungry stare. And when you're detained in your room until you're ready to come out and act your age young man, when you're so bored you start to see things, you look up and He's hanging right there, on the wall above your bed. He's a sideshow, an amazing feat of strength. Blood runs over His feet.

A slap on his arm. "Cut that out!" the secretary hisses. Next to her mouth, she's covering the phone's receiver.

Ollie lets go of the yellow ribbons and frees Snow White.

The secretary hangs up the phone, yanks Ollie back into Uncle Bobby's office, and slams the door.

On the back of Bobby's door is a calendar picture of a hot air balloon over some hilly place. It isn't an ad for anything. There's just some verse under it about resisting temptation and a caption that says, "George Washington National Forest." The balloon is a bright white sail in a blue sky: a sight that is supposed to make people happy, but to Ollie it's scary. Because if you don't keep the flame going, your ceiling deflates and smothers you as you sink.

This is why Ollie wanted to protect Miranda. The rule with the parachute game is that the gym teacher makes you sit on a certain color of construction paper taped down around the outside. Then everyone starts flapping, making waves. When it's your turn to run under the parachute, you can't stop until you find your home color, your match. When Ollie was in kindergarten, the gym teacher walked them each to their square: Lara to the first orange, Gavin to the other. "That's who you run to," she said. And so on with ten colors, ten pairs. But there were twenty-one bodies, and she forgot Ollie. "Shit," she said. She took off her hot pink sweatshirt and tossed it on the ground. "Here. It's your color."

Outside the office door now, the secretary's voice rises and falls in a conversation with another lady. Soon their words disappear down the hall. Ollie eases open the door, looks both ways before he crosses. And then. His feet barely touch down as he bolts toward the secretary's workspace and his hair whips like a chopper blade and his arms are the wings of Houdini's daredevil biplane over the desert and he crashes into the desk, where Snow White waits for the prince to save her. He closes his eyes, braces himself for a heavy hand on his shoulder, for someone to nail him, and he reaches out and he grabs, because heroes need good timing. Get in there, scoop up the hostage, save the fair queen from a life of small men and creepy animals with staring problems. Plush fabric in his hands, sweaty hands now as he whips around, and no time to stuff the hostage up his shirt as he flies back to his safe island. He slams the office door. He lifts the hostage, holds it out in front of his belly. No midnight hair, no snowy skin. Just pansy rabbit ears, pansy rabbit fur. Ollie did not save the queen, but this will have to do.

In his kindergarten gym class, once the silk parachute was rolling and bubbling, and the gym teacher was shouting out names one at a time, each kid skipped or sprinted through to their match on the other side. Ollie pumped from his wrists, his elbows, and when she shouted "up high," he raised his arms. He hoped the parachute would billow high enough to block him from her view. The silk's flap and whir grew louder. A pounding came from deep under his sweater, in his ears, and in his throat. Her voice cut through the waves: "Oliver's turn!"

He let go. He ducked in. It was an ice cave, a time machine, his own personal cloud. The whistle blew. "Crocodile crawl. Everybody drop!" So they all sat around the edge, and then the ceiling fell and the bubbling and rippling died down, because she wanted Ollie to be the first to get down low, to have the least air, the shortest line of sight, and no color to call home. He inched, he grunted, he felt his shoelaces slip apart. *Just get to the other side, out of the igloo*, he thought. The janitor had barely finished mopping before class started, and the floors were wet. Ollie's hands slid, and he breathed the clean floor smell until his nose burned, and his eyes welled up, and the silk parachute stuck to the sweat on the back of his neck.

On his back, and then on his side, curled in a ball, the silk and the chemicals sucked him in. At first he clapped his mouth shut, and his brain gave his heart the red light, but it kept racing. Light filtered through the silk and the other kids' giggles were underwater sounds. "Come out, come out, wherever you are," one of them sang. The teacher barked, "Stop joking around, Oliver! Your turn is over." I'll try, I'm sorry, he couldn't say, because there was no air to make the apology. There's no way to repent when you don't have anywhere to go. It was just him on the pink square. No match, and he couldn't claim the place where he started, because it was just a cotton sheet with holes for arms and head, and it belonged to somebody else. The sounds faded and the chemicals stopped bullying his nose, and under the white silk everything went black, and he found his destination, in that space when his sister was still alive but not yet born. When she was tied up, blind, drowning.

Ollie hooks a safety pin into the rabbit the way Uncle Bobby taught him to nail a trout. And then he holds it out, lets it hang. Because when you're suspended, after a while you forget your feet are dangling, that the blood's rushing down, and you learn how to move, to breathe, while everything inside you is still.

With one hand he pulls the matchbox out of his pocket, and with the other he removes the pin and pets the rabbit between the ears. "Brave little boy," he says. With the bandanas, he binds the rabbit's paws and blindfolds him. The rest of Snow White's colony is out there pretending no one is missing and nothing is wrong, still whistling while the secretary works.

Under Bobby's desk, Ollie finds a wastepaper bin. Behind it is a rectangular glass bottle. Mostly full. Ollie knows its shape, its label. It's the same brand of whiskey Bobby always brings to the house. Ollie unscrews the cap. He sets the bound hostage into the bin and drops the last handkerchief over its ears and head.

Just when he's about to pour the alcohol in and strike the match, Uncle Bobby's feet and voice enter the room.

"Ollie Ollie oxen free!" he says. "Where are you at?"

Ollie pops up and sits in the swively chair. He leaves the whiskey and matches under the desk.

Bobby waves Ollie out of the chair so he can sit in it. "Hide and seek, huh?"

He leans back in his throne and speed talks about his next deal, the big chase for the highest-winning TV commercial spot. "My next meeting starts in five. I need to close with the Jimmer, a guy who sells ad time for this new *Nightline* show. He'll be here any minute, right here, shaking hands with you and me. He knows some hotshots in cable TV, says he can get me straight to them." Uncle Bobby shakes a cigarette out of his pack. He doesn't notice anything at his feet. Phew.

The secretary will be back soon. Ollie wants to split. "Why can't we meet him somewhere else?"

Bobby holds his cigarette with two fingers and points it at Ollie. "When you make an important friend, you invite him to your house, understand? This office is my house, and a deal with *Nightline* is golden." In one motion, he pulls the ashtray from its perch next to the reading lamp, takes the matchbox from it, and lights up. "'Cause if Carter makes his next hostage statement on there, that time slot's gonna take off, and you know what that means." He blows smoke into the lamp and counts on his hand, starting with his pinky. "More viewers choking down Bufferin, and Pepsi." Another drag, another finger. "And smoking more Camels. Yeehaw!"

A young lady in a short skirt walks in and hands Uncle Bobby a note. Bobby makes a face that starts out as a smile, then gets stiff, official.

"Damn," Bobby says. "Change of plans. Gotta make a house call." He flips the note along his knuckles the way he does for card tricks. "We'll swing by the Jimmer's house on the way to lunch. I got to close this deal with him today."

"I'm hungry now."

Bobby stands up, so Ollie stands up. He grabs Ollie by the neck again and leads him out the door. "Complain again and you'll starve."

The company car has electric windows. Ollie commands them: down, now up. He stops them halfway. Through the glass, the bottom half of Ollie's view is a blur of cement and occasional green patches. The naked top half is glimmering skyscrapers and signs, and then, farther south, boarded-up houses and going-out-of-business banners. And soon here he and Bobby are, a Conlan and a Sims in a black Lincoln, rolling right down Halsted Street as if Mr. President himself is buckled into the backseat with Miss America.

Bobby chews on his toothpick as he explains the next big thing: cable television. Soon, he says, *Bonanza* won't have to shoot from TV towers along the river downtown and out to all the rabbit ears in Naperville. "It'll burrow through the banks," he says. Through black sand, it will flatten worms and overturn rocks, rub tree roots raw until they strangle it, and arrive on your screen without the wavy stripes. And through that same cable comes Pass Sports and news from Canada and X-rated movies. "Pretty soon, Ollie. Everybody will watch cable. It'll be a godsend."

As they near the Back of the Yards neighborhood, a police car pulls up next to them at a red light. Ollie looks over to his left, past Bobby. "Is that Officer Joe?" he says. Officer Joe used to stop into Ollie's grandparents' flower nursery all the time. He followed Aunt Joy around, even into the greenhouse, said don't worry, he had both eyes on her place. It was on his beat. That's what he told Ollie: You're on my beat. Now Mr. Vince is there every day, Uncle Vince now, with Joy and Mom, to serve, and to protect, and to take care of the family business so the women can stay with the soil. Vince is all right as a new uncle, but Ollie would prefer Joe.

Bobby's hand is on Ollie's neck again. "Duck," he says, and pushes Ollie down until his head hits the dashboard hard enough to bring tears.

Just like that, the light turns green, so Bobby lets go of Ollie and accelerates. He laughs. "That wasn't Joe. He's a bozo anyway. You don't want to be waving at cops."

Ollie rubs his forehead. "Why not?"

Bobby taps his foot, faster and faster. "They just want to write everybody up."

"I already got wrote up once this week."

Bobby makes a sharp right turn off of Halsted, into Grandma and Grandpa Conlan's neighborhood, and slows down. "Listen, Ollie, I'm sorry you got busted on account of Miranda. I appreciate you wanting to look out for her. You're good like that, a regular hero, but that's my job, 'cause I'm her pop." He looks over at Ollie. Ollie looks over at him. "All right?"

"Okay." All is forgiven now, but Ollie doesn't want to talk about it. He needs to change the subject. Questions do the trick. "Why are we going to Grandma's?"

"We're not. The Jimmer lives just around the corner."

Then Uncle Bobby's off again, staring straight ahead, driving faster now, riding on nerves. He keeps reaching into his trench coat, into the secret pocket, like he's checking to make sure something special is still there. Ollie's dad does the same thing when he wears his trench coat. His secret pocket holds his wallet, with its white and green squares—licensed to drive this, born over there but allowed to live here, and in the back, behind that, a holy card from Ollie's sister's funeral with all the angels and saints that glow and rejoice alleluia: this is who died here, before she ever lived. And now Ollie is supposed to believe that she is up there, hanging from big white wings.

Uncle Bobby slows down as they pass St. Luke's. Ollie plays with the windows again. *Zzzeep. Zzzurp.* And now, the church's top looks more silvery between the shadows, brighter than its muted steps below. Ollie ducks when they pass his school. Right now he should be in science class, the reward for surviving all the other subjects. The thought of science relaxes him.

It's tough to imagine any streets around here with cables under their lawns. The Jimmer's lawn is a dirt square divided by crackly concrete and chain link. As Ollie and Bobby step through it, the sprinkler continues its arc, and the tan surface does not turn to mud, because the soil here is hard packed and gritty.

On the porch, they hold pretend pistols next to their ears as they step to the sides of the door, ready to swivel and shoot when it opens. Bobby is an inside sales agent, and the Jimmer is an outside agent, but it is Bobby who must wait on the porch, in plain sight, after he rings the bell.

"Now hide," Uncle Bobby says. He jerks his neck out, toward the sand.

No bushes, no trees, no furniture on the porch. "Where?" Ollie says.

Bobby rolls his eyes. "Just, just, here." He reaches across the door, sweeps Ollie behind him, and then leads him to the end of the porch, around the side of the house. As he steps back onto the porch, he says, "Keep your mouth shut. I'll be right back."

Bobby pounds on the door.

Three clicks of deadbolts and then a creak. Ollie peeks around the corner.

"Hold it right there, Jimmy!" Bobby's elbows are locked

now, and his invisible weapon points straight out, leads his feet toward the threshold. Bobby is not really armed, and he's not a vigilante or a cop, but he's scarier than a burglar or Officer Joe, who has better neighborhoods to worry about now. Bobby is a guy in a suit holding somebody up, busting in.

The screen door whines. "Take me away," a lady says. "Punish me. I've been bad." Her voice is honey-coated cigarettes. From his spot off the edge of the porch, Ollie sees only her fingers and the silky red sleeve of her robe.

"Gladly," Uncle Bobby says. He steps onto the threshold, and his arms move across it, low, like he is pushing a laundry cart instead of breaking in. The rest of the robe moves toward him until Bobby's and the lady's whole bodies stick together like putty, or magnets. Legs that go forever, the right in shiny nude panty hose—and the left bare all the way into her yellow high-heeled sandals. In her left hand she holds the other leg of hose, lets it hang.

In her right hand, a cigarette dangles. "You're early," she says. Her voice might be scratchy like Grandma's, but her face is still pretty. She could be on TV she's that pretty, even with the scarf over her hair and the yellow eye mask on her forehead and the red sleep marks on her cheek and the black smears under her eyes. She's one of Miranda's Barbies come to life, one of the dark-haired dolls when they're half-dressed.

Bobby's head bends down and he pulls the scarf off the lady's head and they kiss. Not like Ollie's mom and dad kiss before how-was-work-honey or after have-a-good-day-dear, and not like when the husband and wife make up at the end of *Bewitched*, because it's not just the lips that do the work. Bobby sticks his tongue out at the lady with the panty hose, right in front of her face, which would mean detention at school or at least getting your butt kicked by somebody's brother, but she opens up anyway, lets him stick his tongue into her mouth. So rude. The hands work, too, everywhere. They yank at the hair and claw at the back and slide into the robe.

"Cable TV," Uncle Bobby says. If he had a real gun, it would have fallen to the floor. "We're here to sell you some entertainment."

The lady with the panty hose has a funny giggle. Aunt Noreen—Bobby's wife—does not giggle. She doesn't smile at all. "Don't want any," the lady with the panty hose says. "I've been watching the news all day. That's enough to make my head spin." She is still suctioned to Uncle Bobby, her chest and his gut the parts on puzzle pieces that snap in, to fill up what's missing in the other. Bobby must really want this time slot. The Jimmer must be one of his very most important friends, and President Carter's next statement about the botched rescue mission must really turn the dials to *Nightline*. Otherwise Bobby wouldn't let this lady grab him under the chin and suck on his lips until they almost rip off.

Ollie steps forward. He will save Bobby. He will take him away, down the street to Grandma's, or St. Luke's, or to the nursery, and Mom will say, You're a hero, Oliver. You delivered him from evil.

But then Uncle Bobby is entering the front door before Ollie can yank him back, so Ollie rushes in behind him. A voice calls down from the second floor, saying, "I'm waiting up here, wise guy," and Bobby says, "Eh, Jim. On my way."

Ollie doesn't ask why the Jimmer is home in the middle of the day, upstairs, doing his business, waiting for Bobby so they can make their deal. There's no time to ask, because Bobby shoots right up the stairs without a just-a-minute or a be-down-in-ten and there Ollie is, with the half-naked lady. Her leg is bare, just a shine of skin, ready for the hose. She sits on the couch in her short robe and steps into the mesh, just like that, in front of Ollie. Aunt Noreen would never. She stands and pulls the waistband up, looks at Ollie. "It's warm today," she says. "I don't got to wear nylons, but I will." She covers her hair with the scarf again and with her arms up and reaching like that, her robe opens.

He studies the room. Shutters over the windows and a large leather sofa. A full bar in the corner, a marble table, a chandelier. Pretty fancy for this neighborhood.

"You can help me get ready for work," she says. "Come on." She leads him to the back of the house. This is the master suite, she says. It's a big bedroom with a door to the backyard, a sitting room, *and* a washroom the size of the boys' lavatory at school. Ollie knows without asking or looking it up in any library that this washroom has the only Jacuzzi in the Back of the Yards.

She waves toward the sitting room, where three full ashtrays sit on a glass coffee table. The TV is off. "Watch whatever you want," she says.

He lifts the *TV Guide*, flips it over. "No TV allowed when I'm on punishment."

She walks over to the record player. "Well, if that's how you think of following your uncle around, I'll relieve you with music instead." She puts on an album, sets the needle in the middle. Horns blast.

In the bedroom, she takes off her sleep mask, closes her eyes, hums the tune—a hit by KC and the Sunshine Band—and suddenly her movements are part of this song. *She's the life of the party, she's a real sensation.*

The lady tells Ollie her name is Patti Rose, but he will call her Panty Hose. She tells Ollie she comes from a place called Mount Hope, near some gorge, "but I got out of there pronto," she says. "Found a job dancing on a riverboat. That's where I met the Jimmer." She has a faraway smile now. "He was up big that night, kept me on his right side for luck at the blackjack table." She wraps the halves of her robe tighter across her middle. "Now he brings people here, for private parties, and I dance for them. Don't have to go nowhere. I'm stationed." She laughs. "Docked for good. Boring, but it's good money. Can't beat money."

Ollie thinks of his report again and decides that hostage

takers like the Jimmer might be a special kind of magician. Usually they make other people vanish instead of themselves. They do it for ransom or fame: here's my letter, my demands, now run after me. But maybe sometimes they do it for the good of the hostages.

His stomach leaps. He hasn't eaten all day. It's rude to ask the dancer to feed *and* entertain him, but she is not an ordinary hostess. "You got anything to eat?" he says.

"I can't eat before I dance," she says. "My belly's all nerves."

Oh, brother. So he will starve after all. He needs questions. They calm his appetite. He walks to the sliding glass door. The backyard has grass all the way out to the tall wooden fence. It looks nice, but he can tell it is sod. Outdoor furniture—nice, new furniture—is already out for the spring. A vase on the table holds real tulips. Potted geraniums dot the corners of the patio and driveway. Nothing is planted. Even the pool is above ground, a blue sheath over its top.

Ollie can tell from the house and the yard that the Jimmer has a lot of buyers, and that upstairs, his handshake with Bob Conlan is closing a deal for a product too ugly to advertise on TV. That much Ollie knows. He touches the glass and looks up at the ceiling. "Not much of a top seller today, Bob," he mutters, "and not much of an uncle either."

Over the whisper of spinning vinyl comes KC's voice: *She keeps swinging, she's my superpower.* The lady with the panty hose stretches her arms and legs against a chair. Her robe comes untied. Bra and straight wall of stomach, nylons up to the belly button, nude underpants. She wedges the chair between doorknob and floor and then clicks all the deadbolts.

Ollie is sure now that the Jimmer isn't really an advertising man at all, and that on a house call like this one, Uncle Bobby is here to make a deal for something other than a time slot.

But Ollie can't ask this woman questions about that, so he says, "How long are your routines?"

"As long as a song lasts. I don't know . . . four minutes?" She hikes a leg up to the wall. "I have to rehearse soon," she says. "Be my audience?"

He shrugs. What can he say? She doesn't eat. She doesn't even leave this house, just twists and shakes and runs around in it every night. "If you're trying to lose weight," he says, "the Jimmer will have to give you at least seven numbers a night, in a row."

"I'm a fatso, huh?"

"Glycogen," he says. "That's all you'll burn until you get to twenty-eight minutes of cardiovascular exertion." He slows down through egg-zur-shin. "That's when you get down to the fat and it reaches the melting point."

She bends back until her body is a rainbow. "How old are you—seven? Eight?" she says.

"Ten last month."

"Well, happy birthday, smart-ass." The big loops in her ears flip upside down.

He bounces on the bed. He can't help it. What else can he tell her? "Houdini could bend like that, you know." He sits still and cranes his neck to judge the reaction on her face. Nothing. "He bent and bent until he folded himself up."

"Then it killed him," she says. "I'm no dummy." She flattens out on the floor, stretches long, wiggles fingers, points toes. She breathes in, deep, sharp, through the nose, and then she coughs. "Another Jew does himself in trying to be a hero. Old story."

The floor rumbles upstairs. A man yells, "Step up to the plate!" They must be watching the White Sox game, must be doing a home run dance. When the man shouts, "Goddamn!" Ollie jolts up to a standing position. His heart races. A shout that loud means somebody must have hit the ball out of the park, but Ollie can't be sure, because the closest TV is all the way in the sitting room. It would be rude to go in and check the score, to see proof of the miracle.

Panty Hose changes the record to another KC album. Her feet slide and flex and point. They are bony, beat-up feet. Once, in the nursery, Ollie heard his mom and his Aunt Joy call Aunt Noreen chunky. Her job is to bake cookies for Miranda and watch *Family Feud* and yell at Bobby. Not a lot of exertion. This lady is so unlike Aunt Noreen or Mom or Aunt Joy or any of the Conlan women that Ollie is convinced she is not a woman at all. Or maybe they aren't. Maybe it's them who've got it all wrong.

When she enters the washroom, she leaves the door open. She sits on a chair in the dark and sprays perfume. He enters without an invitation. On mirrored trays, more bottles hold colored scents. Clamshell palettes hold paint and brushes, for eyes, cheeks, and lips.

"Get lost," she says. "I need a minute."

She locks him out. Through the door, he hears clacking and a *shh* and an "Oh Jesus."

One-Mississippi, thirty-Mississippi. He knocks. "Miss Patti? I'm sorry I barged in. Can I watch you rehearse? I bet you're real good."

The record has finished its cycle of songs, now that a hanging arm has scratched out its slow spiral, from the outside in, and reached the bald core. *Let's go party, come on in, I'm your boogie man.* As the Sunshine Band fades out, the alarm clock's second hand keeps a new beat. It winds through four punishing minutes. How long will it take for Uncle Bobby's secretary to realize one of her little friends is gone, and will she find it tied up in the trash bin? Will she tell on Ollie for kidnapping it when he was supposed to be in Bobby's office, not touching anything as he memorized the commandments? *Thou shalt not steal. Thou shalt have no other gods before me.* Tick tock. Ollie has to be in the ad agency lobby in less than an hour. And there Dad will be, in his trousers and trench coat, with its secret pocket. Skirts will swish past him as he's reading his *Sun-Times*, waiting for the delivery of the miracle.

"That's my son," he'll tell the security guard. Not my son the kidnapper, the failed escape artist.

Tick, tick. Then a boom on the other side of the bathroom door, as a drawer opens, and then slams shut. She turns the knob, but does not pull back.

"Set the needle back to the middle of the record," she says. "Then come in."

Once he's back in the washroom with her, he looks around. Her robe hangs on a hook, but the head scarf and bra and panty hose stay put on her hair and skin. He counts her ribs.

She takes a cigarette out of her pack, hands him the lighter. He makes fire. *I'm here to do whatever I can*, KC sings. She closes her eyes in anticipation, in pleasure. This will warm her up. When she opens her eyes, the brown irises are thin rings, the pupils big black bowling balls.

He sits on the edge of the Jacuzzi, near the wall, so he won't fall in. "You smell like lilies," he says.

She licks her gums. "How do you know that smell?"

"I know flowers."

"Oh yeah?" As if she doesn't buy it. "What's your favorite kind?"

"Pansies." The song urges now, and the piano reaches a high tinkling note.

She tosses her head back, so the laugh shoots straight out from the throat. Behind her, wigs cover the scalps of three plastic life-sized heads.

She picks up a compact mirror from the counter, claps it shut. She turns around. "Hey," she says. She touches his knee, rubs in circles until it heats up. "It's okay. I won't tell." She smiles. It is a closed-lip smile. "Some of my best friends are pansies."

He stands up. "That's not what I mean. I got busted at school. That's why I'm here."

She swivels back. "Congratulations, big man."

He has shown her he is a man. Now it's time to be a boy again, to act his age. "Is your hair done yet?" he says.

"Oh, God no." She fluffs and punches it through the scarf. "It's a disaster. I do hair after makeup. It takes a while."

"Can I play with it?"

She cocks her head, catches his eye in the mirror. "Well, I don't see why not."

With both hands he peels away the scarf, gathers and smoothes her wavy black hair, and finds the kinks. He thinks about obeying, stealing, coveting, using names in vain. He wants to stretch the blond wig on, pull it down behind her ears. Jackie O. one minute, Marilyn the next. Ollie knows these looks, the dark and the light, good girl and bad.

Panty Hose stands and cups her hands over his eyes. Now it's her turn to touch his hair. It feels like when Mom used to re-verse hug him, holding the back of him against her belly when it was round from the baby and all that water she swam in.

She spins him around, leads him along the width of the counter and back, until he doesn't know where he stands.

"Reach straight out," she says, "and choose a model."

In front of him, the three wigs wait for him to choose. He has studied them already, the looks to match the titles: *Little China Girl*, *Gentlemen Prefer Blondes*, or *Arabian Nights*.

He doesn't have much left to lose. "How about just your real hair? I like that better."

Panty Hose pulls away, reaches for her cigarette. In the mir-ror, the ash grows. She opens a palette, chooses a brush. She tells him to turn off the overhead lights and turn on the gas lamp in the corner, keep it dim. She's got special bulbs around her mirror, to guide her through the final brush strokes.

"You shouldn't see how we pretty ourselves up, you know. It should be a mystery."

Under the light switch, on the counter next to the compact mirror, is the cut-off end of a McDonald's straw, with the yellow stripe and the red stripe. Over a million billion served. *I'm your boogie man*, KC sings.

While the dancer's hands are busy, Ollie picks a cigarette up from the ashtray: the one she lit and forgot about two minutes ago. How many does she burn at a time? He tongues the filter, sucks in, listens for a crackle. He inhales all that's left and taps it out. It's stiff from too much burning, or not enough. She tells him to flip the record over and start it near the end.

More noise from upstairs: an "Oh, come on, already" and a "One more line." Then some walking around, jumping and shouting, a strange dance. Perfume bottles clank down here on the trays. The game must be ending. For the first time ever, Ollie doesn't want to see Uncle Bobby. Not yet. Not until Bobby calms his own nerves. Ollie checks the ceiling. It is one big piece, no tiles or rafters. Sturdy enough, but if Uncle Bobby did come crashing down, Ollie would have to face him.

When Ollie returns from the record player to the bathroom, Panty Hose says, "Look at me," She is done with the makeup, the blues and greens, the black, and now only the slippery parts of her shine up: bra, teeth, whites of eyes. "Please understand." She points up. "They all got deals to make, and it's none of my concern, or yours."

She holds out the pack. "Hurry. My song's coming up."

He gets his own cigarette now, whole and fresh, a clean burn. Smoke fills his head. It swirls around, loops and twists with her warm-up movements and with the song. Smoke makes everything a little easier, a little quieter.

Panty Hose stubs out her cigarette. "All right, little man. Watch me burn some fat." She stands with head down in the silence between songs, behind the smoke, and then she emerges from the dirty dark.

The dance begins. *You can, you can do it very well.* Her arms and legs clutch and wrap around things—edge of counter, towel rack, stool—and the parts of her twist in disagreement, until she arches again, knots up. *You're the best in the world, I can tell.* Then she is all tail for a minute, a fish on a hook. *Shake, shake, shake.*

In the middle of the song, as the chorus builds, she places Ollie's hands on her hips to prove that she's really exercising, really working hard. The muscles flex and relax, flex again. The bones roll around in their sockets.

When the song ends, he returns to the record player, flips the album, and plays side one for her. It starts with a slow love song, one Ollie always skips on his own record, but she keeps dancing fast, and he can hear it now: the clank of wrist on towel rack, the bang of hip into drawer, crack of ankle, shush of stocking feet against tile in the spin. Without enough volume on the band's music, the show loses its magic. Ollie's eyes have adjusted to the dark.

There is no clock in here, and time is running out. Ollie's dad is going to be in the agency lobby soon. Bobby has to finish his meeting with the Jimmer, this long fast of a lunch hour, then get Ollie back to the office in a flash, like it never happened: all that business, all that fun.

"This song I can't do," Panty Hose says.

"No, keep going."

She scrunches up her face. "Pick a new record. Something fast."

Ollie races into the sitting room once more. With his thumb he flips through album covers, and with his finger he races through song titles. "Brick House," "Black Betty," "Queen of Clubs." Today the Sunshine Band sounds better than usual, but he should pick something new.

And in that space between songs, between the last strum and the first strike, Ollie hears feet moving down the stairs and toward the back of the house, closer and louder. Bobby yells from the other side of the bedroom door. He garbles and mumbles and then roars his commands. "Open the door, girl! We got business. I'm here on important business." On the last word he erupts into giggles and another voice laughs out a high note. Must be the Jimmer.

"You gotta let me in, girl . . . Patti."

Ollie fumbles with the records and sets the needle down, somewhere in the middle. This will have to do, fast or slow. *Wrap your arms around me. Come on, come on.*

"Listen to me, Ollie. We'll leave," Uncle Bobby says. "Just let me seal this deal first, buddy. Let me in."

Ollie turns up the volume until KC's voice drowns out Uncle Bobby's. *Don't waste no time.* He steps back into the washroom and finds his way to the tub's edge. He does not want to go out there and have the toe-tapping, knee-slapping, neck-snapping good time that Bobby offers.

Panty Hose—Patti Rose—clicks the locks, so that Bobby is two doors away now. When she starts dancing again, she does a lot of bouncing, a lot of repetitions of just a few movements. She turns in a circle, leans into the counter. She has lost her groove. She winces and grabs her wrist. It is bare, and Ollie thinks a watch should circle it.

The record stops, but this is not the end of the album. Ollie knows the order of the tracks. Bobby must be in the bedroom now, standing at the record player. Just like that. He can walk through walls and bolted doors.

The smoke clears and her eyes burn Ollie's with that shine, with the mirror's glare. And here it is again: the explosion in his gut, the pressure in his chest—her terrified heart in his chest, in his ears, a hammer in his neck. Uncle Bobby spikes up the volume—*Wrap your arms around me, you're what I want*—and then the song cuts out. No more vocals. No piano or horns. But the drums in Ollie's chest keep playing.

The dance continues. She taps and sways and squeezes to the beat. She does not hum, does not sing the rest, now that the horns and piano and guitars have quit. She does not even snap, because the percussion goes on: heavy fist on the bathroom door, a kicking, and then broken vocals: "Ollie Ollie oxen free! Tell me who's your favorite uncle, huh? Come out and tell me."

There's a thump of what must be Bobby's forehead against the door. His voice is lower now, close to the floor. "The only one you listen to, huh? Who's that? Oliver, Oliver, tell me who keeps your secrets."

Finally Uncle Bobby is here—Uncle Bobby, the only

grown-up who understands or listens or knows how to have fun—but the time has run out on their one-day vacation, and Ollie does not want to face him.

Panty Hose's hands shake as she turns the lights off and the Jacuzzi faucet on. She whispers in Ollie's ear, "Listen to me, and listen good: hear what you need to hear, and tune out what you don't." And then she lets go, pulls back, starts a staring contest with him. She points up, into the empty sound waves. "There is only this, what you choose to play, right now."

He concentrates on all the colors that aren't the shades of her face: the black air behind her, the white-blond of the wig.

She picks up the yellow sleep mask and slips it over his head, pulls the elastic down behind his ears. Now that she's blind-folded him, she takes his hand and guides him toward the tub, tucks his arms and legs inside, balls him up like his sister, when she was swimming, drowning, because if you hide your hostages, hold them, and keep them safe, they will be yours forever. Ollie wants to parachute out of here, but this will have to be an underwater mission. He will make it through one hundred Mississippi. The water is warm. She crosses his arms over his chest.

Through the blindfold Ollie can only see shadows and hints of color. Over the sound of the water, he hears Panty Hose unlock one lock on the door, take a few deep breaths, and though Ollie can't see it, he believes that her hand is poised over the other lock. Just when Ollie is sure she's nervous enough to go out there and do the dance for Uncle Bobby in the master suite's sitting room, where sweat will sprinkle over skin while bones roll and veils fall away, he hears a whimpering and a wheezing series of breaths, the lock clicking back into place, and her feet sliding toward the tub.

The water is really filling up now. Ollie slides down deeper until his pants are soaked. Panty Hose squirms in behind him, and the meniscus rises up past his belly button. She does not turn on the jets. With one arm she holds him in a reverse hug. With the other she pulls the robe over their heads, and a pink canopy seals them in.

THE LOST BUREAU

The district picnic is a hell of a way to end Andrea's first week on patrol. At the table, the folding chair next to her stays empty. Cop, wife, cop, wife, empty seat, female cop. "Who's your husband?" is a broken record by six-thirty. That's when she pours her first and only drink. She has thought about this all week: beer is too masculine; choosing it would suggest she thinks she has a shot at becoming one of the boys. White wine is too dainty. Liquor, if drunk too fast or with the whole hand clutching the cup, signals too close a friendship with what's inside, as if she stays up late laughing and crying with it every night. She chooses a red from the cluster of bottles at the center of the round table. She will sip it slow, for composure, and because her swing shift starts in three hours. She will leave here early, but until then, she will focus on the positives. Positive No. 1: She's a patrol cop now, hunting one of Chicago's dirtiest pusher-pimps. Positive No. 2: Her sister, Trina, is safe at home.

After dinner, at the other tables, women take their positions. Lieutenant and captain wives there, black wives over here, old ones there, with a couple of rookie wives salted in at each table. Old hands—the same hands that once raised signs in front of Police Headquarters, protesting a decision to let their husbands patrol with women—hold young hands now. *Welcome dear, and congratulations. What a life you will have.*

The other lady officers who have shown up are the ones still on office duty and married to male cops. Andrea envies that kind of security, but she'd rather be out on her own beat. For the first time, she misses the girls at the police academy, misses the way the strong few, the finishers, never spoke to each other. The silence kept them separate, safe, because together they would fall.

At Andrea's table, every other chair is empty now. The men are at the beer coolers, where they joke about the week's news, about how the bullet must have softened Reagan "like Cupid's frigging arrow, and turned him gaga for Sandra Day O'Connor." The wives fill their husbands' empty seats. In order to hear each other over the music, they have to huddle close together, until Andrea becomes home plate and they are the arc of the outfield.

"You're Leoni, right?" one of the wives says, pointing a finger at Andrea.

Andrea nods and holds her breath.

"I hear you're a good shot."

"Oh, thank you," Andrea says. The rest of the wives inspect her sundress, her necklace, her neat brown drape of hair. "Whoever told you that is too kind."

"It was my husband, Alan. Alan Serano." She blushes. A proud wife, a fearful wife.

Andrea nods and reaches up to smooth her hair, which she has worn down but not teased. She spent hours deciding what to do with it. The outfit she wears is also the result of deep worry. Too flattering would draw attention. *She's over the no-good husband*, the wives would think. *Now she wants ours, or a promotion, or the hand of one of the bachelors left on the squad.* Too concealing suggests a lack of interest in men, period, and they've already worn out the names for that.

One of them stands. "I don't know about you girls, but my kid's got school in the morning, and my mom is a pill about babysitting past eight, especially on a Thursday night." She shoves in her chair. "Toodle-oo."

They check their watches. "My mom's the same way," another wife says. She looks at Andrea. Her frown announces a realization that Andrea has no kids, no pain-in-the-ass mother. "No offense," she says. "We don't mean any offense."

Positive No. 3: At least Andrea doesn't have to wake up and see Serano's mug on the pillow, or Parker's, not Accardi's or O'Malley's either. Andrea sleeps only with her husband's .32. Unloaded in the thigh holster, Frank's gun reassures her, lulls her to sleep. She pities the other cops' wives. At home it must be all shoeshine and billy club and wait till your father comes home. The officer everyone wants to see. What pride is higher than that?

"No offense taken," Andrea says. She stands in what she hopes is a ladylike way, and then she addresses the whole table. "My kid sister," she says. Their eyes open wide. "Not Cindy. My other one, Trina. I gotta go help her with her homework." She nods. "Evening, ladies."

In the parking lot, a clammy hand grabs Andrea's wrist. "I'm sorry."

Andrea turns around. It's O'Malley's wife, Nicola. "For what?" Andrea says.

"You know. For Frank and your sister. For what happened. It was just—" She clicks her tongue, and her hand settles over her heart. She chokes up. This is practice for the crying she'll have to do as an officer's wife, because with the pride comes the worry. Imagine. Everything can go down out in the field. Nicola's eyes, behind the mascara and the shadow, will never see what Andrea will, or even what she has seen already. The wives' hands will never close around steel, fingers won't clasp, and elbows won't lock as every angle of the body aligns with the target.

"Don't be sorry," Andrea says. "I'm the one who's sorry. I let it happen."

"No. Do *not* blame yourself." Nicola tightens her grip on Andrea. "Tell me something."

I keep a secret duffel of my dead sister's stuffed animals in the trunk of my car, Andrea could say. *I lug it out of the house with the rest of my gear before each shift, because who knows when you might get a chance to take afternoon duty at the shelter or on South Western Avenue? When you could have a fifteen-year-old runaway cry and hug you—actually hug you first—and make real, sustained eye contact when she tells you her mama never gave her dolls?*

"Shoot," Andrea says. "Ask away."

"Tell me if you think this is funny," Nicola says. "My daughter. Two years old and she wants to be a cop!" She leans in to deliver the best part. Barbeque sauce on her breath. "When her daddy goes to work she cries 'cause she has to take off his cap." She lets go of Andrea's wrist to lean back and laugh at her own joke.

Yesterday it was Officer O'Malley's hand on Andrea, in the ladies' locker room. She was unwinding her braid and humming, *Make me a channel of your peace . . . . where there is darkness, only light*, when he came up from behind her and said, "Grandma's hymns and holy cards ain't gonna save you now." His hair held the goat stench of teenage boys, like Frank's White Sox cap.

Andrea froze up.

"You're a lousy shot," he said. Everyone had heard about how she more than nailed the proficiency test at the shooting range last week, but he took it the hardest. "A broad in the Supreme Court, another one for mayor, and dykes on patrol."

She knew better than to talk back.

He asked her to cover his Friday shift so he could take Nicola up north for their anniversary. This Friday is Trina's birthday, but covering it would mean another chance for Andrea to nail Billy Green, the pimp they've been after all week. The warrant is close.

"What's that? You say yes?" O'Malley said. "Good, 'cause I already settled it with Sergeant Pinkerton." O'Malley reached up Andrea's pant leg, pulled the pistol out of her ankle holster. It was her backup weapon, and so far, no one else had noticed it. "Damn, Leoni. Thanks to Mayor Byrne, I could fry your little can for packing this."

"It's Frank's. He bought it before the ban." To keep him company on the walk from steel mill to El platform to house to pool hall, where he'd bought it, wrapped in a paper bag.

"Didn't take it with him when he left ya? Is he even your husband anymore?"

Andrea didn't answer. She closed her eyes and pictured the headlines that would've run if Frank had taken his .32: "Innocent Brother-in-law of Cindy Marino Found in Ohio River with Own Gun."

O'Malley dangled the weapon over her head. "Cover my Friday afternoon or Sergeant Pinky finds out about your unregistered gun."

After the picnic, Andrea's sister, Trina, lights a candle in their kitchen. Next to it, she slouches over a textbook.

Andrea straps on her gun belt. "Test tomorrow?" she says.

"Pop quizzes," Trina says. Light flickers over one eyeball and flashes up a tooth.

Andrea lifts her cap off the rack. "Good," she says. "You deserve the torture," but Trina doesn't laugh.

Andrea hates the swing shift, hates leaving Trina alone in the house from nine-thirty at night until dawn, with only the neighbors' dogs to stand watch. But it's patrol: no more office duty, more time with Trina.

"Sorry," Andrea says. "You know what I mean." She picks up her work shoes. They hold a gloss. "Hey, who went and shined my shoes?"

Trina shrugs. She is thoughtful. She would make a loyal friend.

Why don't you call up one of the girls from school, Andrea

doesn't say, because she knows what girls are into these days. Better not to have friends. Just each other. Tomorrow, if Pinkerton lets Andrea punch out from the afternoon shift at eight p.m. instead of eleven, she and Trina will do each other's hair. They'll read *Seventeen* and listen to records. Catch a movie, then stay up late and watch the comedy shows.

Trina turns the page of her biology textbook and out pop the illustrated fallopian handlebars, ovarian grips. She hasn't grown at all in the past year, hasn't bled yet. What if I'm not a real woman? she has said. Woman will come, Andrea told her. And when she does, you'll want the girl back.

"That's the end of the book," Andrea says.

"I like reading ahead."

Trina is bored with endocrine and nervous. She wants to know about the reproductive, the circulatory. The chromosome chapter will be an easy one for a girl like her, who got hair so light it's almost blond, clear skin, straight teeth, *and* brains. Top of the double helix. But she stutters here and there, just enough to leave her without a boyfriend to kiss or girlfriends to show her how to use Cover Girl and dance to the Bee Gees and all the other skills of teenage life that Andrea does not have time to teach.

That's why they'll do something grown-up for Trina's birthday tomorrow—hair, makeup, nails—before they catch the new Freddy Krueger movie, something Frank would have taken Trina to see. Then home for cake.

A few months ago, on Andrea's birthday, they made ziti. Trina wheeled the TV into the hallway and the sirens of *Hill Street Blues* drowned out the boil sizzle pop. Andrea gushed over the male officers and studied Lucy, the take-no-shit lady cop. Look, T, she said. Look how they walk, like all that weight's no weight at all. Look how they flash the badge, how they question, how they run. Yeah, yeah, Trina said. I got eyes, too. And with that, Andrea flung a spoonful of tomato sauce toward Trina's mouth, and just to fight back Trina opened wide to catch it—as if to say

Fine, try to shock me—then spit it out, and it dribbled down her chin, and they laughed. It was a sound and a twitch in the gut that caught them both by surprise. They kept going, kept painting each other red and laughing, because it felt good, and because they knew the laughter would bring tears.

Trina closes her book. "What do you do when boys are laughing at you?"

Jesus. Wouldn't Andrea like to know? She pictures the rookies entering the meeting room at the station—Serano and Parker, Accardi and O'Malley—in jackets too big for the shoulders inside. Arms swat tops of heads, mouths make animal noises. They call each other girls.

"You laugh right back," Andrea says.

Trina says the boys at school call her washboard, chalkboard, diving board. It's worst at her locker, where they stand outside the shop classrooms. They growl and throw metal scraps at her. "And some of them are big now, after the summer. They could crush me."

Andrea stiffens up. She recalls the weapons trainer's voice: Be the tree. The first and last line of defense. He'd reached out to his sides, and the cross tattoo peeked out from under his sleeve. Arms apart, so you're not aiming at them. Not at first. Stare them down, and when you see them hurt anybody, blam. Shoot for the middle. But when the time comes for Andrea to bring Billy Green to his knees, she will choose a shoulder or a leg instead. Because even though he is an animal, she is humane, efficient, a flawless shot. If you go for the gut, the fight's over. All they can do is surrender.

"No. They could *not*," Andrea says, pointing a finger at Trina. "Nobody can crush you. You hear me?"

"Yes, ma'am. It's just—" Trina says, fighting tears now, "at fourteen you already had Franky." Finally, she makes eye contact with Andrea. "You had protection."

Andrea beckons Trina over to her and pulls her into a hug. Over Trina's shoulder, Andrea sees this kitchen now as it looked when she was fourteen, as she leaned back from her post at Cindy's crib and glanced down the hall: Mom stirs a steaming pot while, at the table, under the hanging light, Pop's rolled-up sleeves hover above Trina's spelling list.

In bed on her wedding night, Andrea cried about having such a tiny ceremony. It was just Frank's dad and brother along with Andrea's sisters: Trina and Cindy. Frank curled around Andrea, the arch of his foot on her ankle. "We don't need friends," he said, "just you and me and the girls."

Andrea combs Trina's hair with her fingers, loosens the snarls. She releases the hug and reaches for Trina's cheek, but Trina slaps Andrea's hand away.

"I'll break out," Trina says. "That's all it takes, just a fingertip of oil."

"You're spotless. You're beautiful. Relax."

"Am not."

"Are too."

Trina's lips curl up, almost into a smile. Not enough to show her teeth, but Andrea knows she has broken through to her little sister.

Off duty and on, Andrea carries Frank's piece as her backup weapon. She has rehearsed showing Trina. This is how you load. Click, smack, flip, point. And this is how you fire.

She's drawn a crude anatomy chart of her own and pinned it on the inside of her closet door, where she aims her unloaded gun each night. Perfect target practice. On the blank figure's arms she's drawn tattoos, and on his face she's given him the same shape of nose that belonged to the man who killed Cindy.

The first time Andrea voted was two years ago, on February 27, 1979, and it was for Mayor Jane Byrne. It felt so good that she punched the card three times in the same hole: for Mom, for Pop, for her. The lady mayor has done a lot for women, especially those in sensible shoes, and she has done a lot for black folks. She's practically a Kennedy, but for this new gun law: reregistering every two years. If Andrea's ever questioned about the .32's expiration, she could bat her lashes and say, I think my husband took care of it and put it in my name. But a quick sift through the L row of files would reveal him as a murder suspect—a cleared, innocent suspect—who went missing after Cindy's case finally closed. Boom goes the file drawer as it reaches the end of its rails. Hands in the air. Put down your weapon.

Before each shift, as Andrea winds up her braid, she imagines eyeballs in it. Tonight they peek through the plaits. On her mirror, the St. Monica prayer card shows one outstretched finger. Go, my child. Protect.

Andrea laughs. "You're a card." She crosses herself, kisses it, and she's off.

The drive past Billy Green's house is a chance for excitement. Parker and Serano drive there in one car, O'Malley and Leoni a few blocks behind them in another.

O'Malley grips the wheel tight. "If we hang him," he tells her, "that makes me a hero in my own neighborhood." Right turn onto Western Avenue. "You, too. Our Lady of Mount Greenwood."

Each night of this week, Andrea has bounced to a different partner. They all take the same kindergarten-teacher tone as they point out: Those are the shipments, those are the bundles of cash, unmarked guns. And here come the girls.

Over the CB radio, Parker calls out, "Hey, ladies: this goes out to you." O'Malley cranks the dial, louder, louder, and through static Olivia Newton-John cries, *Let's get physical!* "Yeah! How about a piece of that?" Parker says. Serano giggles in the background. Andrea feels a hot flush in her cheeks. "Ladies" includes O'Malley and any other male cops bored enough to listen in, but the term does not refer to Andrea. She chews on a hangnail while the men sing along. Of course they all want a piece of the singer. She has advertised herself well on her album covers. Andrea ignores the radio and stares out the passenger window. She maps the terrain: every liquor store, drugstore, covered-up storefront. Every shopkeeper, bum, every Joe on the street. Glass is all that stands between her and them.

Serano on the radio: "Billy Green ain't his real name, you know. It's a long dago tongue twister, starts with a *G*. Primo Guido, that's what I'll call him."

"Roger that," O'Malley says. "We should have Leoni go in undercover, huh?"

Parker's voice now, in a tin can. "Yeah, Drea, tell Green you're a girl looking for work."

It takes everything she has not to close her hands around a throat—through the radio and the airwaves around five blocks to Parker's throat, or across the seat to O'Malley's—and shake it six times: I. Am. Still. A. Married. Woman.

A month into the academy, she was ready to drop out. She'd had it with the sprints, the books, the stare-downs. Then she read about the first policewomen in America, whose chief duty was to look after kids. They counseled troubled wives and mothers, steered wayward girls straight, and took charge of the Lost Bureau: all those letters asking, Please, find my missing person. That was seventy years ago. In this decade, because of leaders like Sergeant Pinkerton, a lady officer can spend her shifts getting to know every sidewalk crack and pharmacy and wino on her very own beat. Later, maybe in her thirties, once Andrea has paid her dues by nailing enough Billy Greens out on patrol, she can specialize in youth policing, hold wrinkling hands out toward the visitor's chair, and make promises she's ready to keep. Everything will be okay, she'll say. You're safe here. He'll come home.

When Frank took off to the pool hall each Wednesday night, Andrea didn't worry. If he wanted to keep bringing home those union paychecks, he'd have to fit in at the mill, become one of the boys on the clock and off. "Fine with me," she said. It would help keep the money coming in, and it would give her more time to get her sisters' lunches packed, homework checked, piano practiced, and the house cleaned, laundry done, church shoes shined. And when Cindy tugged on Frank's pant leg and begged to go with, well, who could resist that little face?

"I'll clip her to my belt, Drea," he said. "Give her Shirley Temples, money for pinball. Sue behind the bar—she can mind Cindy sometimes, too, while I'm sinking eight balls. I'll stand at the washroom door while she pees."

"But she's always in your periphery." Andrea raised a finger to the tip of his nose, led his eyeballs all the way right, and then left, to test him.

His teeth snapped at her finger, and then he kissed it. "Always. Home by nine."

And he was. Every Wednesday, with a full report. Cindy's a whiz at pinball, he'd say, and then later, Sue taught her to play dice. Or, Tonight she shot stripes, when I was in a slump. She sunk one.

On Wednesdays, Trina and Andrea trudged easier through algebra, outlined Napoleon's conquests, and decoded the mysteries of thirteen-year-old boys.

One week, Frank and Cindy came home waltzing and high-fiving. Late. "She buried the eight ball!" he said. He kissed Andrea, twirled her around the kitchen. "Won me twenty bucks!"

The final report comes in dreams, one dream that speeds or slows, appears in Technicolor or shadows, depending on what kind of day Andrea has had.

Frank zips up at the urinal. "You there?" he says. Ear cocked toward the door. Sure am, Cindy says. Hands turn faucet. Still there, Cini-mini? You bet. Paper towels. How 'bout now?

That's when the front door of the pool hall bursts open, and when thick, tattooed arms sweep Cindy up, away from the men's room, outside, and underground. To nail Frank for winning so much of their money, they destroy his lucky charm. That was the first story Frank told Andrea, and she didn't buy it.

Dreams are hard to trust after your husband has let your youngest sister tag along and the streetlights come on and dinner congeals and Johnny Carson says good night.

When the dreams run out, you start to rely on facts, Exhibits A and B. A story you can touch, through the sealed plastic bag, with the permission of men in suits and the armed guards that lead you to them. This is all you can do once a train has tripped over your sister and your husband has hopped a different line, Grand Trunk or Greyhound. When the facts creep up on him—about all the other wagers he made and lost to those guys without telling you—maybe he snorts them away, swallows or smokes them. Or maybe the change in scenery is all he needs in order to forget. He calls here and there during the first few months, to apologize or to cry and to give you five or six words at a time: "I'm in the Blue Mountains," "mosquitoes like you wouldn't believe here," or "been sleeping in my cousin's barn," but the rest of the words, the important ones, are still lodged in the subway tunnel, snarled in your sister's hair. So you breathe into the receiver, the two of you, until you expect a snoring sound, his arm across your ribs, the arch of his foot over your ankle. Then comes a crackling, and the operator's voice: your time is up, goodbye.

You don't know what to believe. You know the cousin is an invention, because Frank only has relatives in Chicago, New York, and Italy, and he never kept touch with any of them. The only people he knows from anywhere else are the guys who came from Kentucky and Tennessee to find work and then lose it at the mill, but he has to keep his distance from them now. He tells you he found work pumping gas, and you decide to believe that part, because it's easy to picture him crouched in a gas station phone booth, scratching the bites on his arms and then squeezing a wad of dollar bills in his pocket. A far cry from the paychecks he used to bring home and wave above your head as the two of you danced around the kitchen table.

Now that you think of it, you're not sure you believe what you've been told about the train either. Sometimes it rattles and chokes in your dream, and out come thick feet, attached to the arms that want their due. Cindy must have escaped their first grab, and then taken off, along a narrow platform, until shoelaces slipped apart, a pipe dripped a small pool, and balls of feet, on soles with no tread, lost ground, and gravity arrived with the punches and the kicks.

Eyes at church, eyes at the grocery store, drugstore, eyes along Thirty-First Street. They had all read the headlines. "Girl Lost," then "Girl Found." The prints and fluids on and in Cindy were not Frank's. Those demons are locked up for good. It's just Frank who's on the loose.

During the case, the thought of him as a real suspect had not crossed Andrea's mind until some inane woman at St. Anthony's whispered the possibility to her. It was a Eucharistic minister, the same one from her parents' memorial service. "The blood of Christ," she said, with chalice outstretched, and as Andrea amened and took the wine, the woman's words came: "Thank God he didn't shame you on that level."

On maples and on elms, green leaves give way to yellow and red. The garbage truck hogs up the usual street Andrea and Trina take to the high school. Andrea detours. The alternate route is just another square of South Side grid, but even this small change is a chance to discover something new: a different saint featured in the lawn statues, a new color of Nova waiting in the drive.

Hopefully tonight Andrea can cast the mold. That is, if Trina lets Andrea straighten or rat out her bronze curls, lets her raise eye pencil or makeup brush. "Little Sister Allows Big to Paint Lids, Cheeks. Big Sister Layers on the Years."

As they pass St. Anthony's, Andrea takes a deep breath, and

church language fills her. Be the pillar, the rock, the tree. She grips the wheel and tells Trina she had to take an afternoon shift last minute, but she'll beg Pinkerton to let her off early, in time for her and Trina to catch the late movie. "Worst case, we have to skip hair and nails."

Trina tugs on the strap of her book bag, rolls it tight. "Easy. I'll just cut it off."

Andrea slows down as they reach the high school. "That's not funny."

"No, because it isn't a joke, Drea." Trina's eyes narrow now, and aim at the school's tennis courts, where punk rockers smoke and stare out at the road. These are kids who will find answers to biology quizzes over the shoulders of girls like Trina. They grow larger as the car moves closer. "I'm done with hair," Trina says.

"If you can't beat 'em, just become one of the boys, huh?"

An eye roll and headshake from Trina, as if to say, Takes one to know one.

Not even fourteen yet and Little Sister knows all of Big Sister's secrets. Nothing gets past Trina—not the fact that Andrea straps an extra gun to her ankle before going to work and sets Cindy's stuffed animals in the trunk of the patrol car. And now the extra shifts to prove her loyalty to Sergeant Pinkerton, even if it means missing Trina's birthday and leaving her home alone all night. Maybe Trina would cheer up if Frank would fill his pockets with dimes and call to wish her a good birthday.

Andrea pulls up to the curb, switches off the ignition, and hikes the gearshift. Parked.

She is glad now that she didn't change out of her uniform when she got home from work an hour ago. Through the halls of the school, Andrea's one hand stays on Trina's shoulder, and the fingers of her other hand splay over the hip holster. She nods to the hall guard who knew her as Frank Leoni's girl, to the ancient guidance counselor, the stooped janitor. And there they are: her old teachers and principal. Staff and students turn to get a load of her hat, her blues, the star over her chest, the fixtures on her belt, and the metal they hold. The boys probably check her ass, and she doesn't blame them. The girls, she knows, picture their own asses, tiny but to them enormous, in the uniform slacks, and their polished toenails secure in black shitkickers.

If only this school were Andrea's beat. She'd escort Trina all day, scoop up wayward kids from hallways and doorways, bleachers and tennis courts. Do what parents are too tired to do. Why can't more boys be the way Frank was? Bad enough to escape ridicule, good enough to win her parents' approval.

She presses her thumb into Trina's shoulder to stop her arm from sliding down, her hand from taking Trina's. Their walk ends at Trina's locker, in a dark cove by the auto shop, wood shop, and metal shop. While Trina wrestles her lock open and heads turn, Andrea slips behind the end of a row of lockers. She listens to the whispers about Trina and about better, curvier bodies that pass by in this hall or that.

Footsteps grow louder, and a boy's voice says, "Hey, Muh-muh-Marino." He puts a straw in his mouth and aims it at the back of Trina's head. He is ready to fire the spit wad.

Andrea steps out from behind the lockers and stands between him and Trina. One hand on her service revolver, the other on the billy club now, with her head down, to exaggerate the presence of the hat.

The boy steps closer, cocks his head, and gives her a once-over. The straw falls from his mouth. He darts back into metal shop.

Andrea nudges Trina, to tell her goodbye. She backs away. Under the clang of the first-period bell, she hears no voices. She sees only Trina's perfect teeth, all of them.

Three hours later, the phone cuts into Andrea's sleep. Sun gushes in through the curtains. She picks up the receiver and holds it over her head a second.

"Cini-mini?" she whispers. "Mom?"

Male caller: "You want some action?"

Female cop: "Pardon me?"

"They've found him."

"Franky?" Her voice is soft, the way it hasn't sounded all year. Frank hasn't called in four months, not even on her birthday. Where the hell was he now?

"What? Nah. It's me, Rick Pinkerton. We got a warrant for Billy Green." He giggles. "O'Malley'd eat his heart out right now up there in Wisconsin. If only he knew." She hears a smacking noise, and knows it's Sarge's notebook hitting his desk. "Green, Andrea. We're gonna get him. Three o'clock, once he gets back from visiting Granny in the nursing home."

The clock on her bedside table shows almost noon.

"That's good news, sir." She covers herself with the bed-spread, as if he can see her.

"You got that right. After all this hunting for him in thunder-storms, tripping over rats in alleys, and crunching down roaches in hallways of the projects, it's time." He clears his throat, drops his voice. Serious now. "Having you out there will make us look even better after the victory."

So victory comes now, does it, after the field training officer made sure I spent the rest of my first year behind a desk? And now you must wonder how you could keep an arm like mine at a typewriter or draped around a crying woman.

She rubs her eyes and shakes her head. "Victory, Sarge?" she says.

"I promise. Go on now, get some rest."

She's wide awake now.

Officer Leoni opens her closet door, stands at the opposite wall with feet spread wide, elbows locked. Ready. She stares down this eyeless creature until the silence comes, washing out the neighbor's barking dog, the passing cars.

When she's done, she closes the closet door, stores her weapon, and sits at the mirror where her mother did hair and makeup. And there, tucked into the mirror's frame, is St. Monica the protector.

"I won't disappoint you," Andrea says.

In the garage, she slides extra weight onto Frank's barbell and pumps it twice. Easy. Three Mississippi, four Mississippi. Eight, nine, ten. Then she picks up the dumbbells and pumps those a few dozen extra times. She massages her arms. Ha. Make them look better.

It's a longer route to work. After a few minutes, she's so caught up in the show through her windshield—pink and white tunnel of hedge flowers, yellow wave of maple leaves, clear song of robins—that she doesn't hear the crackle of the radio at first. She recognizes Sarge's voice pushing through the static: "Don't dally once you hit the station, because we're about to make the Hundred-and-Third Street hustler kiss it all goodbye."

Turn, and the scenery changes. Pachysandra gives way to thorny rose stalks, browning oak leaves to a willow's open jaws.

A lady cop, the residents' faces say. They stare from porches, from driveways and doorways. Or, inside, they lean away from the glow of TV screens and glance through picture windows, where two panes separate them from her.

In Pinkerton's office, all ten members of the team lean over the map of Green's property.

"Leoni, you're on yard duty," Pinkerton says. The light through his window whitens one side of his red face. "Ride alone behind the unmarked cars and pull up from the other end of the street."

In the car, Officer Leoni sets her weapon on the passenger side and leans into her seat.

Turn. A whole new scene. You don't have to go far. Andrea wonders now if Frank has changed direction and made it all the way west. In Hollywood, she's heard, someone rides a bike to change scenery, so it looks as if the car or train or horse is really getting somewhere. But then you spot that shrub again, or that rock with the gouge, and you think, *So much for spinning wheels. He's pedaling us nowhere at all.*

Eighty-Ninth, Ninety-Ninth, 101st Street. Sweat under the brim of her hat. Protect. Serve. Keep the Billy Greens of the world away from girls on the verge.

She passes 102nd, and more saint statues. Hands clasped, eyes rolled. Exalted, defeated, dead in the name of service.

Slow onto 103rd. Two cars park at the other end of the block, and four officers approach Green's porch: Parker, Serano, and two older cops she can't name. She knows they pray for backup, for rescue, not from the guys in the outfield posts around back, but from a steady arm like Officer Leoni. It feels good to know they are counting on her talent. *Ha*, she thinks. *Turn and get a load of me.*

But this kind of pride is low. To show it now is lower than waltzing around the kitchen because your husband made good money at the steel mill or won even better money at the pool hall, lower than faking modesty when the officers' wives tell you what a damn good shot you are.

She creeps toward the side of the driveway, behind a bush and a shiny Mustang. Eyes over the hood, aimed at Green's front door from a forty-five-degree angle. Banging now, and, "Open up! Police!" and all elbows are locked, arms streamlined with each pistol.

She reaches for her hip. Empty holster. It's too late to go back to the car for her service weapon, so she checks her ankle holster. Loaded. She is ready to back them up if Green runs loose.

Tick, tick. Sweat runs down from the hat, into her makeup. Andrea squats until the backs of her knees feel sticky and her quads burn. She sits and looks around. No one on the street, just a Doberman behind a fence and a few eyes in the gaps between curtains, because what else can you do but watch when the cops are already here, not doing a thing?

Yelling inside Green's house. Yelling from the officers. Andrea kneels. A thud of the door's bolt, a rattle of chains. Five clicks as each officer raises his gun, braces for Green's exit.

Out with his hands up and a halo of sun around him. Billy or Bruno or Artie or whatever he was before he became this, has a scar above his eyebrow. His shirt, clean and buttoned and tucked, hangs from narrow shoulders. He's not covered in tattoos, not wielding any weapon up high, and there's no funny hat on his head or harem of tricks on his arm. Head low. Hands clean.

Andrea forgives, and the gun is an anvil in her hands now. But she stands, takes a deep breath, lifts her weapon. Defend, protect. She squints and realigns herself with the target, so that her head and chest and hips and toes point at him. And here comes the silence. Ready. Aim for a shoulder. Aim for a leg. Slow down, little boy. Easy.

Another body sneaks out behind him. A girl's body. She's standing close to Green, so close that nailing him becomes impossible. Her thin arms reach for him. Because the girl's always there, in his periphery. Despite her revealing clothing, she might make a good wife if Billy gives her the chance. He turns toward her. "Get inside, girl!" he yells. She won't budge, won't listen. Surely she is a girl who wouldn't listen.

He points. "Get inside!"

The girl takes a step back and her blond fringe swings.

Andrea doesn't like the way he yells at the girl or the way he grips her shoulder with one hand and reaches his other hand into his pocket. That's it, right there, the intent to hurt somebody, probably a whole bunch of somebodies once the hand pulls the weapon out of the pocket. Blam.

So Andrea squeezes the trigger. Her barrel is right on Green's shoulder, she knows her fire's heading to that, and in a second the bullet will sear into his left deltoid from this, her forty-five-degree diagonal over the car in the drive, just the way they taught her to hit the torso, just the way she hated to do so right *on* in the shooting range, just like the geometry problems Frank did for her until she could figure them out for herself, like the way he lined up for the touchdown pass, so sure it's a touchdown this time, the way you'd whip a ball to first base for a tag out, the way you'd line-drive it at the pitcher's shoulder, to bring in the no-good backup, to take the league title however dirty or backhanded, and now the bullet hits with a pop and the blond hair is what whips and the white tube top is what's seared because the suspect swiveled out of the line of fire and the girl goes down, and in the wings, on the lawn, Parker and one of the older cops tackle Green because Green was already running from the bullet out of Frank's unregistered pistol and here comes the grind of handcuffs over there, and here, where Andrea's feet stop running, the girl is down.

The girl's chest pumps—a shake up and then down—as her white top, white skin turn pink and soon, cherry red. "Where did you come from?" Serano says, and Andrea doesn't look or answer, just takes off her uniform shirt and wraps it around the girl's middle. Andrea is down to her undershirt here, in front of this pimp's den, and she is fumbling over this girl whose belly is a busted pipe, and someone says, "Call an ambulance," with a burst of expletives, and then, "Who made you queen, Leoni?" "Really, Drea, when did you fall out of your tree? You're gonna get cooked," but Drea shuts it out because the girl's eyebrows come together and her mouth opens, she is going to speak, please speak, please forgive me, I was trying to save you.

"Just stay with her," Serano says.

He runs off, and here Andrea is, on hands and knees, tending to the wounded. "I got you, honey," she says. "What's your name?"

"Jenny."

"You're gonna be fine, Jenny." Andrea hopes she sounds convincing.

The girl nods and winces. She does not ask where the bullet came from.

He turned, Billy did. That was it. The turn back to the girl, and the pocket and the fear and Andrea's hands and the trigger and the revolver and the bullet—as it raced toward a spot too far below the shoulder and well above the leg—spiraled in a ballerina's twirl, became a torpedo.

"Jenny!" It must be Green talking. Andrea's back is to him, and she can't bear to turn around. She imagines his wrists behind his own back now, red under the handcuffs. "Baby, you okay?" His voice wavers enough to show that he knows the answer, knows Jenny can't deliver it. "I'll be right back," he says.

The girl's eyes move sideways, but her neck doesn't turn.

An engine starts, and one unmarked car is gone.

Andrea touches Jenny's middle, and the blood soaks her fingers, her palms. Despite the red hands, Andrea decides, the scar above Billy's brow might be the kind of thing you overlook once you consider the way Jenny must have walked in stride with him, his hand on the small of her back. And the way she might have sat next to him in his hot Mustang, his arm around her shoulder, both of them high on *mine*. Imagine she's so in love she doesn't ask where he goes every night and where the cut came from that later scarred up his face. Or maybe it was already there when they met at a church fair before the school year began, where fourteen meant almost a grown-up and a Tilt-A-Whirl car fit her and Billy. Instead of screaming, this girl here, the girl down, might have smiled and squeezed the ring on the finger of Billy Green, who might have been Bruno or Artie or Antonio then, because if he squeezed back, the crush would keep the burn of nausea from rising up her throat, stop her belly from flipping. The girl told him, Drea decides, on the night they met, at a fair filled with girls who might seem to Billy to be just as pretty or as controlled with their stomachs, "My pop taught me to clean guns," and Billy said, "Be my family. Be my girl." "Proudly," she said. That meant packing a piece of her own, keeping the curtains drawn, losing her own family. Being his girl scared her to death.

Officer Leoni wants to go home and cry this all out to St. Monica, the way O'Malley will do to Nicola, for not having been there, for missing his chance. Serano and Parker will curl up in the laps of their wives or mamas. Little boys after a day of playing Man.

So after a while Billy probably came home with more cuts and duffel bags Jenny'd better not open, and sometimes he flat didn't make it home. But it was her—"It's you, girl," he said. "Just you and me, doing business so I can take care of us"—and business meant one gun in the glove box and one zipped into her old musical teddy bear. Work meant sleeping light, ears on the door, eyes poking through the blanket Grandma knitted.

The girl's breathing slows. Andrea squeezes her wrists to feel a pulse. At home, or later, behind bars, Andrea will pray for Trina's forgiveness, but Trina will not forgive. Why should she? She will let go, say Andrea's failure today didn't shock her at all, tolerate four years of state custody, and then live a decent life alone while Andrea and Frank burn together in their separate hells. Even Jenny, if she doesn't survive this, will fry, too, because she let Billy Green take her underground.

But then the floor fell out in that Tilt-a-Whirl, and he squeezed her, and they spun, and the few facts Billy knew of Jenny—Evergreen Park High, too pretty to have friends, mother with a full house of holy cards—swirled together and he drank them all in. The beginning of an everlasting drunk.

She loved what he was, too, under the surface of him, the tough guy: scar over the eye, one gold ring, baseball bat under the bed, gun in the zipped-up spine of a silenced toy. A boy who turns girls into beasts and sells them as women. That's just the cover. What he really was was a dimple under the eye, dumbbells, bony arms, spinning cup.

It wasn't supposed to be this way: the swivel, the wound. Because the bullet missed shoulder and leg completely. It was a wide turn, so Andrea's shot hit a torso with less muscle to dig through, after the thin tube top and before the ribs, and the guts that exploded and the heart that Andrea wrapped the shirt toward, to hold it all in. She grips the shoulders now, pulls the skirt down to cover the legs. Jenny's body shudders again. Lips darken, eyes fix on Andrea. Voice: "That's it. I can't luh-love him no more."

Her eyes close and her breathing grows louder. Andrea cups the girl's face in her hands. Sixteen she is, tops. Small and blond and perfect.

"Talk," Andrea whispers. "Tell me what you've seen."

The paramedics arrive and Andrea steps back.

She figures Billy still loves Jenny for what she is, probably, too, under her surface: the skinny legs and straight hips, and the one mangled pinky. Maybe he loves her for pitching to him so he could hit a few balls out onto the train tracks. And she doesn't ask questions during Bears games, and she knows how to clean a gun.

Jenny has always been a bright girl. She knew this day would come, the end of Billy Green. The end of her life as his woman. No more pestering or admiration from Ma. No more of Pop's sad faces. But she kept loving Billy, kept being his girl, even after he hollowed out her teddy bear. She knew she would never be Mrs. Green. If she made it back to Evergreen Park High, she might become a new, modern woman, a working woman, but she'd still sit by the closed curtains each night, light a candle, watch for shadows on the other side of the glass.

Jenny is on the stretcher now. They figure she's got a chance. Andrea is hopeful that Jenny will make it home and back to school. She will no longer be pretty enough—the boys will call her used up, smacked up, blown up, and spit out of Billy Green's beast factory in a wheelchair—and this ugliness will save her. She will be left alone to study algebra and biology and pass the right answers to kids with stiff hair who might otherwise drop out and become the beasts they paint themselves up to look like every morning.

Andrea will ask the youth policing officers to put in a word to Jenny's principal, asking him to let Jenny finish.

In the event of a miracle, Jenny will answer Andrea's letters, which will tell the girl she can still save her, even from inside the women's jail, where Andrea will undoubtedly do at least a year. That is, if she can get a good letter to Mayor Byrne first. She'll have to beg Pinkerton to write it. If he tells her no, that he can't stick his neck out that far, and that he's sorry, but she'll just have to do the maximum time, Andrea might have to write the letter herself. She'll tell the lady mayor that she respects the gun laws, even if she didn't show it on this particular day. She will admit that she is not one of the boys, that she never deserved to wear the star on her chest, and she will ask for leniency on account of Trina, a fourteen-year-old girl with a future who needs the stability of family. Big Sister is the only family Little Sister has left, which is why Andrea's sentence must be kept short. Too long in state custody, and Trina would completely unravel. This town can't lose another bright mind to the streets, can it?

Andrea stands over Jenny for one last moment before they load her into the ambulance. She looks down at her own bloody hands. With her thumbs she paints red streaks on the girl's forehead, around the eyes, over the cheekbones. And now the stretcher is raised up and locked in, hurrying off.

It's a long drive from Evergreen Park to the jail, but Jenny could visit Andrea once in while. If Jenny will allow it, Andrea will have one more chance to be the sister she can't be to Cindy anymore, or to Trina, who will never forgive this, never again believe anyone who promises to make her birthday happy.

Over the next year or more, Andrea will think about all that she can do for Jenny, all she can say to Jenny's parents and to Jenny herself, to make up for what went wrong. *You don't need girlfriends or boyfriends. Just us,* she'll write in her letters. *Together, we'll make it.*

She will smooth down her hair and show up early at the visitation table where the girl will meet her. "I meant to kill Green," Andrea will tell her. "He was no good for you."

If Jenny accepts that apology, Andrea will reach out and take her hands. Save one of them for me, she will say. Small and beautiful and smart, like you. Find her and tell her I'll be out in time for her sweet sixteen.

REPRESENTING THE BEAST

In the living room, Keiko finds the TV on and muted. Words roll along the bottom of the screen and "Kobe Earthquake" is the constant caption at the top. Another caption, "January 17, 1995," sits next to a ticking clock. Scientists make estimates. Seven point two. A park overflows with people in nice pajamas and overcoats. Some stopped to grab hats or shoes before leaving home. A highway overpass has overturned. A shrine smolders. Each time the city shakes, the frame rattles, and Keiko sees things off to the side that the TV camera means to hide. A barefoot boy runs screaming through the edge of the park. A woman in a T-shirt makes a tourniquet with her jacket and ties it around a man's arm. Another man in a suit sits on his briefcase with his head in his hands. He rocks back and forth.

As images of the day's ruin flash across the screen, Keiko scans the Japanese symbols on fallen signs. She is able to make out *car, caution, train station, downtown, telephone, please.*

Keiko's cousin Ayaka goes to Kobe University, but she's in Osaka now, staying with her mother so she could audition for the ballet company there yesterday. Osaka, the captions say, isn't feeling the same toll. Still, the screen pulls Keiko's chin closer, until she feels the weight of those fallen buildings on the back of her neck, those steel meteors that split the pavement.

She can imagine herself not as someone who fell or burned or got caught under a train, but as the ground itself. Keiko would split into cracks so deep that all the people not ready to be crushed could step down into her, backwards, like they would into a root cellar or the deep end of a pool. She would hold them.

She walks down the hall, past eighteen years of photos showing her with Ayaka on their summertime or Christmastime visits, and she stops at her parents' bedroom door. They're not usually awake at this hour, but the phone woke everyone up. Keiko thought it was Ayaka calling to tell her she nailed the audition.

Behind the door, Keiko's dad says, "Come on. Sit up."

Her mom's crying is a series of shallow breaths and squeaks. "How will we tell her?"

When Keiko nudges the door open, she sees the back of her dad's head, the geometric shapes on his robe. Her parents are kneeling in front of the bureau, side by side but still facing each other so that her mom's knees and her dad's toes all face the door. Her mom has buried her face in her dad's chest. A sunbeam shoots in through the blinds and glides over his hair as he rocks her.

Keiko's mom will take the next flight to Japan so she can help Aunt Yumi take care of Ayaka's cremation and other details. Then she will bring Yumi back to North Carolina so she can keep an eye on her.

"My sister can't be alone anymore," Keiko's mom says, shoving clothes into her suitcase. "She asked a stranger to drive her as close as they could get to Kobe, and then she walked the rest of the way. Through the smoke and aftershocks. Alone." She presses the clothing down to make room for more, and then she looks up into Keiko's face. "All day she wandered around in that mess, asking people, 'Have you seen my daughter, the dancer?'"

Keiko turns away and studies the pattern of crackly lines in her mom's raku vase.

Her mom continues. "Yumi even brought a bag of warm clothes to hand out to people sleeping in the park." She points to a drawer in the bureau, so Keiko opens it, pulls out two handfuls of socks, and tosses them into the suitcase. Her mom closes the suitcase and zips it up. "She collapsed on the sidewalk, so the police put her in a van going back to Osaka. Who knows what she'll do next?"

Keiko wants to go and help, too, but her mom won't let her.

"Go back to school," she says. "Work hard, and get into a halfway decent dance company as soon as you can. That's the one thing you can do for us, Keiko."

On the bus from the airport in Denver to the college in Boulder, Keiko watches snow hit the ground. When it piles too high, the plows will push it aside. Since October, and especially since she went home to North Carolina for Christmas break, layers of fat have piled on Keiko and wrapped around her in a Michelin Man style, puffing up her thighs, hips, stomach, forming pouches under her chin and eyes. Seventeen extra pounds of soft coating that she can't push aside. She hopes that, like melting snow, the fat layers will drain into her, flatten out, and disappear.

Until the weight gain, everyone told her she was big company material, just as Ayaka had been, but Ayaka was a year older, a year better. Tokyo, New York, you name it, and she could have leapt right into their best academies. For now, Ayaka was only auditioning for Osaka because her dad hadn't been dead long and she wanted to keep an eye on her mother a little longer. Then she would move on to bigger companies. Keiko pressed her forehead to the window and let the cold glass numb her. Ayaka's kindness and sacrifice were as great as her talent. Keiko never had to compete with any of that until now.

One day in practice a week after the earthquake, her teacher,

Roberto, pairs Keiko with his favorite male student. The guy's hands slide and start to give way under her. He grunts when he lifts her off the ground by her waist, and in the mirror she sees that his elbow wobbles under her weight.

"No, no!" Roberto says. "Lift her all the way up. Up!"

It's bright in these studios. No shadows to crawl into, backwards and down, until you disappear. The male dancer puckers his lips and exhales until there is no air left in him. He mutters a string of curses. He swallows and gasps. Keiko teeters in front of his forehead until he lets her down.

Roberto stares the dancer straight in the eye, bends at the knees, and sweeps his arms up to exaggerate the lifting technique. He looks away without acknowledging Keiko. Everyone is rusty after Christmas break, he says. They will change partners more often.

Toward the end of class, Roberto calls Keiko's roommate, another freshman, to the front. She rushes up there, swings a pointed foot behind her, and bows. Most of the girls smirk. A few cross their arms. Her smile is not gloating, like Keiko expects. It's just a wrinkle in a white sheet of hair and skin. Roberto sets his hands on his own hips and says, "Well, are you going to show us something or not?" She holds her breath for a moment before she begins.

Keiko has heard Roberto call her roommate his little Russian bird. Last semester, he used to call Keiko his exquisite machine while he rubbed her calves. He had summoned her to the front of the class many times. Let Keiko show us the poise we need for this move, he would say, or sometimes, Keiko, could you lead us into this sequence? He would wrap his hand around her waist the same way any of the male dancers did, but lower, tighter. He would wait until she met his gaze in the mirror, and then they would begin. The other girls would exchange looks before imitating her form. He started asking her to stay after class and practice with him in Studio A. By November, he was arguing with the male dancers because outweighing Keiko by fifty pounds shouldn't keep anyone from jumping as high or as long as she does.

When tonight's class ends, everyone else files out like they have somewhere better to go, but Keiko takes her time getting to the dressing room. She lets her hair down and stretches a while longer in the main studio. Her right foot burns. The pink seam of her pointe shoe has turned red. She peels her shoe off and touches the line of blood over her toes.

As she enters the dressing room, the last pair of sophomores is leaving it. They used to be a trio, always terrorizing freshmen together, but one of them didn't come back after Christmas. Keiko still sees that girl in her accounting class, but failure is contagious, so Keiko keeps her distance. Everybody gets pushed out of the circle eventually. It's just a matter of knowing whether to elbow your way back in or scamper off.

They back up to let Keiko through. "You look different," one of them says. "Haircut?"

Keiko shakes her head. Behind the sophomores, her roommate keeps her head down, because Keiko hasn't spoken to her all week. She picks up her gear and rushes out of the room, turning not toward the exit but toward Studio A, where Roberto waits.

The sophomores cross their arms over their washboard fronts and give Keiko a slow once-over, counting every ounce of fat. "I know," one of them says. "Color contacts. Blue."

Keiko can't see well in the dark, even with her new blue contact lenses, so on her walk home, she follows the lines in the middle of the street. It feels good: the pierce of cold air on the roof of her mouth and the danger of finding her way alone. She wants a ghost to pop out from behind a tree and lead her back, down the Colorado River, into a gulf, across an ocean, into Osaka Bay. The ghost would walk her through the streets of Kobe. *Look*, it would say, *there's Ayaka's train station, her campus, her apartment building, her favorite noodle shop, the site of her audition with the Osaka Ballet Company. Step into her pointe shoes and follow.*

But no ghost floats onto the road. There is no river here, no liquid at all aside from the promise of melting snow.

The phone keeps ringing in the middle of the night. Every time, Keiko thinks it's Ayaka calling. To hell with the time difference, Ayaka would always say. I need you now. When Keiko answers, Aunt Yumi's voice is just as urgent. She prattles on about some news story she's heard, or the weather report, but never about Ayaka or the earthquake. During one call, Yumi tells Keiko she'd better get the leading role in this semester's production of *Othello*, because Yumi heard about Keiko's performance as Kitri in last semester's production of *Don Quixote*, and now she wants to go all the way to Boulder to see her perform. Keiko lies and says she will get the leading role.

"Where are you in the dormitory?" Aunt Yumi says. She is very awake.

"I'm in the bathroom." Keiko checks the mirror. Circles around her eyes, puffed cheeks, dried lips—imperfections that any monster should expect.

"No. Too dangerous. Stand in the doorway while we speak."

Keiko pinches her cheeks to wake herself up. "I don't need to take cover. There will never be earthquakes in Colorado."

"I'm in the doorway of your room here at the house, so go stand in the doorway there. If we can be in the same type of safe place at the same time, we can pretend we're together."

Keiko does as Aunt Yumi tells her. Neither of them speaks as they stand there for a moment, at their thresholds.

One Sunday in mid-February, when Keiko's dad is at a conference in Denver, she borrows a car from the sophomore who dropped out of the dance program so that she can meet him. The sophomore approached her one day after accounting class, and they've studied together a few times. Now the girl is offering her car as an olive branch, or some baton of sympathy, from one has-been to another. This girl had been the star freshman the previous year, before Keiko joined the program and had her one semester at the top. Rumor has it that when the sophomore was a freshman, she was destined for a big city company, and why did a girl like that need to finish college, but auditions didn't go as planned, and when she returned to the program in the fall, Roberto was disgusted with her for not doing him proud. He was on to bigger and better possibilities like Keiko. The sophomore withered in practice last fall as Keiko bloomed, but she didn't blame Keiko. She's a local girl, so she could keep living with her parents, stay enrolled in school, and land a spot with a small dance company in town. There were, of course, plenty of stories of girls who'd quit dancing completely, but when you rise as high as this girl did, it's a harder fall.

When Keiko reaches the sophomore's house, she wants to run away. Before she's halfway up the front walk, the sophomore opens the door and steps onto the porch. She wears a white sweatshirt with the hood up and her long, black hair spilling out of it. The indoor lights glow behind her. She smiles with her mouth closed. Keiko has seen pictures of her in costume, under the lights. It's no mystery why Roberto favored her.

When the girl hands Keiko the keys to her car, she also hands her a book. There's one word on the cover: *Cahiers. Notebooks*, in French.

"What's this?" Keiko says.

The girl pulls her hood down. Under it, she wears a red skull cap. "The truth."

Now that Keiko sees her up close, she notices facial scars and circles around the eyes.

The girl tells Keiko the book is a French translation of Vaslav Nijinsky's *Notebooks*. It's the new unabridged version of the great dancer's diaries, only available in French. "It's got all the stuff his wife took out, even the dirt about sleeping with his director and losing his mind." She tilts her head back and smiles, baring lots of teeth. Her incisors are larger than they should be, and the enamel has worn away in some spots. Her nostrils flare and her lips curl as she lets out a full-throated laugh.

The hotel lobby in Denver is a drum of ringing phones, polite laughter, and voices saying, car, please, downtown, thank you, come again. When Keiko's dad steps out of the elevator, he looks so Japanese: round black-rimmed glasses, hard-shell briefcase, department-store shopping bag. Over the breast pocket of his sport coat, he still wears the conference name tag.

He has a lot of gray hair—more just since last month—forming wings around his temples now. The circles under his eyes appear darker, deeper. When he sees Keiko, he clamps his mouth shut.

Finally, he says, "You look different." He means fat. He pauses. "Older."

He motions for her to sit in a low chair. From his shopping bag he removes a box and passes it to her with both hands. She opens it and finds a pair of fleece slippers inside.

"From New Zealand," he says. "Molly Jacobs's mom brought back a pair for each of us."

The Jacobses live down the street, and Molly used to dance. A lot of girls used to dance. The slippers are suede and stuffed with wool. Keiko checks the size. It is a large number, measured in centimeters, maybe, but the slippers look narrow.

"Try them on," her dad says.

Keiko removes one of her boots, and it hurts her heel. She slides one slipper on, tugs the open back of it. It doesn't get past the ball of her foot.

"Try it without socks," he says.

No luck. Her foot is red and puffy, with a budding bunion and corns. Where the tendons and bones used to splay under the skin, her feet, now square, give way to toes that have no shape.

"Maybe they will fit Aunt Yumi," Keiko says.

"No. You're just swollen from today's practice. They'll fit you tomorrow. Besides, Yumi does not—" He turns toward the window, and then faces her. "Sorry."

"What do you mean? She doesn't what?"

"Forget it. Let's eat."

They have dinner at the same restaurant where they ate last August with her mom.

"We're looking forward to your visit home at spring break," her dad says over his menu. "Yumi is eager to have the memorial service."

"How is she doing?" Keiko asks, because it's hard to tell from Yumi's phone calls.

Her dad tells her about things he can only say in person, because he's afraid her mom or Yumi will eavesdrop if he tells her over the phone. One thing is Yumi's late night stirring around Keiko's room, where she is supposed to be sleeping, and another thing is her morning walks, sometimes a dozen circles of the same block. "She doesn't wear a coat over her robe. The Jacobses say she walks up their driveway, kneels on the ice, and talks to their dog through the fence."

Keiko pictures the Jacobses' German shepherd lying down to listen, his nose poking through the chain link as Yumi strokes behind his ears.

Keiko's dad sets down his menu and tells her that he and her mom are running out of ideas. So far the only way they've found to bring Yumi back to life is to lead her into another disaster, so her dad's been taking her with him to work at the children's hospital, where she paints his patients' faces in the oncology unit.

"She didn't tell me that," Keiko says. "Lead her into another disaster? What's wrong with you?"

The waiter arrives at the table. Keiko orders the first salad on the list. She doesn't wait for the waiter to leave before she tells her dad that bringing Yumi around so much sickness and death is asking for trouble. "She's fragile, Dad. It's a bad idea."

Her dad looks at her as if to say, *Yumi may be fragile, but she's stronger than you.*

Keiko lifts her water glass and drinks. Throughout high school, she had turned down more than a few opportunities for part-time work or volunteer service credit at the children's hospital. She could have dressed up in costume and visited the patients, which would help to promote her performances, but she wanted nothing to do with the place. One day when she was fourteen, she was moping at home about a bone fracture and all the dance time she'd miss, so her mom dragged her to the intensive care unit to visit kids with real problems. On the car ride there, Keiko planned what she'd ask the kids, safe questions that they'd be happy to answer: what was their favorite TV show or sport, did they have a pet at home, and did they like music? That would get her mom off her back.

Once inside the hospital, Keiko took one look at a sick boy's face and felt a tremendous weight on the back of her neck. He had some kind of lung problem and hadn't gotten enough oxygen, so his skin was a color that Keiko couldn't describe and didn't want to remember. He was one of hundreds of patients that had come all the way from Bluefield or Huntsville or Lynchburg to see specialists like her dad, away from home and school and every other place a kid should be instead. She wouldn't ask this boy about sports because he probably couldn't exercise. He'd never know how good it feels to sprint or jump, to leap or pirouette or feed his ego with applause. Before she had a chance to say hello, he pointed to her crutches and asked if she was okay. Keiko rushed out of the room then. Five years later, she still hates herself for being comforted before comforting, for turning her back on someone stronger than her. It was the only thing she was ever too ashamed about to tell Ayaka.

But Yumi. Yumi is like that sick boy, with nothing left to fear. She marched right over the cracked streets of the earthquake, and delivered warmth in a park full of screaming, bleeding families when she was the widow and mother who needed comfort.

And now she wants to visit a pediatric oncology unit to draw cat eyes and bunny noses and clown smiles on the faces of the suffering.

Keiko tells her dad that she doesn't see how the little bit of help Yumi gives is worth the pain she must feel just from being there.

Her dad shakes a sugar packet and rips it open. "The face painting gives Yumi a purpose," he says, pouring the sugar into his coffee, "and it's something she can do without having to understand much English." He stirs. "Besides, we can't avoid trouble completely. On the days when she doesn't go to the hospital, she won't eat or bathe or change clothes until your mom forces her." He says she spends the evenings smoking brown cigarettes and watching television: horrific reenactments of the civil war or shipwrecks or apocalyptic science fiction.

"No wonder she's up all night," Keiko says.

The waiter brings their entrees, and then he holds out a cheese grater. "Parmesan?"

The last time they ate here, her dad said, "Oh, come on, K. It's so good." He turned to the waiter and did what her mother usually did. "My daughter here is a dancer," he said. "Eighteen years old and she's already studied at the American Academy of Ballet, the Martha Graham Center, and now at the university in Boulder." Keiko's mom told him to be modest, but she was smiling. "She thinks she needs to starve," her dad said, "but I tell her 'No, enjoy the food.'"

This time he tells the waiter, "No cheese, thank you."

He eats his elk burger while Keiko makes mountains out of the greens and nuts and sliced pears on her plate.

After a few minutes, he moves his silverware around on the table, lining it up and then spreading it out in disarray. "I've wanted to tell you something else, too." He leans forward. "Something your mother and Yumi cannot find out about."

Keiko's tired. "I don't want to hear anything more about what you plan to do for Yumi."

Her dad takes a deep breath, and his shoulders slump as he lets it out. "Remember the blood test I had the nurse give you at the holidays?"

Keiko's cold hadn't let up for two weeks, so her dad made her come in to the hospital for a quick checkup. "Yeah, she said you wanted to make sure I didn't have other infections."

He takes her hand. "Did you learn about the thyroid in biology?"

"I don't think so. What's that? Do I have cancer?"

"No, no. Nothing like that." He squeezes her fingertips. His eyes well up as he explains the thyroid, that slothy beast behind her Adam's apple. Hers is extra slow. "Since I saw the results of the blood test, the feet swelling makes sense now," he says. Now she can blame the lazy thyroid when she can't concentrate in the studio, in the classroom, or on the phone with Yumi. She can blame it for all the nights she has sat in front of the TV or photos of Ayaka and known she was supposed to laugh and gasp and cry, but felt nothing. "Also," her dad says, "your backaches and creaking joints aren't just from carrying extra pounds. They're another symptom of thyroid disease." From now on, he says, she will gain and lose, gain and lose.

Before she can ask whether she'll have to quit dancing, he says, "I've brought medication for you. It will stabilize your weight."

He lifts her hand above her head, as if he's about to twirl her, but she pulls her arm down, because they're not in a ballroom. They're in the corner of a restaurant known for its big game.

"We have to keep you in your dancing shoes," he says.

The next week, Keiko's roommate breaks the silence. She says she is invited to a prestigious summer stock dancing program. It isn't the Martha Graham Center, where Keiko went last summer, but it's almost on that level. Keiko tells her she is happy for her, and it's the truth. She won't let herself fall into envy. After all, it's almost spring, a good time to get back on speaking terms, back on track. There is reason to be hopeful. Her weight is down and things are looking up.

Even English class is tolerable now. All she has to do is choose a few books from a list and write papers about them. Nijinsky's *Notebooks* isn't on her English professor's list, but Keiko convinces him to make an exception. She admits that her French could use some work, but she can handle the challenge. When he asks why she doesn't just read the abridged English version, Keiko tells him she wants to know the truth about Nijinsky, wants to read about who he really was under all the pretending.

Her professor laughs and thanks her. "That's the boldest thing I've heard anyone say in this course yet," he says, "so if you're up for the challenge, then go ahead. Why the hell not?"

She gets started right away.

Nijinsky's diaries begin on January 19, 1919, written moments before his last performance. The diaries end seven weeks later, when the asylum took them. January marked the beginning of his crack-up.

"You will understand me when you see me dance," he wrote. His forte was representing the beast. That's what people understood, a beast that channeled God. He stopped dancing after he went mad between world wars. Blood, he said, was war. He often saw blood on his feet when he stopped dancing. He stood on an earth that he believed was an inferno, and he welcomed earthquakes to remind him that the inferno breathed.

One day in late February, Keiko's mother calls with an idea. "Forget about the auditions you missed for summer stock dancing programs," she says, "because there are two left, and they're both during your spring break: North Carolina Dance Theatre and Asheville Ballet." Across the room, Keiko's roommate smiles into the mirror. She brushes her hair, turning so the light hits her earrings, her teeth, her manicured nails. Everything sparkles. Keiko's stomach churns. "Don't worry," her mom says. "The Jacobses are on the arts council. They'll make sure you get in."

"Come on, Mom." Keiko doesn't want to point out in front of her roommate that Asheville is the company she started with in middle school, so she uses only Japanese during this call. Speaking terms or not, she won't give her rival the satisfaction of knowing she is so desperate. "Molly Jacobs dropped out of dance in fifth grade, Mom. What could the Jacobses possibly know about companies?"

"All right. So it's not Ailey or Mansfield or the American Academy," her mom says, "but this is no time to be picky. Impress these companies in summer, and you'll have a shot at a long-term spot. A *career*, even if you have to start out small." Keiko stabs the bureau with her eyebrow tweezers. "There's still time, Kei-chan," her mom says, her voice wavering, "just not for the big ones. This is a lucky last chance. I changed your flight—" She chokes up.

"Mom, I'm not doing it. There's no use." Keiko stops short of mentioning the blood test. "It's time for me to bow out."

Her mom switches from crying to laughing, but on the phone, it is all the same shallow burst of air. "Oh, you want pity now? A vacation from the competition? Well, try again." The rest of it comes out in one breath: "I didn't raise you to be dramatic—or lazy—so if you want to be a peach *and not a princess* for once, you'll work harder to climb back to the top. That means getting your butt to the airport when I tell you to be there." When she is out of air, she hangs up.

Keiko walks outside and sits in the snow behind the dorm. She was already planning to go home for Ayaka's memorial service, but now the rest of the week will be taken up with practice and auditions. It is the only way her family will let her help.

She removes *Notebooks* from her bag and examines the pictures of Nijinsky in costume. In some of them, he's covered in paint, to play the Blue God or the Golden Slave. Unlike Keiko, he reached a point when he didn't have to follow orders anymore. He was not the idiot savant people thought he was, either. Far from it—he read Tolstoy and knew about all kinds of art. Keiko opens to the page where God tells Nijinsky to lie down in the snow, so Keiko lies down and lets the snow soak into her hair. She searches the sky for a cloud, but it's full sun today, plenty of reading light. Her last English paper was on a book about Vermeer, the painter who used an upside down camera to get the right lighting for his pictures. And now Nijinsky steps in. The real him, not the surface Nijinsky she'd always heard about. Keiko has nothing to lose.

She's not afraid to go deeper into his madness, so she presses on through the dancer's secrets again, finally authorized by his daughter, who never saw him dance. If Nijinsky hadn't brought the diaries with him when he went to ask the doctors about his nerves—to ask why, if he was dance and love and God himself, was everyone out to get him, to derail his career?—he might not have been diagnosed or locked up. He could have continued his violent, soaring acrobatics.

She feels good the day before she leaves town for spring break. The short number from *Othello* that Roberto assigned her includes exploding leaps and spins, just like the routine she has planned for the Charlotte and Asheville companies' auditions. After practice, she stays another minute in the studio, to try a difficult jump, just once more, and then she walks down the hall to Studio A. Through the window in the door, she can see the mirror. It reflects her roommate's profile, with arms outstretched, ready to start, or resume, the routine. Her roommate is playing Desdemona: the lead role in *Othello*. Roberto grows larger in the mirror as he approaches his position beside her, and a step behind. He holds one of her hands and wraps the other around her waist. The music begins.

The next day is the first Friday in March. Keiko's dad picks her up at the Charlotte airport and drives her to the hotel. She wants to tell him she's quitting, but he and her mom have gone to all the trouble to get her here, so she will roll through the motions one more time tomorrow, and then she will tell them it's time to hang it up. There's no spot for me next fall, she'll say. I haven't been losing the weight fast enough.

The next morning, she wakes up with swollen feet.

"Sometimes it happens," her dad says, "even with the meds. You have to fight it."

When he turns his back, Keiko starts to cry. "My feet bleed on the studio floor, Dad. I've slept through a lot of morning practices. Let's face it. I'm hanging by a string."

"Do you think I don't know the symptoms? You're bigger than this!" he says, pointing at his Adam's apple. "Every teacher and judge is over the moon about you. I've seen it. When are you going to wake up and learn that your whining is what's hurting your chances?"

Keiko wipes her tears with the back of her hand. She is out of chances, but for today, she will keep pretending and surrender to Yumi, who's back home, waiting for her do the same routine next weekend. Nijinsky was against medicines, but Keiko forces down the rest of her bottle of ibuprofen and ices her muscles all morning. Still, the numbness does not come. He said an artist must sacrifice everything, so Keiko will put her body on the line once more. Her mind races as her fingers and heels tap along to her warm-up music. Nijinsky said the public doesn't like to see an artist who isn't nervous. She pulls her hair into a bun, dusts on makeup, chooses a black outfit. Another day at work.

When she takes the floor at the North Carolina Dance Theatre audition, something happens to all those nerves. She forgets the swelling and bulging and lost chances. She flies across the stage in diagonal patterns, twists and pumps her arms with all the finesse of the little snowflake she played in her first Nutcracker. She falls to the floor at the thunder of kettledrums, and after a pause she springs up and glides into the next sequence. Instead of the simple leaps she had planned toward the end, she throws in one *grand jeté* after another, Nijinsky's signature move. She floats high above the stage, high as he had, it seems. In the air she feels still. She cannot hear the judges cough or scratch their pens on clipboards, and she cannot hear her own feet kiss and then hammer the ground to facilitate each soaring, gliding flight. She does not wait for the song's cues or stop to think. Her body knows this number. It is a violent number. When the last drum pounds she hears a rush of waves. They say his long thrown leaps looked like someone floating over a pile of dead bodies, casualties of war. Russia was his mother, he said. With each jump he lingered above his brothers and sisters as they slept on their mother, and he made the ground below him rumble, crack open, let the bodies in, and rock them. The inferno still breathed.

In the first entry of his notebook, he wrote, "I will dance when everything is calm," and then he was all nerves. "I danced terrible things."

On the drive to Asheville, her dad sees the book. "Reading a whole novel in French, *ne?*"

As she reaches to turn down the heat, her back, shoulder, and arm throb. "Yup. For English class." They laugh. She flips the book closed, so he can see the cover.

"Nijinsky?" he says. "The second greatest dancer in the world!"

"Oh, stop," she says. It's nice of him to flatter her, but like every compliment these days, it falls hard on her shoulders. She forces herself to sit up straight. "This book is more about who he was off stage. He was pretty messed up."

"Mmm." Her dad squints out at the road, slick with new rain. "He was a renegade, not someone we ever wanted you to follow too closely, but you're old enough now to learn the truth and judge for yourself."

This is her chance to tell him she's quitting, but she hasn't decided on the best way to cut her losses: she could drop out of dance and stay in Boulder to finish her schooling, or she could drop out and just not go back at all, stay at home and look after Yumi, maybe take classes at a local college in the fall. Either way, there's no use in going through with another audition. It is time to scamper off.

"Dad," she says, "I'm not Nijinsky. And I'm not Ayaka." She studies the side of his face for a flinch, a grimace, anything.

He turns up the speed on the windshield wipers. "When I had to memorize muscles for an anatomy course," he says, "and your mother and I were dating, she would quiz me with photos and drawings of Nijinsky's poses. Messed up or not, he was an artist's ideal." He rubs his chin. "Mother's, too, I think." He takes a quick breath and holds it in, to conjure up the memory. "She'd shine a flashlight on the parts of different pictures. 'Lateral deltoid,' I'd say. 'Flexor, adductor, gluteus.'" He giggles. "His face was exquisite." He holds up his hand, tracing the detail in the invisible photo in front of him. "Exotic. In school he was called 'the little Japanese.'" He brings his hand to his mouth and blows warm air on it. "So, you did well today?"

Keiko opens the book, because it's a long drive to Henderson County. "I didn't fall."

"When do you think you'll hear from them?"

Out the window, blue-green hills hug the fields, walling them in. "I won't hold my breath."

The book tells her that Nijinsky does not exist in motion pictures, and no picture was ever snapped while he was in flight, on stage, under the lights. That's why Nijinsky's legend lives, so we can wonder. Keiko wonders what would have happened if Vermeer and Nijinsky met—painter and subject, eye and body—in a dance studio. Add to that meeting a camera and movement. Vermeer would capture Nijinsky beckoning his earthquake in natural light. It couldn't be much different from showing Vermeer's woman pouring water or standing under Cupid. It would be an action shot, easier than the usual still poses, held until the point of aching, cramping stiffness. Although Vermeer and Nijinsky lived centuries apart, they were both men ahead of their time. Maybe Vermeer would have gotten it right in the future, with a smaller camera, and offered a glimpse of Nijinsky turning ballet upside down with his *Rite of Spring* or *Afternoon of a Faun*. Vermeer would have been the only one to show what Nijinsky's action did to his viewers' nerves, by capturing the pain that kept him moving.

"You know," Keiko's dad says, "Mrs. Jacobs said we could watch your audition in Asheville next weekend."

Keiko has nothing to say. She rubs her ankles and continues staring out the window. It has been a mild winter. The fields are a wash of mud and fallen branches under gray sky, all of it moving past her, behind her.

"It would be good for Yumi to watch you dance," he says.

On Monday, a monk from the nearest Buddhist temple does a private memorial service in the backyard. The guy doesn't know any Japanese, so Yumi doesn't understand a word. He doesn't even pause long enough for anyone to translate. When he finishes, they all walk down to the creek at the end of the property and scatter a few pinches of ash into the water. Mom holds Yumi, and Dad holds Mom. The monk walks Keiko away. When she is finally ready to face what's under all the pretending, the man there to guide her is giving her an out. She hates him.

"I've known your parents a long time, Keiko," he says.

"That's odd. They've never mentioned you."

He ignores the insult and looks back to the huddle. "They're deeply concerned about your aunt. It's important that you carry out her wishes."

The promise of spring lifts Yumi. She sleeps more, talks more. She smiles whenever the sun shines in through the windows. It is warm enough now to move around outside. Keiko's parents won't let Keiko go back to the hospital, so when she's not practicing, she joins Yumi on her walks. That's when she gets to hear Yumi talk as they walk, about the patients, the parents, the nurses, all the wonderful people she has met. Keiko leads her out beyond her usual route, a little farther each day. By Thursday morning's walk, Keiko is determined to break the news to Yumi that she will not do the second audition on Saturday. But Thursday is when Yumi finally mentions Ayaka.

"The night before the quake," Yumi says, her voice cracking, "Ayaka and I were so high from the Osaka Academy audition. I think it was our happiest night. It was like she knew it was her last performance. She just nailed the hell out of it." She loops her arm through Keiko's. "They let me watch. I wish you could have seen it." She stops and stares into the air in front of her. "I never thought that she could dance one number, and with each turn or spin, I could see my daughter as another array of color and light, another shape, each one revealing the very best of her. I knew then why I let her destroy her body for something she loved so much." Yumi takes a breath and starts walking again, but slower this time. "In that moment, the injuries were forgotten, and the pain, all the things she gave up."

Keiko follows in step with Yumi. "All the things you gave up."

Yumi ignores her compliment. "Her body said it all that day, and everybody heard."

Keiko kicks a loose stone and tries again. "I'll bet her hair looked its best, too."

Aunt Yumi has always credited at least half of Ayaka's success to the perfect makeup and hair that Yumi has done for her before auditions and shows. It is the only thing she has ever congratulated herself on, and the family allows her this one indulgence in pride.

She stops and sits on a fire hydrant in front of the elementary school. From her purse, she fishes out a brown cigarette and lighter. *Tick, tick, hiss.* She sucks smoke in until her cheekbones form cliffs and the rest of her face two concave walls beneath.

After a few drags, a fog shrouds her. She props her feet on the hydrant, draws her knees to her chest, and wraps her arms around them.

The cigarette teeters between Yumi's knuckles, and ashes fall onto the ground. The gray flakes dance a little on a leftover patch of snow.

"That night I wanted to stay up and celebrate, but she wanted to go to bed early. She knew she was going to quit school as soon as she signed on with the company, but she still insisted on getting up early to catch the first train back to Kobe as planned." Yumi chokes on the last few words and buries her head in her knees. When she lifts her head up to take another long, shaky drag, tears jump off the edges of her cheekbones rather than crawling down her face. She is that thin. "Damn her," she says. "Ayaka never took one moment to congratulate herself." Yumi stubs out her cigarette on the fire hydrant and drops it in the melting snow.

The nights are still cold. Under her pajamas, Yumi wears Ayaka's leotards and leg warmers. By the time Keiko climbs into bed next to Yumi each night, Ayaka's pointe shoes, tied together by their pink ribbons, swing from the hook on the back of the closet door and brush against the wood. When Mom went to Osaka, she helped Yumi burn everything except Ayaka's dance gear, which Yumi has arranged in Keiko's closet, with the urn of ashes. The room is so heavy with Ayaka that Keiko is sure a ghost will pop out from a sheet, a robe, a white sweatshirt in the closet.

On Friday night, Yumi is already under the comforter when Keiko crawls into bed. She finds a photograph on the nightstand. It shows Yumi with a little, bald white girl. Yumi has painted a purple butterfly across the girl's face. They look happy.

If Yumi were to paint Keiko's face, she'd probably draw her as a bear or tiger or wolf, a beast that doesn't know how to channel God or anything good at all. Yumi places her hand on the back of Keiko's head. They're both numb, from the grief and the thyroid disease, and Keiko wonders if Yumi expects an anvil to crush her, too.

"How do you do it?" Keiko says. "How do you face it like you do, when you know it's going to swallow you whole?"

"It's easy," Yumi says. "I have you."

When Keiko wakes up Saturday morning, she has waited much too long to quit. She has to tell Yumi now, but Yumi and the pointe shoes are gone.

Yumi and Keiko have planned to prepare for the Asheville audition in Keiko's parents' room. It's early when Keiko walks downstairs, and she hasn't put in her contacts. When she nudges the door open, Yumi looks over at her the way Vermeer's woman, standing under Cupid, peers out of the frame: *Come in. Have a seat in this empty chair.* She wraps Keiko in Ayaka's white dressing gown. Keiko sits next to her and watches her arrange cosmetics cases on the counter in front of the big mirror. Yumi opens all of the cases except one, and then she starts combing Keiko's hair.

Keiko corrects her posture and catches Yumi's eye in the mirror. "Wait," she says. "Before you go any further, I have to tell you—"

"Shh," Yumi says. "Just let me take over."

Keiko leans back. She runs her thumbs along the satin lapels of the dressing gown, and along her collarbones. She stops her fingers from moving to her throat. For the first time, she doesn't mind the way her bones blend in with the rest of her now, rather than jutting out and drawing attention to themselves. She leans forward, staring into her irises, her imperfect lenses, so brown they have to be called black.

Next to the liquid eyeliner on the counter, Yumi lines up tweezers, brow pencils, rice powder foundation. She will paint Keiko white. Still, Keiko wonders what colors and tools await them in the unopened case, what possibilities it holds that no one has yet considered.

Yumi keeps running between the mirror and the bed on the other side of the room, where she digs through more bags. The only one she doesn't touch is the white silk bag, which shows the outline of Ayaka's pointe shoes inside. Against the brown bedspread, it is a flag in a barren field, begging for sun.

The bag should be dirtier by now. Every night for nearly two months, Aunt Yumi has pulled it out of a drawer and loosened the drawstring before removing the shoes and hanging them by their pink ribbons on the hook behind Keiko's bedroom door. The bag might get dirty in the mornings, perhaps, when Yumi has to force the shoes back into it and cinch them in. Maybe in the mornings, Keiko thinks, Yumi wrestles with the bag and pulls it, clutches it, punches it, and then stuffs it away, out of sight.

"Ayaka," Yumi says. Her voice sounds lighter, younger than usual. "Do you want black or silver hairpins?"

Keiko doesn't correct her. There's no higher compliment than being called Ayaka's name. She considers how the stage lights might bounce off of the silver and make her sparkle as she spins. "Black," she says.

Yumi walks across the carpet and stands behind Keiko. In the mirror, Keiko can see the dimple below Yumi's eye: the same one Keiko's mother has, and in exactly the same spot as Ayaka's dimple. Keiko doesn't have it.

Yumi sets her free hand on the back of Keiko's head to soften the yank of the comb. Her eyebrows knit together and her lips pucker, as though she will be judged for the look of the hair, as if all eyes will bore into her rather than the dancer.

There is a knock on the door. Keiko's mom asks how they're doing. She has agreed not to open the door because she knows it disrupts Yumi's process and Keiko's nerves. They ignore her.

While Yumi pulls and scrapes at Keiko's scalp, Keiko squeezes her hangnails and peels at their frayed ends. "Please stop," she says. "Look at me." Yumi places the last pin in Keiko's hair before she stops and looks. "I can't—"

"What is it?" Yumi says. "You can't what?" She is smiling and admiring her work. She is so full of hope.

"I can't believe you did such a great job on my hair."

During his crack-up, Nijinsky made drawings, too. They are mostly of eyes, watching him, waiting for him to leap higher but knowing by that point in his illness that they'd see him fall. They couldn't watch him anymore, because he locked himself in a room, to spill his mind out all day into his diary. A mind so alive but too sick to send his body to work.

Maybe there's another way to bow out, Keiko thinks. You don't have to elbow forward or scamper away. Maybe you can stay right where you are and face the beasts of grief and shame, with their puffy eyes and aching backs, bloody feet and numb fingers. You can drop your shield.

Keiko decides to stumble onto the stage and through this one last number today, because it would be good for Yumi to see her dance. For three minutes on stage under those lights that add fifteen pounds, Keiko will be applauded for her flawless hair, if nothing else.

"Time for makeup," Yumi says, her voice shaking. She scurries back to her bags on the bed.

Keiko turns to watch, and the dressing gown slips down her arm. She feels a draft, but she does not cover herself.

Another knock on the door. "Let's get a move on, ladies," her mom says. "Tick tock."

Yumi mutters about not being able to find something. She sniffs. "The hair looks exactly how I want it," she says, "but can I have a break before makeup?"

"Sure," Keiko says.

Yumi flops onto the bed. Her hands and feet twitch.

Keiko wants to spring up and wrap her arms around Yumi, tell her it's okay. I'm worried about you. I miss Ayaka, too. Really. *My pulse is an earthquake. You will understand me when you see me dance.*

Yumi's whole body shakes. She stretches her arms over her

head. Her hands pull the brown comforter with her as she falls onto the floor, knocking over the raku vase. The lip of it hits the wood floor and a small piece chips off. Keiko will glue it back on as soon as they get home from the audition. Her mother will never notice, and Keiko will pretend it didn't happen.

Keiko wants to wrap the comforter around Yumi and hold her until the tremors stop, but there's no time for that. It's time to stand tall one last time, spread your arms out wide, and face it. For that you need a little protection, a mask between your skin and what's coming at you, so Keiko opens the last of Yumi's cases and finds the face paints inside. She picks up a blue grease stick and runs it over her cheekbones, her jaw, around the brow line, across the eye lids, and then she colors in the rest of her face.

THE MUSIC SHE WILL NEVER HEAR

On the way to the mine, the historian lets Jace control the radio, if there are any stations out here at all. After listening to some fuzz, the historian says he wishes he had some tapes, some of his son's tapes, lying around. He laughs. "What is it that they say? 'Not your father's music'?"

When he asks about Jace's music, Jace reaches down into his backpack and pulls out a pirated album. He tells the historian that the band isn't on the radio much, that they are called Phish, a concert group, a live phenomenon, how they played at Red Rocks and you just wouldn't believe the sound. How the beats and chords blasted out from the stage in the half shell, that orange-pink cave. He has to stop himself from getting carried away.

"Guitars and drums and keyboards, but it's not rock?" the historian says.

"More like fusion. Jazz, rock, bluegrass, maybe, a lot of improvising. I guess it sounds like rock to people who don't know it, or it looks like it from the long hair and the clothes."

"Sounds a bit like that Garcia fellow and his tribe. Hell's Angels and all that business."

Jace has to choose his words carefully. He's tired of people making that comparison, and referring to Phish as Baby Dead. "It's not exactly like that, Dr. Sims," he says.

"Go on, let's have a listen," the historian says. "I like it already."

Jace pops the tape in. While it plays, the historian glances at the tape deck. On this field trip, the historian wants to know about more than just heavy metals. He has called in Jace to tell him about the harder stuff. Carbons. Mites, tites, rites. Complex bonds. School me, kid, he said when they spoke on the phone. Give the teacher a lesson in rock.

After a few songs, he turns the volume down and smiles at Jace. "How about your outfit? What kind of music do you play?"

"My band's not playing now. I'm drums. Brad, my uncle, he's the front man, sings and plays lead. Keiko, his girlfriend, she got bored and picked up tambourines, then took over for the keyboard player when he split. We lost our bass player, too, so maybe she'll learn that." He laughs.

"What's so funny?"

"Girls can't play bass."

The historian glances at Jace. His face looks red, like he's heating up. "What about those all-girl groups?"

"That's different. She doesn't get along with girls." Jace rubs a threadbare spot on his jeans. A hole will form there soon. "Besides, Keiko likes to hide on the platform, only show the top of her. Thinks she's fat."

"Ah," the historian says. "Yes. You're behind your instrument, too. All of you are."

Jace turns back toward the window. "Didn't think of it that way."

The historian's hands shake as he drives west. They enter a tunnel. Jace imagines that a stone door closes over the entrance behind them, and then an animated roadrunner pumps TNT ahead, to force a rockslide over the only way out.

Now the historian's face twists up. "Keiko? One of those in my world survey course."

"One of what?"

"A Keiko. She came to my office last week. Falling behind, she said. Otherwise I wouldn't remember the name. It's hard to pick out a face in a class of hundreds."

"Sounds like her. But she'll get there. She holed herself up all weekend to cram for midterms."

"Right. So, Keiko and *your uncle?*"

"He's only a few years older than us. My grandma said they needed extra time to recover from raising my mom before they could have another kid." Jace laughs. The burst of air from the back of his throat surprises him, and then he has no air left.

"Your mum. Where does she live?"

"She doesn't."

They stop for breakfast. Once the historian's stomach is full and the coffee kicks in, he taps his thumbs on the steering wheel. A pebble clinks the windshield. Then there's a shush of light rain and the swish that wipes it away. Jace twirls a pencil, a stick of soft graphite he uses to sketch impenetrable carbon bonds of diamonds, those bastards that last through the worst heat and pressure. That was how it started, the twirling and spinning, the drum stick tricks, over his muffled snare and in front of heavy metal music videos, to imitate the stunts those drummers could do, the way they nailed not just the skin, but the rim and hi-hat. They struck with their whole bodies, all the force they had. That'll kill your ears, Grandma always said. Jace didn't care about damaging his hearing, but he couldn't lose it completely. The silence that followed the final crash would hurt more than the loudest pound.

One day Grandpa brought home an entire drum set, arranged it in the basement, behind Brad's microphone stand and amp, and along the stream of cords. He tacked foam rubber over the walls, the egg carton shaped stuff his buddy at the radio station had told him about. You could yell all you wanted, pound the daylights out of a room, and the sound waves would still stop there, lodge into the grooves between a thousand eggs. It made the space smaller, but it promised to absorb every vibration, strike, kick, and squeal of electric strings. Grandpa slipped the guitar strap over Brad's head. He tossed Jace one stick, then another.

Brad and Jace tried a few bars of something generic, and it felt real, felt good. Brad took off into one of Grandpa's favorites, some jazz standard Jace couldn't keep up with. Grandpa sliced the air to say stop, and he faced the invisible crowd. "Ta da!" he said. He held his arms up, then down and out, toward both of his boys, but mostly toward his son, the lead. He held his arms up again, toward the kitchen above. "The music she will never hear."

Jace tries to make getting to the mine fun. "You said you have children, right, Dr. Sims?" he says.

"Sure, though sometimes I forget. My son, Ollie, he's good at disappearing."

Jace has no answer.

"My mates at the School of Mines said you're quite a whip in the geology lab and I should request you as my guide," the historian says. "Lucky for me, isn't it?"

"I don't know. Guiding's a job. It's not bad."

"Jace is an unusual name. What does it mean in Japanese? You must be half or—?"

"My name means moon, and I'm not Japanese. I'm white, and Ute." He mumbles this last part, because it's none of the historian's business, and because Jace is not used to the topic. His association with Keiko confuses people, but at least the historian won't ask any more dumb questions about names and groups and who came from where.

The historian nods. Origins are his business. "My wife and I, we look different, too. She's what you call black Irish. White skin, black hair, dark eyes. Her family wasn't too thrilled when I came along. Another English invasion."

"Yeah, I know what you mean." This is a bullshit comparison, but the old guy is backpedaling. He is really trying.

"But before long, the differences fade away. Life will get easier for the two of you."

"You mean for my uncle and Keiko."

"Right. For them." He checks the rearview mirror. "It will get easier for you, too."

The tape has reached its end. The historian punches the stereo's power button. Tell me some mine legends, he says, so Jace indulges him. This is the true work of the guide. It's harder this time because this client is not the tax lawyer or the curious senior-citizen tourist group, trying to escape through a cave, to be kids again, in the dark. Jace asks if the historian knows the one about John Henry's hammer versus the steam engine, if he knows how the tunnels were made. Of course he knows that one. The historian says his head has been in the Old West for years now, and he's touched a lot of the remains, but this mine, the one they're about to reach and one of precious few that isn't closed off, is a first for him. How many times has Jace been through this one? Twenty-seven. Will it look like the historian imagines, like the books say? Darker. Sound like? Twenty-seven leaky faucets. No, as many second hands, Jace tells him. Tick. Tick.

The historian says he moved his family out here from Chicago because his specialty is the mining era—the magnetism of the gold and silver rushes—what brought whom to the Rockies and why. Hunger, greed. And what kept them panning. Starvation, pride. So Jace wants to tell him not about wet caves and what grows within, but about other phantoms in tales he has learned outside of the School of Mines, echoes in a darkness for which the historian's research money isn't meant. The historian will think this myth is passed down from Jace's elders, that Jace actually knows his elders, rather than from old smelly books he dug up in the library.

"You ever hear the one about the moon versus the coyote?" Jace says.

"Can't say I have."

"The moon wanted the living to bury their dead, but his enemy, the coyote, was for cremation. Since the coyote was right on the ground, it was hard to stop him from swaying the living. Eventually the moon gave in."

The historian responds, but Jace doesn't listen. Out the window, below the interstate, in a valley town where even the trees are trucked in, the taller pines lean down, shelter the new growth as best they can, and their highest eaves rest on the halt of power lines.

Sometimes you can learn everything you need to know just by checking a window, looking through it past your reflection into what you can't see from any other angle at any other time. If you leave the blinds open just a crack, a moving object—say a rock, or a snowflake, or a man, a stranger—might come at you from the south, from the bus station. Or maybe he hitched. Maybe he walked, just wandered off. Maybe he parked, sat, waited. Just around the corner.

On a day in eleventh grade when Jace stayed home from school, the man had walked the way only a messenger can, or the way of a guilty child awaiting punishment. His hands were full, which made his steps slower, and his concentration more a part of the movement. His face tilted up to check address numbers, and as he came closer, he appeared taller, the curves of his hat more defined, the thing in his hands more bag-like than box shaped. Jace knew where the man was headed. He grew larger on the sidewalk until he cut a right angle and made his way up the cement path that split Jace's front yard. If Jace opened the window he would hear the man's boots: click, tap, click, tap, click. No scuffs or drags. The bag lay flat over the man's palms, and Jace imagined him presenting it to Grandma. *It's a beautiful covering for the box*, she might say. *A nice way to wrap up my daughter, but we prefer urns. Have you people kept her in a little box all this time?*

After the man disappeared under the cover of the porch, Jace dressed without making a sound. He wanted to get downstairs in time to hear Grandma say it, but what do you wear to accept your mother's ashes from your distant cousin or would-be neighbor or uncle? How do you prepare for a moment you'll have to remember and retell for the rest of your life? It was a Thursday in 1993, he'd say, eleventh grade, when I was out sick from school, so sick I'd lost my voice, and I was wearing my Rockies jersey or my red T-shirt or Brad's flannel. Not boxers. That wouldn't do.

At first all he heard from downstairs was Grandma saying, "Do you need a ride to the station?" Then, through the storm door, came the man's voice, the upward pull on the middles and ends of words, so that each statement sounded a dozen questions. It was that intonation, that tongue which to Grandma sounded foreign enough to wince at, that put Jace at ease. Perhaps the women on the reservation, women besides his mother, sang baby Jace to sleep with that very pattern of rise and fall. Perhaps Grandma had to change his tune when he found his voice.

Jace threw on the best shirt and pants he could find. As he zipped up, he raised his head. A figure moved in the corner of his eye, through a crack in the blinds, down on the street, away. The man was leaving already.

Even with his hands free of the bag or box, the man constricted his movement. He shoved his hands into his pockets, and he still hunched over. His hat hung by its string around his neck and onto his back. Jace could see the hairline now, just a slight receding, nothing like Grandpa's low tide, and a black crew cut. And then he saw the ears: tiny brown coils. Just like Jace's ears.

Jace opened the window and listened to the man's steps. They were not clicks or taps at all but thuds. Hey, he wanted to say. I know you can hear me, Dad. But that day he had no voice.

At the kitchen table, once Grandma couldn't stand it anymore, she made Jace open what the man delivered. Jace untied the bag and pulled out the box.

"What is it?" she said. "Feathers? Beads? Turquoise?"

Jace opened the latch and held up the treasure: a rose quartz. Its mount had separated from the chain. The crystal was chipped and soiled but still shined pink.

Grandma brought a hand to her mouth and backed her chair away from the table.

Once she had made it to the driveway, Grandpa said, "It was the last thing they argued about. Grandma didn't want her wearing it. She didn't want your mother doing a lot of things."

Jace knew this, knew how it all must have sounded to the neighbors: a good girl, a nice Arrowhead Academy girl, trying to civilize those people. And if that isn't enough, she goes and lets one of them work his charms on her.

Brad is Keiko's official boyfriend, and he is, officially, Jace's uncle. It's October now, and neither Jace nor Keiko has seen Brad since July, when Jerry Garcia reached his deathbed. Brad called Keiko last week to announce his visit. If she hasn't failed out of school yet, Keiko is still on the historian's official roster of students. The historian is Jace's client this weekend, who pays to have a guide with a permit, someone who knows rocks inside and out, to take him underground. Jace is the guide. But these labels are all coincidence and fail to explain the actual roles each of them plays.

When Jace and the historian check into the motel at the end of the first day, the historian stares at the key in his hand and looks toward the east wing, where a bed waits. "I'm knackered."

"Okay. I'll get settled in my room, see what's on TV."

"Sure. Do as you please. It's your holiday, too." The historian reaches for his wallet, pulls out three new bills, and rubs them together until they squirm apart. He stretches his arm out, toward Jace. "Get yourself something to eat. This should be enough for a haircut as well."

While the historian sleeps, Jace dreams. All of last summer was a dream. Every day he spent with Keiko glimmered, even in the pouring rain. Pitter patter, rat-a-tat. Besides counting beats, and pounding them out of course, this is what Jace can do: judge a stone by its color, cleavage, hardness, and by its specific gravity. Sometimes you can find two stones in one. That's what his rock guidebooks say. Hold a purple stone up to the light and you'll notice the golden glow of citrine inside. One day on the Phish tour, a day when clouds threatened while Keiko slept, Jace opened her bottle of thyroid medication. No capsules inside. Not two, not one. Without them anything could happen, any expansion or contraction of cells, tissues. It would show in her middle and in the glow of her skin. Her disease screws with her weight so much that she had to give up ballet, and it screws with her hormones, too. They need the meds as a special transmitter, a daily call, to send signals to those eggs stalled out on the sides of their roads, their pathways into the dark tunnel, and then outside. By October the signals sit stagnant with three months worth of blood. *Wash me.* She keeps saying it's just her thyroid messing with her cycle, but Jace wonders if a new life is starting to grow.

But that's now. This was then: the summer Phish tour, the stolen moments alone with her. Like the day when Brad was off trying to score concert tickets in the parking lot of Red Rocks Amphitheatre, while Jace and Keiko snuck into the cave on the side of the pavilion. The going rate was getting higher, and in there they could climb and pull and crouch and enjoy the show for free. No one would know. It was harmless. They just sat there, enraptured by the music, and stared into the golden-coral-pink-blue-everything-is-possible sky when Brad was nothing and nowhere, like everyone else but the two of them.

That's what it was like last summer when Phish played at Red Rocks or Mud Island or Finger Lakes. Once the music starts and you grease up and all your cylinders kick in and the pistons are really pumping and you sweat and pulsate and start dancing around, you're not just one pathetic little engine anymore, you're on the superhighway: thousands of individual bodies moving as one amoeba.

When the tour took them through Kentucky, Keiko rested her head against the passenger window and said, "Looks like home."

Jace had heard her talk about home before, so he expected her to flip out the closer they got to it. Home for her, she'd told him, was some town on the border between the Carolinas near the Blue Ridge Mountains, where a mother poured a father's money into a ski lodge in the Rockies, just so they could tell their friends they were spending Christmas on the slopes in (near) Aspen. It was so convenient when Keiko got a ballet scholarship to a college close by. Another excuse for Mother to brag.

But something else happened to Keiko. When Brad stopped the van at a gas station in Kentucky, Keiko sprung out the door, pranced into the grass, held her arms wide, and spun around, tilting her face up. And there it was, the other side of her, the dancer she had locked away, still alive, and set free for this moment. Jace followed her. He took her hands to steady her. She was breathless, dizzy. He loved when she got like this. It was contagious.

She smiled and inhaled deeply. "It's like home, Jacy. Same rock faces, same smell."

He pulled her close. "The gasoline smell or the bathroom smell?"

"No, the tree smell, the humid air." She ran her fingernails absently down his arm. "It's the trees you miss the most."

A few days later, Brad promised Keiko a detour to North Carolina on their way back from Vermont, where Phish's tour would end. She sat on his lap and plastered kisses all over his face. Thank you, thank you, thank you. It's perfect timing, she said, because her parents were in Colorado, and they'd left her aunt in the house alone. "It's only my aunt that I want to see anyway," she added. The aunt had lost her marbles after the Kobe earthquake and moved in with the parents. "She won't tell my parents that I'm road tripping with two guys. She won't even tell them I visited. They think I'm busy with summer classes."

On the night after Phish's closing show, when it was late, but no one was tired, and gone was the novelty of card games or hacky sack, Brad grabbed his flannel, just like he'd done every night for the past week. "Going beer hunting," he said. Brad wouldn't be twenty-one for a few months, so he had to use his fake ID when any of them wanted a drink. He was always whipping it out like a pistol.

"Hope your weapon backfires," Keiko said. She did not look up from her knitting.

She and Jace knew by then that Brad wasn't going on a beer run, and he wasn't going to follow through on his promise to take her home, because he had stopped following through on everything. She was plotting her escape, and Jace promised to help. The next morning, during his driving shift and Brad's sleep time, Jace would detour to a town somewhere off Highway 81, where Keiko could catch a southbound bus. Then it would just be him and Brad alone in the van.

The last thing Keiko said before she fell asleep that night was, "When you meet my Aunt Yumi, whatever you do, don't tell her I quit dancing. It would crush her."

It didn't make sense anymore, now that Keiko was going alone to visit her aunt, but Jace promised to stay quiet. He ran his thumb over her forehead. If she didn't get away from Brad and go home, Keiko was the one at risk of crushing, not her aunt. Jace stayed quiet about that now, too. He always knew to stay quiet for Keiko. She had spent so much of her life on stage that she relied on a certain amount of make-believe.

A few hours before sunup, in that slice of night too late for activity and too early to start the new day, Jace heard a hum from the edge of the parking lot. It was the engine of whoever dropped Brad off, some floozy or dealer he met last week maybe, when he ditched Jace and Keiko to go to some nearby Grateful Dead shows. They had expected him to disappear for at least a whole day, like he'd already done twice that week. Jace bolted upright, slithered out of Keiko's sleeping bag and into his own on the bench seat. It was a cold night, so he was already back into his clothes. Keiko did not stir when he peeled away from her.

Brad rolled open the door and grabbed Jace's foot. "Dude, wake up. Jerry's tweakin'."

Jace lifted his head and rubbed his eyes longer than necessary. It was a good act.

"It doesn't look good," Brad said. "The rest of the Dead tour's canceled. They're talking Betty Ford Clinic." He squeezed Jace's toes on that last part, and then he leaned onto the feet, rested his chin over the ankles. "I should have seen it coming. The way he kept the volume down at Giants Stadium, and how all those chicks cried and clapped when he was barely making any noise at all. Just leaned onto the guitar pedals, like they kept him upright." Brad straightened up and let go of Jace's feet. "If things don't get better, they'll send him back to California. A bunch of us are gonna meet there no matter what. So we gotta get going. I gotta get you guys home and be on my way."

Jace climbed into the front passenger seat as Brad started the engine and pulled out. He expected Brad to be too high to drive, but Brad sounded more sober than ever. Hearing the bad news must have kept him from shooting up or dropping tabs or whatever he was about to do with his new Deadhead friends, so Jace didn't insist on driving right away.

"I might need to take the semester off," Brad said, and Jace could hear it in his voice then: ten years of an older sister's records fading out, another chorus lost, another groove scratched.

"I can graduate next year. School seems like such a joke now, compared to this."

Jace couldn't listen to it anymore. While Brad rambled on, all Jace heard was a ripping sound, a split between him and Brad, and a great *whoosh* as Brad flew off to some aquamarine planet where everyone let the job of being a music fan distract them from making their own music. Jace wanted to bring him back to reason, but Brad was already too far gone. He'd have to come back on his own, to sew up the split. For now, only Jace was able to keep perspective: It's not like it was a member of Phish on that hospital bed. Their band would still go on. It was just the old guy from the Dead, and old guys croak all the time, but Brad couldn't go on without the music's front man, the voice inside all that vinyl.

On the tour, Brad barely ever let Jace drive. Usually he would ask him to navigate instead. That night, on the way home—a somber night because they'd just gotten word of Jerry Garcia's hospitalization—Brad just needed Jace to keep his mouth shut and stay close by. Once Keiko was up and in shotgun position, Jace sat on the floor between the front bucket seats, listened for the tempo changes or never ending drum solos on the tapes. At this spot, Brad could elbow Jace's shoulder when they reached a bridge, as the strings rose in pitch and speed, and the vo-cals held onto a note. And Keiko could cup the back of Jace's head as he nodded on the accentuated beats. Sometimes she thumbed the edge of his ear, circled around toward the center until it tickled and he jolted away. On the floor he felt the bumps in the road.

It was during that return trip, the don't-worry-everything-(especially-Jerry)-will-be-fine movement west, that the pound-ing slowed to a thud at the right front of the van. Brad pulled over. No cussing. No words at all. No kicking, and very little sound as he walked to the back. Then the click of the tailgate.

Keiko opened her door and whipped out of her seat, but

she didn't tilt her head back and spin around this time. She followed Brad. Jace took his spot on his bench seat and faced the back. He set his chin on the headrest and curled his fingers over it. He watched Brad shove blankets and duffels aside, and pull up the trap door. No jack. No spare tire.

"Where the hell is it?" Keiko said. One hand dug into her hip, and the other sprung out.

No answer from the driver. The spare tire pit held only a quilt, the old pink one Grandma had threatened to burn. It protected something square. Brad looked up at Jace as he lifted it. It was heavy enough to strain his face and neck muscles, but Brad made the bundle look weightless. All that time it had been there, in the van's belly, and through a steel sheet it felt every splash, every bouncing rock, the wind below. Brad let Keiko unwrap it and reveal a stack of early Dead records, imprints of half-planned riffs and spontaneous jams. *Anthem of the Sun*, *American Beauty*, *Wake of the Flood*. Tracks useless to moving forward in a cassette and CD era, but necessary to remind them of their precursor, their source, their uncle father sister mother of sound.

When Grandma had finally cleaned out her daughter's room, Jace was old enough to get out of the way. It was a curse, she said, for anyone to wear a dead girl's clothing or shoes or earrings. Grandpa boxed and carried and dumped all of Jace's mother's things into the trash, but when Grandma wasn't looking, he placed one stack of records under each boy's bed, with a set of headphones to the hi-fi in the basement. There they could sift through what she had left behind.

Keiko didn't touch the records. She didn't whine about her escape plan or take off running west to the junction of Highway 81, just a few miles ahead now. She set the bundle down and held Brad.

Jace shoved his hands into his pockets and hit the road. Eventually there were signs. Not just the green of this route or that, the white of watch your speed, the blue of filling station or rest area ahead, or the red of you'd better stop, but brown signs indicating an interesting turn off.

It was a cold and quiet walk at that hour, as the blue-black sky gave way to lavender. Glass shards twinkled on the shoulder. A stray dog zigged and zagged and then disappeared behind a rock wall with watermarks at its base. Water was here, then one day it fell away, down chutes of dirt and stone, into pools, through valleys, and eventually released into the sea. Gone. And it left dried remains with sediment lines to help us remember a time we never knew.

With his thumb pointed up, Jace trotted backwards on the shoulder. He stopped, jumped, blew on his hands. A car pulled over. Behind the wheel was a fat man in a beige jacket. The passenger window was down. Jace leaned in. The man offered a price and stroked Jace's hand.

He walked another mile, maybe two. Head down, the chill burning him now. Lights poured over him and passed him by. Eventually a station wagon sputtered onto the shoulder ahead of him, crunched rocks, flashed one taillight. An arm appeared out the driver's window and waved him forward. It was chubby, a white blob against dark pavement and sky, with dark fingernails.

When he told the driver how many miles he and his uncle had covered and how far west they were headed, she let out a low whistle and picked up her CB receiver. "You're gonna need a good tire. Up here's an honest mechanic, sells quality parts. Normally on a reservation, they'd bleed you dry, but not these people. Got the fear of the Lord in 'em." She made the call, woke up the man in charge. He would leave the door open. "Ten miles ahead," she told Jace.

"Thanks."

He scanned the interior. A bumper sticker on the glove box said, "On the eighth day, He listened." No radio. No tape deck. The backseats were folded down, with boxes on them.

"What's in the back?" Jace said.

"The Good Word. That's what I got to give, or sell some-times. On my way to Burning Man now. Those kids frying in the desert, they need some inspiration. They're a tough crowd." She raised a finger, wagged it twice, and then held it still. "But at every concert I hit, I always catch a few before they enter, reel them back out. Return to sender."

When they reached the gas station/garage/general store, Jace carried in a soiled and tattered sheet of paper with the tire's diameter written on it. The door creaked open and then slammed shut behind him. The lights buzzed. Two employees, husband and wife probably, spoke in chains of inflections until it was settled. A price. Behind the counter, the wife rubbed her eyes and said, "It must be quite a trip, to drive through the night like this."

When he stepped outside and loaded the tire into the back of the car, the sky was more purply-pink than blue. The driver was pleased. She honked and waved goodbye to her friends as she peeled out of the lot.

"It's going to be a fine day," she said, "like the days when I sell my lucky Bible; you know, the last in a box."

Jace bought her last three Bibles for ten dollars. She dropped him off a few exits from the van, where Brad and Keiko waited.

"Good luck at the next show," he said. Now, as dawn broke, he noticed the amulet that clutched at her throat. It was round and white and it stole the light from her skin.

Jace can't sleep. If he's going to try to win Keiko back, he should use the historian's money to buy her a gift. Across the street from the motel is a shop in a long barn, shined up and ready for traveler's checks. On its roof, a billboard-sized sign shouts up to the interstate: "Precious Gems." Jace enters the store and un-zips his jacket, a heavy jacket that makes him worth watching. His hands stay in his pockets as his eyes scan the merchandise. He does not enter the shopkeeper's blind spots.

He peeks out the window, through the blank space between

signs. The last slice of sun sinks behind a peak to the west. On the other side of it is the resort town where Keiko studies now, in her parents' ski lodge, where she begs her cycle to end, or to begin again. She is waiting for something to crack, to break down and pour out.

He passes over the dross and toward the shiny rocks. He finds a stone that looks just like the one in the driver's amulet: pearly, opaque, but too clear to call white. The shopkeeper tells him it's a moonstone, a gem whose main element is wind. It's known to transmit magnified emotions, lunar energy, psychic perception.

"It's a third eye," she says.

Once the shopkeeper unlocks the case, Jace holds the moonstone up to the light and tests its weight with a dip of his arm. Solid and full of complex bonds. Impossible to break. He sets it on the counter, and it clanks against the glass, as if to tell the stones below, *Hey, up here, look at me. I'm free.*

Jace removes his billfold and separates two notes from the third. "She'll love it," he says.

The shopkeeper wraps up the moonstone and hands it to him. "Lucky girl."

As Jace and the historian return to the mine the second day, the historian hands Jace a stray branch. It is pointed on top. "Here. You're the guide."

They walk for a while, crunching dried leaves until their feet fall into step. It takes a while for the bird noises to find his ear. There is a quiet that follows the tour, even months later.

Above them, the moon hangs low with a blue blanket tucked over its middle. Pines keep their limbs down, but near the bottom, some reach straight out and curl up. The branches stretch wider down low, away from the trunk and its waterways. The needles brown and crisp easily this close to the dirt and the roots below.

The soil hardens as Jace and the historian climb. Slate chips away and slides around. Their toes break it off, and their heels skate back a little on tiny sleds of it.

A hawk blinks, casts one eye down on Jace. He wonders what kind of view it has from its perch, if it can make out the whole mountain range or see what's ahead.

"Jace, over here," the historian says. He waves a hand and points to something important on a rock wall, a scrub tree sprouting out of a crack where stone meets dirt. What Jace notices is a carving off to the left, above the sediment lines: "100 years come around, 100 years underground—1988 and where's my mother lode?"

The historian says he wishes his wife, Gail, were here to name this sprout. "Gail really knows plants. So the trees, the soil, that's not completely foreign to me."

Up top, there's never enough traction underfoot, but below, in the mine, that's the world Jace can sink into. He knows it by feel and by ready-made notions of what the underground world should be. Caves, holes, mines. Stalagmites, biotites. Lights on helmets. Chisels and scythes. Tracks, trains, engines. John Henry tried to beat the machine with his hammer underground. That's what they tell you in school. What Jace knows are tough rocks, knows what makes them burst, give way, tumble, and hide under their neighbors. The historian wants to find out what's inside, what's bubbling and spitting, what's pulling them down.

Before they go in, Jace scans their surroundings, imprints the image: white aspen branches cast out gold leaves. Below them lies a wash of dirt slopes punctured by slouching telephone poles—crosses falling over train tracks. Jace knows the wires they carry, how they hug the old trunk lines that lead the interstate along and then swizzle away. But these telephone and telegraph wires always veer back, always return to parallel the streets. They are, as the historian told him over poached eggs yesterday, the same routes to the same destination, but they stop now for shopping centers and resorts instead of bridges and county seats. Still, they follow the same rivers. These phone and rail lines guided Eisenhower's construction, and now his roads have made them obsolete, but they stay as Western flavor: an attraction, a reminder of how far we've come.

The historian stops Jace. He is short of breath from the altitude and the excitement. He can't wait to start a day of time travel, to fill the gaps in history books. Maybe Jace will get a thank you in the fine print of the historian's next book.

He pats Jace on the back and motions toward the mine. "Artifact is history where there is no memory," he says. "All that ever happened or might have been lives inside of something we can touch. It must, or else it never was."

Maybe it's the coffee pulsing through him, but Jace wraps his head around this. Yeah, he thinks, we feel a surface, judge its heat, blame its simplicity, praise its usefulness, its place in the evolution toward what we want need gotta have can't live without today. Right on, old guy.

Jace swings an arm around the historian's shoulder and leads him in. He is ready to move Dr. Sims beyond the basics of rock. Igneous, volcanic, metamorphic. Mites, tites, rites. Those are easy. Jace is here to tell him about what else is down there, what can distract or obstruct, what can console. And he does. He leads, listens, and nods at every question, even if it's too dark for the historian to see him. In here, Jace does important work.

When the historian asks him to pound, Jace says, "We're not supposed to, Dr. Sims. Mine access permits are pretty strict."

"I'll take the heat. Just find a spot and nail it." He pauses as he hands over the instrument. He does not have to show Jace how to use it. It is the guide's tool, and Jace has been here before.

Jace finds a target and taps. The historian steps away and finds his own spot. They pound in unison for a while, and then their paces stagger, like a gang of hammers forcing spikes through railroad ties and into dirt or slate or impossible rock below. Clink clink. Clink clink. For a long time nothing breaks, but they make a rhythm, tap out a pattern. Veins bulge above the historian's brow. Sweat slides down his neck. His breathing offers a loud wind accompaniment, but it can't keep tempo with the percussion.

"I'll try over there," he says, and points around a bend. The words barely come out. He smiles and grips Jace's arm. "Feels good, doesn't it?"

Jace stares at the wall in front of him. They are supposed to be taking samples, photographing the site, getting a sense of the everyday reality of the prospectors' search, like they did yesterday. His boss told him that's what the historian is known for: sniffing out the real story behind the mining myths, getting into character. Jace is just paid to identify stones, explain formations, point out hiding places of gems that may have been passed over. He is here to demonstrate the safe spelunking practices he absorbed from expert geologists. Some guide he is.

When it happens, Jace is just around the corner, pounding the daylights out of a certain groove, as the historian instructed. He stops, doubles over, and hears only silence. The dripping has stopped, and the steady beat of the historian's hammer is gone. No echo. Done. Over. This is what Jace will tell the paramedics when they arrive.

In the darkness, he reaches for the historian. He kneels next to the old guy's body, and he takes the moonstone from his own pocket. Jace presses it to the historian's pulse points at the left wrist and then the right, moves it over his torso, over the cavity of organs to upper chest, holds it over the place where he thinks the pounding happens, where the blood landed once it reversed its flow, where the force begins and, if he doesn't do something quick, where the force might end. He knows he should press hard, should lean onto the historian and smother him with a chance at resurrection, bounce him back to life. And so he removes the stone, pushes and pumps, covers Dr. Sims's lips with his. Puff times three. Jesus. They made it look so easy on *St. Elsewhere.*

He runs away. Through the tunnel, down the slope, a wet and muddy sorry excuse for an exit, and then he's back on the trail, where he hurdles erupted roots and he ducks under branches and shrubs sprouting from rock. He hears only feet and breath, feels the downward pull of the historian's wallet and keys in his pocket. Each step stays on the ground too long, each stride too short, wasting time, wasting air, losing another minute, second, instant. He is not supposed to hear the slap of feet and breath, not supposed to concentrate on his own sound at a time like this.

He stays upright all the way to the parking spot, where he finds a cellular phone in the historian's glove box. He punches the buttons, gasps under the beeps. "Come on. Answer."

The paramedics appear like a hologram. They work their magic—one two three one two three, listen, again—and they blow used air into the mouth from which the history flows, oxygenate the blood that stills in blue trails beneath graying skin. They beg life from this stranger, give him breath, help him draw in and expel the stuff on his own. But the heart takes its time in responding. It slows as it comes down from the fight, the return of blood to its sender.

They say Jace was right to let the historian lie, to resist the urge to drive him away, that a miracle kept him alive. That it's not every day you see a cardiac down in the hole. Not anymore.

The ambulance shrinks as it rushes toward the nearest hospital, a hospital that fixes a lot of heart problems, in the closest of Colorado's resort towns. Lots of old guys feel the pressure on the chair lift or in the hot tub or by the fire, where the blood starts to boil, hits obstacles, bottlenecks between buildup on the walls of its paths, its closing tunnels, and rushes back home, overflows. So they keep specialists close by to clean up the mess.

Before the paramedics left, they told Jace to call the patient's family, to follow the ambulance in the historian's vehicle. He knows the way, right? But instead he stays, lets his feet sink into the mud as he watches the ambulance shrink away and as the rain pastes his hair over his face. It feels slimy, and it narrows his view. In the distance a train gives warning. *Here I come. Fear me.* Jace is supposed to move faster, to hurry up and follow the historian to the place where he will heal and come out a better man.

The moonstone. Before Jace gets in the car, he has to go back down into the mine, to find what he left there. It is a slow walk—no hurry now that the life is saved—so he has time to notice that out here the aspens have dropped most of their yellow leaves and to feel the chill that carries a warning of impending first snow.

In the mine, the darkness swallows him, and the air thins exponentially. He wheezes as his fingers travel along walls and ground. Beams of headlamp and flashlight bounce and swing, revealing the usual debris: shreds of rope, pencils, loose pennies. It's too dark in here to retrieve any object that might slip out of hands or pockets, especially if it's brown, yellow, or copper.

Jace stands where he stood just minutes ago as he pounded the wall. It was foolish and illegal to follow the historian's whimsical orders. He walks around the curve, into this alcove the historian found, and where he pounded until his heart stopped. Jace kneels down into the mold his knees made earlier, beside the indentation that the historian's back left in the dirt.

This is where he set the moonstone down. It was a silent release, softer than you'd expect at a time when your heart is an Allman Brothers drum solo at a million decibels, to compensate for the other guy, who's lost his volume, his treble, his bass. Jace holds it up now, and his headlamp draws out the gem's pearly coloring, that shade between clear and white that's so hard to name, even in full light.

Keiko will hold the moonstone under a lamp, too, once he gives it to her. She'll either say, What kind of gift is this, or she will say, Oh, Jacy, you know me so well. She will embrace him and stroke his ear with her right hand and rub the stone with her left. Together they will hold it, test the weight of all it offers: lunar energy, a third eye. But it will still feel light after all, because, as they will remember without saying, the moonstone's main element is wind.

Right now, he thinks, she must be sitting by the window, watching the last of the aspens' gold eddy down, away. Maybe the altitude will affect her cycle and apply some pressure to her stubborn female organs.

Outside again, Jace dials the people in the historian's address book. No answer from Gail, the wife. The son, Ollie, is at work, working on a Saturday at a fancy restaurant where they play classical music to pacify callers on hold. Jace waits. The music does not calm him. Frantic violins and cellos burst above the kettledrum's thunder. It is a tune to be performed live so that the musicians in the pit can strum and strike with the appropriate violence in the neck and fingers, and on stage a ballerina can dart here and there in a fury. Keiko would know this tune. After all the running around, she would finish with a slow, soothing flourish. He is sure.

Over the phone, the historian's son stays composed. Just a low "Jesus Christ" and a "Shoulda known this was coming." He sighs and gives thanks to Jace, the witness and rescuer, the messenger of this not shocking news. It's lucky, the son says, because the hospital is close to his workplace, a restaurant in a hotel Jace has seen in glossy advertisements. The son will be there in no time.

"Drive yourself home in my dad's car," he says. "Call us at the hospital, and tell us where to pick it up. Might not get there for a few days, but don't worry, we'll pay you for your trouble."

As he starts the engine, Jace pictures the historian's son behind the wheel instead, a miniature version of the father: short and wiry with curls more gold than silver. He is driving his father home. Gail is a small, dark-haired woman who stares out the passenger window, knitting and crying small diamonds. They fall into her lap, shine up to her face. She turns around to check on her sleeping husband until they approach their house at the end of a dirt road. Maybe it rests on a hill, sitting apart from the others. Maybe it is humble, or maybe it's dripping with ornate artifacts as proof of the historian's life spent sifting through forgotten days. It is a bi-level with an entrance down below, or it is a colonial with two shuttered bedroom windows for eyes in its face and blinds open just a crack.

When you're on the road, like Jace is now, alone in the historian's car, you think about other travelers. It's the trees that bring you back. You think of those who've gone before you, through this canyon of turning aspens, and those who've veered off here or at that exit back there, and you wonder whether they strayed from their routes or continued over the pass, and where they ended up, if they made it, and who they thought about along the way on this road or that.

The last thing Brad said to Jace was a hook, because he wanted to fight: "What can I learn at school that I can't pick up out here?"

It's been a long time since Brad has played or sung. He must be ready to burst.

In order for Brad to visit Keiko, he has to skip Phish's Phoenix show between the northwest and southern legs of the band's fall tour, where things are really blowing up now, because since Jerry Garcia's death, the Grateful Dead tour is off. All those fans need somewhere else to go, so Baby Dead has really hit pay dirt. Brad stays close to the action to see what's inside, but he has a day or two to spare for Keiko. He probably can't wait to tell her all about how Phish has changed, bigger and more popular, but still better, to assure her the sound hasn't lost its magic, that it was okay for the band to sell themselves out to MTV just once— it was worth it for a song like "Down with Disease."

Brad travels light. That much Jace knows. Some practical

and some useless items sag in his backpack with the photo of Keiko, taken a year ago, when she still danced. In costume, in position, under the lights. She looks away from the camera to something higher, out of reach. Since doctors committed Jerry, and Deadheads called Brad in for support, the moon has cycled three times, but Keiko's cycle has stilled, frozen up. Without regular cues, you lose your rhythm. Jace thinks that tonight, on his way back from Oregon Washington British Columbia, Brad drives with the photo propped on the dash. He taps a beat on the wheel and serenades the photo as he drives, tells it that he's almost home, that he's okay, that everything will be different now. Keiko's photo stares back and says, *I'm dead. It's a new me that awaits your return and swells with new life. Maybe.*

The historian's glove box vibrates, and a high-pitched ring shakes Jace back to right here, to this road. He answers the call.

"Hey, it's me, Ollie," the son says. "The old man's still ticking. He's had a heart condition a long time, and he's not supposed to go into those mines."

Now it's Jace's heart that stops. He's never had a client threaten to sue before. He hasn't been trained to deal with calls like this. "I'm sorry," he says. "He didn't mention any of that."

"Sounds like my old man all right. Always working, no matter what." Ollie tries to laugh, but something catches in his throat. "Look, none of that matters now. We want to repay you."

Jace hasn't been trained in how to turn down gifts either. "It's nothing, really."

"Some other time, then." Ollie sounds offended. "Hey, which class are you in? Nineteenth-Century American?"

"I'm not one of his students. I go to a different school, in Golden, for geology and chemistry." But he takes the bus to Boulder every weekend, and sometimes he helps Keiko with history.

"Chemistry? That was my thing. Now I lean over a stove all day. I love it, but it's a killer, too." Ollie pauses. He doesn't have to give Jace his time right now. He should be rushing to the hospital, reappearing when his family needs him. But here he is, trying to say his thanks to Jace. "So don't drop out like I did," he says. "I predict you'll get hell from the old man if you do, and I sure don't want to hear about that."

The son grew up here, after his father left home, migrated west. Jace heard the difference when they spoke earlier, but something in the intonation, in the way a guy not much older than him could sound like an old English historian, put so many years between them. Something protective and concerned and underscoring the shoulds and sures sounded a rhythm learned early on, through regular listening. Repetition and imitation. It was a natural pattern, an imprint.

From the south, the mountain moves closer. So tall and official and useful now. It still blocks Jace's view, hides the town of heated sidewalks and patient lovers. *Respect me*, it says. Snow blankets not just the mountain top but its face, too: white and opaque and silent. The cover is highly anticipated, and around here it falls harder and faster and earlier than anyone can predict.

When he arrives at Keiko's ski lodge, she is not sitting by the window. Brad's van is not parked in her driveway. It could be in the garage, but Brad's the type that likes to announce his presence.

Jace pulls in. As he raises his fist to knock on the door, Keiko opens it. She's been crying.

Brad's boots aren't in the foyer, and his voice isn't rattling through the great room. He is nothing and nowhere. There is only Keiko, waving Jace forward.

In the kitchen, when she is searching through the freezer for a quick dinner, Jace holds the moonstone out to her with both hands. Keiko closes the freezer and accepts the gift, carries it to the middle of the room, under the light. She does this without question, without any words at all, and this does not surprise him. He knows her so well.

"It's just us now," she says, eyes fixed on the glowing rock.

It is so light in their hands. He worries that one of them will let go, and it will shatter on the wood floor, but it is solid, full of complex bonds.

He bounces it. "Unbreakable."

"That's lucky."

They sit at the front bay window in silence. He thinks of popping in a tape, but this isn't the time for music. He doesn't fill the air with stories about what happened today to her history teacher either, and he doesn't ask what kind of test she's been crying over, or if her cycle has sped up. Not yet. For now, they make no noise at all, no movements, as they watch white flurries spin around on the other side of the glass.

"It's beautiful," she says. "I haven't thanked you yet."

"You are now." Jace leans back and lets out a long breath, relieved that she likes the moonstone, that she accepted it at all.

"I mean for all of it," she says, finally looking at him. "The whole trip. What you did last summer. I was ready to crack, and you kept me in one piece." She leans forward and slips her hand over his shirt cuff. "Thanks."

In the window's reflection, her eyes look wet, her lips curved into a smile.

"No trouble," he says.

He cranes his neck to take one last look at that same mountain top before the storm closes it off for the night. By tomorrow, this town will boast a foot of fresh powder up there. It is the impromptu high, the call to action, the moneymaker. The sounding: come forth and conquer the Rockies. *They're all yours*, the ads say.

Jace slides closer to Keiko and holds her there, ready to stay like that all night, waiting for her to speak, forgiving her when she doesn't. He touches the moonstone to her middle and looks beyond gray clouds to a swatch of purply-pink sky, remembering the possibilities. *Name a star for your sweetheart up there*, or here, name a peak or a ski run, or just one little mogul, after yourself.

CENTER OF POPULATION

In here, loss is different. I learned this on my first visit. After I stomped the snow off my boots and signed in at the front desk, I passed by a waiting area, where a pregnant woman sifted through hunting and car magazines. Next to her, an older woman inspected the fingernails on one of her hands. She rested her other hand on her prosthetic leg. I had done taxes for some retired navy, for flight attendants, and small business owners—I'd seen loss. In the autumn months, I also taught fitness classes at Curves, and that's why I was here at the VA hospital annex to do a favor for my cousin, Mark, their resident exercise scientist.

I continued down the hallway, which is painted in loud yellows, reds, and whites. The only decoration is a small statue of the Roman soldier, Cincinnatus, on a plant stand in a corner. He doesn't stand tall and proud like the other statues of him around this town. The armor weighs down his gumpy frame. That first day, I noticed his big ears, too. Despite the blank eyes and long nose, his other features are soft. Nothing juts out. He looks like a scared kid in boot camp.

The day before, when Mark had asked me to take over his

kickboxing therapy class, I said, "You want me to teach a bunch of GIs to dancercise?" "No," he said. "*Exercise.*" It was the middle of tax season, but I agreed to fill in for him, because I hadn't taught a class in months. I wanted to hear ankles crack and breath hitch and hips pop out of socket. I wanted to turn faces red.

When I reached the martial arts room, I took a deep breath and walked in. It was hot inside, with no windows and unmoving ceiling fans.

"Fan blades won't spin," one of the guys said. "Fuse blew." He was looking where I was looking. I flipped the switch anyway. *Clack.* "Good luck," he said. *Clack clack clack.* Nothing.

He squeezed a tennis ball and brought his free hand up to the Bengal tiger face on his orange T-shirt as he introduced himself—Eric—before pointing toward the others: Tony (blue T-shirt) and Raphael (white shirt). They looked how I expected young marines to look, but with longer hair and skin gray from the circulation condition I was there to cure. They stood up, and when I told them my name was Delia, they called me ma'am. Although I kept my dangly earrings on that day, I wore baggy sweats, pulled my hair back tight, and skipped makeup. I wanted to be taken as seriously as a man, as seriously as they take Mark, but in the mirror, I looked like a twelve-year-old girl.

While I laced up my cross-trainers, I watched the marines do towel stretches to aid circulation to their feet. Mark had told me that they had to finish these before I could start the class, and that they'd just spent a month with braces on their feet or splints under their hands. Winter, he said, was a tough season for healing. I watched them grit their teeth as they pushed against the resistance. Eric clicked his jaw and Tony grunted, but Raphael stayed calm. His features were more relaxed. Maybe he didn't have it as bad as the others.

I didn't want the marines to catch me staring at them, so I looked around. I noticed an equipment room with a wooden shim holding its door open. Was it any cooler in there?

When I turned back to the marines, I noted a receding hair-line on Raphael, a slouch in Tony's posture. These guys looked older than their years, after guarding some snowy mountain in the Hindu Kush—an empty peak at the center of the world's population—where they sat and waited for action until their toes turned white.

After an hour of action in here, I'd go home to an empty place, too, a house so much darker and colder since Nico and his daughter, Maggie, had moved out. Nico's glasses wouldn't slide down his nose as he cooked dinner, and Maggie's curls wouldn't bounce as she set the table, nodding through one two three forks, one two three knives.

The marines snuck looks at me while I set out my stepping blocks. I don't have my cousin Mark's muscle or his height. In their eyes, I didn't measure up. Mark's mind is always on his work, his mouth always spouting out jargon: interminable cap-illary damage, sustained recovery, surgical intervention. That day, I was supposed to take his kickboxing routine and mix it up with my step aerobics routine. "As long as the fingertips show some coloration during exercise," he had said, "we won't have to cut them off. Or anything else."

When Eric, Tony, and Raphael were done stretching, I popped my aerobics remixes CD into the stereo. *Music*, Ma-donna sang, *makes the people come together*. I led the class into a march, and then I told them to plant their feet wide. "Bend at the waist," I said, "reach right, left." We straightened up one vertebra at a time. "Time to loosen shoulders and necks." *Music mix the bourgeoisie and the rebel* . . . Our heads rolled.

Mark hadn't included a warm-up in the plan he gave me. Did he begin like I began? Was his practice as good as his theory?

I decided to stop doubting Mark. After all, he's a king in this place, not just for fixing people using exercise, but also for helping the cognitive behavioral doctors figure out some new virtual reality therapy system for the combat veterans. He said it's like a video game, where bombs explode before their eyes and special sounds and odors trigger their memories as they drive imaginary Jeeps through the battlegrounds in order to get past them for good. It's the most successful form of therapy yet, a godsend during this flood of new patients.

We finished the warm-up, and the marines shook out their hands and feet. I tried to imagine how they had felt, half-frozen on that mountain, and wondered if I had it in me to cure any-one, to help them retrieve what they'd lost.

I led them up and down and across the stepping blocks and then into a spin move called "knees around the world." The con-stant motion would bring more blood to the feet.

The young marines obeyed. Step two three, step two three. *And when the music starts . . .* Madonna sang. They breathed louder.

"The next step," I said, "is called revolving door."

I demonstrated the step and the sequence that followed. Eric and Raphael did just fine, but Tony shuffled through a few rep-etitions and then lay down in the center of the studio floor. He stared up into the still fan.

"I don't know when to turn," he said.

"Just think in eights," I said. "The intervals are always eight beats long. Turn at the end."

"I don't think in eights."

Madonna faded out. The next track was a short instrumental version of "Disco Inferno." I threw in some jumping jacks be-fore the next stepping sequence. My earrings jingled.

The song's cymbal sped up. *Snic, snic, nic-a-nic.*

For a while, Eric stepped over Tony instead of the blocks. Then he picked up a block and hurled it across the room. "Large muscle exercise, ma'am," he said. "Mark said that's important for controlling my temper."

A chill shot through my middle. I remembered the steps of the grief process then, from the books my aunt had made me study. Anger was unavoidable.

"Fine," I said. "Then we'll box."

Tony crawled into the equipment room and shut the door.

I ignored that and led Eric and Raphael into rhythmic up-percuts. One and *two* and one and *two*. One *two* one *two*. *Nic-a-nic*. I was using Mark's routine now, but things were getting weird. I had reason to doubt his theory and his practice. He had once invited Nico to join his jiujitsu therapy class. I couldn't believe it when Nico had changed out of his shined shoes and his pressed scrubs to study martial arts from my cousin, the violence doctor. Afterward, Nico came home cursing. He never cursed. The class was an hour of yelling and grunting and sharp movements, he said. "Mark used me to demonstrate a leg sweep. Almost broke my back. How does that heal people?"

Once the marines had practiced enough uppercuts and hooks, I added jabs and kicks. Instead of punching an arm straight up, the way I would in a Curves class, I punched straight out. I had to make my moves sharp for these guys, like video game moves, so I didn't swing my hips either. I was all forward movement. *Snic, snic*.

"This song sucks," Eric said.

"Yeah," Raphael said, "and boxing just freezes up my hands all over again."

Eric turned off the CD and switched the radio on. When he landed on a rap song that said *run the jewels, run the jewels*, there was a pounding noise. Tony's face appeared in the equipment room door's little window pane. Raphael trotted over and let him out.

Tony rejoined the group. His body and eyes held a new focus, like a toddler rehabilitated after his time of punishment, grateful for the chance to start over, to do as he's told.

The three young marines postured in front of the mirror, leaning back with arms crossed, and then gripping an imaginary steering wheel. *Can you feel it?* They jerked their shoulders and hips around, but they didn't punch. They followed the rapper's command to wave their hands in the air like they just didn't care.

Behind them, I checked my reflection: big frown, lines on my forehead, redness in my ears, cheeks, neck. In all the photos of Nico's dead wife—even the hidden ones he thought I hadn't found—she never frowned or blushed. Not even in laughter, before the sickness whitened her for good. She had a way of holding herself—hair pulled back in this photo, no makeup in this one—concealing a certain amount of her beauty in each picture so it didn't blind you all at once.

Can you feel it? The rapper asked again. The class wasn't slowing down. They were just fine without me. Eric led Tony and Raphael from jumping jacks into down-ups. They huffed and cursed at him between reps.

I switched the CD back on and cued it to the next sped-up pop song. I took the floor and stepped slow. Right, left, faster. Soon the marines formed one horizontal row, and the tips of their noses showed the slightest color.

It was time to raise the intensity, to force the blood to the edge. I kicked, and the marines kicked. They looked terrified, but they kept following me.

My feet were set in that rhythm, but my mind was still two years into the past, when I first met Nico. He was a referral from an old Greek lady who was a client and a regular in my Curves classes. She knew him from church.

He showed up at my office door carrying two trash bags.

"Let me take care of these," I said, reaching for the bags.

"Sorry for the mess," he said. "At least I didn't wait until the fourteenth of April, huh?" Aside from some faint lines on his forehead, he looked youthful. We were close in age.

We started out slow, sitting on the floor next to my desk, where we dumped the bags out and sorted the papers into piles. The medical bills quickly towered up and slid into a heap.

I was careful in calculating the toll of his wife's health care, and in itemizing deductions for this or that expense Maggie had required. I wanted to land Nico on a refund, however small. His was a difficult case, but I only charged the base rate and threw in a discount, because I felt so bad for him. To thank me, he and Maggie took me out to dinner at his cousin's pizzeria.

"Greek pizza's your favorite, Miss Manolis," he said. "I can tell."

"You're right," I lied. I'd never had it.

In the pizzeria, while Nico hugged and high-fived his relatives and handed Maggie off to the only female cousin, I scanned the walls. It was almost Valentine's Day, something I hadn't thought about until I saw hearts taped up behind the counter. Customers had paid a dollar each to write their name on a heart that carried the name of some disease awareness organization. I always wonder how much of that money makes it to the patients. How much is spent on dyeing the paper red and cutting it, printing the logo on, shrink-wrapping the hearts into heavy piles, and trucking them into a place like this? You think of these things when you run a business.

Finally, Nico introduced me as his accountant. I could tell by his cousins' smiling and head-to-toe gazing at me that I was the first woman he'd brought to them since his wife died. There's a responsibility that comes with being the first.

The wall along the booths was covered in customer photos and murals showing mythological characters in action. Nico sat facing the kitchen, and I faced the door. He kept glancing behind me, as if taking cues from the cousins. He would occasionally straighten his posture or force himself to smile, to do as they told him, directing him from behind my back. When I glanced behind him, I saw a small statue of the goddess Artemis.

One of the cousins arrived at our booth and said, "So skinny." He was serving up a bottle of wine and a pizza we hadn't ordered. He smiled at me. "You need to bring this knucklehead in here every night so we can fatten him up."

Nico turned red and patted his stomach.

While we ate, the cousins continued fussing over Maggie and busying themselves with the few other customers or the football game on TV, but mostly they snuck looks at us.

"Isn't football season over?" I said.

"Don't tell them that," Nico said. "They record the games and watch them again and again all year."

He told me about his job at the dermatology clinic, his daily routine with Maggie, and all the help he gets from sisters, aunts, cousins, in-laws, church ladies.

"Sounds like you have a great family," I said.

"Forgive me. I'm talking too much. You already know my social security number and how much money I make, but I don't know the first thing about you." He picked up his glass and then set it down, leaned forward, closer to the overhead lamp. Perfect skin, perfect teeth. "Pardon my manners. I don't get out often." He sat back. "Mostly I talk to Maggie. We shoot the breeze about Big Bird a lot." We both looked over at her. "It's a wild Friday night at our place, let me tell you." He raised his glass to me and took a sip.

It felt safe to laugh then, so I did. "Your manners are just fine."

"She's getting a good vocabulary now, but nothing along the lines of amortization or charitable contributions, capital gains. We talk it up all right, but I can't jam with her about stuff like that yet." He returned to his pizza and bit off a long string of cheese.

Most women run away from a guy who talks about himself for a half hour before asking a question about her, but I stayed put. Eventually, he did ask. I didn't want to create a competition of suffering, so I ambled through the questions, glossing over my childhood and my parents' death, letting him know I considered my aunt and uncle to be my mom and dad. No loss at all, really. What I wanted to say was, I was lost just like Maggie. I can guide her.

Just then, the cousins all shouted, "Who Dey!" and Maggie repeated it. They called Nico over to the TV to watch a replay of a Bengals touchdown. He joined them, and then they rewound and watched it three more times, celebrating every step. There seemed to be a lot for them to talk about and relive, so I got up and walked closer to the door to get a better look at a painting of Hera blinding Tiresias. It was an embarrassingly large and gaudy mural that my aunt would have winced at. Germans would never exaggerate a story like that, she would have said.

Among the customer photos, I spotted Nico, with a perfectly chiseled young woman and a baby. Maggie.

I made my way over to Maggie and the female cousin, who would have thought me rude if I didn't take this chance to talk with her and Maggie.

Before I reached their table, Nico found me and guided me back to our booth. "Sorry about that," he said. "Our team's up, and getting ready to win by a landslide."

When we sat down again, he offered a more pleasant subject: the old Greek lady, our mutual friend. "I forget which church she said you went to. Maybe we know more of the same people."

"None," I said. "Not anymore." I cut into my pizza.

"But when you were a kid? You had to be baptized somewhere."

I mumbled the name of the Catholic parish where I spent most of my childhood, and then I lifted my fork, stuffed a large bite into my mouth.

He set down his slice. "*Delia Manolis?* Last time I checked, that was a Greek name."

I told him that technically, I am Greek—aren't we all, when you get down to it?—but only half. My mother was from Greece. Her brother was Mark's dad, and when he and his German wife adopted me, he didn't want me to walk around with my dad's last name, some North German name you hear on every other street in this town. He didn't want people thinking I was some orphaned ragamuffin from Over-the-Rhine (that's how he said it), so he gave me his name—my mother's maiden name—in order to avoid the questions.

That was the only parenting decision my uncle every got to make. My aunt sent Mark and me to Saturday Greek school off and on, but we spent more time in catechism classes, and I never ate Greek pizza or learned to cook lamb. It was too soon to explain all this to Nico. He was having enough trouble with the news that I wasn't Orthodox.

Another cousin returned to the table to refill Nico's glass. I hadn't touched mine. I never drink a drop on a first date, or a second or fifth or sixth, especially not one where the guy brings his kid. If your thinking gets cloudy and you make the wrong decision about somebody, you gamble away not just your own time and his kid's hopes, but once you let it continue, you're wasting the hopes of all the kids and parents and grandparents in a forest of family trees. You're pulling the cord of a chainsaw if you make the wrong choice.

The cousins cheered again. Nico watched and laughed as they broke into a touchdown dance.

"They're clowns," he said. "It's why I love them. They did this serenade for me one night, a real troubadour act, to get me to—" He stopped.

"Get you to what?"

He bowed his head. "To ask their cousin to marry me."

I lowered my fork. "These are *her* cousins?"

He stuffed a chunk of crust into his mouth and spoke while he chewed. "That makes them mine, too. Always will be."

I didn't eat another bite. Nico didn't just have an old olive tree with deep roots to worry about. He had a whole orchard of them, gnarled and twining together until there was no way to tell where one set of branches and roots stopped and another began.

Most women would also run from a guy who took her on a first date to his dead wife's family restaurant the week of Valentine's Day, so he got the hint when I didn't return his calls. But then, when I woke up on April 16, I saw an opportunity in him and his family, a chance to give of the innumerable parts of me—even my time, which was suddenly infinite.

The trip to France last fall was to celebrate one and a half years together, and more than two years through Nico's grief process.

I know about the grief process from the book my aunt gave me, written by a German expert. We studied its theory, one chapter a month, as soon as I could read at that level. I was in the fourth grade, and this was my therapy three years after watching my parents die in a car crash. I'd write down definitions of depression symptoms or methods of coping, traumatic effects that death could have on children weaker than me, prone to even worse night terrors, and then I'd have to match them to the correct stages of the grief process, all according to the book. My aunt would praise me after each chapter test by saying something like, "You've mastered Denial and Isolation. Next month we move on to Anger." After one year of retroactive grieving, I had studied hard enough to recover from my trauma, and I had accepted my loss. We never spoke of it again.

All couples dream of celebrating in Paris, Nico and I decided. "Let's be different," he said. "Let's go to the South." The food would be better on the Mediterranean, and the old walled cities, he said, with a dreamy smile, and the cathedrals. We'd have a better time down there.

I was ready for a better time. With Nico I was always coaxing, tiptoeing, and waiting for the safe moments when I could crack a joke or suggest an ounce of intimacy—even the sharing of secrets, however small. Sometimes I'd dig something up and offer it to him. One for one, I figured. One for four or five, at least. So I'd hook a series of fat, juicy confessions on the end of my line and start casting, waiting as the flesh dangled there, just under the surface. I told him about my flaws and embarrassing moments, the pedestrian secrets of my past: eating disorder, abortion, minor lawsuit from a client for a mistake I knew better than to make. Cast, wait. He would sometimes bristle and sometimes nod, never looking up at me or touching my hand, just processing the information, squeezing his eyes shut as he tried to forgive my many trespasses. Cast, wait. The only bite I ever got on my line was when he told me he'd almost gotten fired for calling in sick on all the days when he was supposed to help treat a patient with skin damaged from cancer treatments. That was the closest he ever got to flames.

It was a fishing method I'd learned from the grief books. How to guide through loss: an easy five-step plan toward leading your loved one to acceptance. The books promised it would bring us closer, but they were no help. Only Maggie could build a bridge between us.

This trip was the first time Nico had been away from her longer than a weekend, and he did well. The first few days, we had fun admiring the architecture and paintings, but it was quiet without her. No tea parties or toys or sing-along songs. He managed to only call her every other day and look at her photo a few times. I was proud of him for that.

He relaxed so much he even said the trip was making him think of becoming a Catholic. "So much feeling," he said of the art. "That *passion*. They aren't afraid to show the suffering."

I took a step back. It must have been the strong coffee talking. Had he forgotten his Orthodox family and what they would say to that? His parents had already retired to Florida, so I hadn't met them. I pictured his mother the way I usually pictured mothers: as an older version of my own dead mother, or better yet my aunt, plucking a Madonna cassette tape out of my boom box and wagging it at me: *No more of this trash. Study in silence.*

On the fourth day he was feeling brave, ready for some wide open space, so when he suggested we visit some old battle site, I agreed. It was a spontaneous addition to our itinerary, so we'd have to wait until the next day for the last museum, and finally, the big cathedral with the view everyone had told us about.

The battle site marked some World War II action that was part of something I'd never heard of called Operation Anvil. The field pulled him in. He took off his glasses, walked to the middle of it, and squinted out at the horizon. I hung back while he sunk to his knees and felt around on the dirt, then lay down on his stomach with his arms out wide. He rolled over, reached into his wallet, pulled out a photo, held it up, and stared into it.

"I miss her, Delia."

That night when we went out on the town in Marseilles, he was looser. There was actually a hint of romance in him. As we had danced under the voice of a lounge singer, he closed a necklace around my neck and said, "Maggie adores you. I adore you. Thank you for bringing me back to life."

I didn't want to talk over the music and the singer's voice and the sounds of people around us having a good time on their night out. I could have said, "You've come so far," or, "I'd do anything to help you get over your loss," but that would have made Nico feel proud of himself, and pride would disrupt the grieving process, which had taken him the prescribed two and one quarter years since his wife's death to get as far as it had. I didn't want to set him back, so I touched the necklace and said, "I adore her, too."

The next morning, we boarded an empty bus at the terminal and sat near the back. The driver stepped out and walked into the depot to warm up before his next departure. A woman entered the bus and chose a seat in the middle. She was the lounge singer we'd listened to the night before. Was she going where we were going, to the center of town?

I nudged Nico, and he squeezed my hand. Here was the woman who had provided our happy soundtrack, now looking too plain to coax anyone onto a dance floor.

Two teenage boys stepped onto the bus. One was puny, with big ears and a long nose. The other was huge for his age, with shoulders bulging under his leather jacket and a tattoo crawling up to his ear. The larger boy covered the singer's mouth and yanked her up. He dragged her toward the front of the bus, where he wrestled her into a stranglehold. The smaller boy grabbed her bag and ran out. The larger boy snapped her neck, dropped her, and left.

Nico and I ducked behind the seats in front of us. The boys moved so fast, they probably didn't even notice us, but we still stayed down. A dozen people must have been milling around inside that depot. If the boy had shot the singer, they'd all be running out, following the sound, but this was a silent killing.

The bus felt so much colder then. Nico was still squeezing my hand, but I didn't feel it.

As the only witnesses, Nico and I had to explain the crime to the police. His French was better than mine, but he made me do the talking. When I referred to the singer as "*la femme*," Nico scowled. "Madame Bonet," he said. "She had a name; it was Jenna Marie Bonet."

The police said the boys were working toward gang initiation, that this gang problem was the damn war this town was always fighting, and the boys had probably been told to jump the first lady they saw. It could have been me.

Across the street, a group of elderly people were dancing in the park. How could they be so joyous in a place like this? I turned my back to them and told the police that after the larger boy broke Madame Bonet's spinal cord and ran out, Nico checked her vital signs. I left out the suffering and passion: the part of the story where he takes off his gloves and reaches for the dead woman, and I restrain him so he won't leave fingerprints on the victim, so he puts his gloves back on, shakes her, calls her unrepeatable names, and yells at her to wake up.

I didn't have the French words to tell the police how much prettier she had been in life than in death. She had worn dangly earrings the night before, and while she sang, they had sparkled up her long hair. But the next morning on the bus, her hair was pulled back tight, and nothing on her shined.

"What are you doing in this city, anyway?" one of the cops asked me. "Americans are supposed to honeymoon in Paris."

"He wanted to go south."

That day, Nico didn't take me into town and to the museum as planned. He didn't take me up to the cathedral. The only time he said more than two words to me the rest of the trip was when the plane was about to land. He kept looking out the window, studying Cincinnati's winding grid, and then he asked me, "What are rents like on the other side of Pleasant Ridge?"

There was a whole world of Nico's loss that I'd only glimpsed, when he would brush Maggie's hair too hard, or when he woke up and walked out into a storm without a coat, or sat with his foot on the brake through a green traffic light. I said nothing at those times, because who was I to tell him to put his foot on the accelerator?

And who was I to guide Maggie? I barely remembered my own parents, the way Maggie would barely remember her mother, aside from the happy pictures that adults put up on the walls of a little girl's world. Much less pleasant images came to me then on that silent return flight, so I leaned my seat back, closed my eyes, and replayed those crashing leaps into the end zone, when you brace yourself for the bones to break, the joints to pop out of socket, the neck to snap. The clock stops, and there, on the ground, you see your dad, your mom, your boyfriend's wife, a beautiful stranger, pulled from the game. Watching it again and again was the least I could do for Nico.

I turned thirty-five just before we took that trip. I'd never gotten this far with anyone to the point of taking an overseas trip together, moving in, playing at Mommy. I thought I was doing right by Nico, by all of us. But as that plane landed, I felt the pull. It was always work, always the gravity of numbers, that kept me down. Too busy, I'd say during tax season. No life. I'm buried in papers.

I'd always thought that under the deadlines and forms, there was a weightlessness, a floating to the surface, where the pressure to marry and mother was gone, washed away. In that sea of phone messages and appointment books, 1040EZs and returns for single filers, I could tread water. I could keep my head up. I could breathe.

When we got home, we had time to sleep before Nico's mother-in-law brought Maggie back to us. Nico didn't get anywhere near our bed. He didn't eat the lunch I cooked for him: lamb and some spinach pie that his mother-in-law had put in the fridge while we were gone. I knew that moving in with Nico would mean a steady stream of relatives coming over, even when we weren't home. After a while, I decided I would let them, and why not? I had already allowed them to size me up, and I had passed their tests. I might even be willing to let them douse me in holy water on their Orthodox altar if it meant they'd invite me back up there again soon to become Maggie's permanent new mother.

That day, Nico didn't unpack his bags either. Instead, he spent the whole day on the computer and then in his car, making phone calls. He drove off right before Maggie was due back.

When she and her grandmother arrived, I told them that Nico had gone to the store and would be home soon. Naturally, the grandmother wanted to know how I had enjoyed the trip. She smiled, and barely a line showed on her face. She looked so young that sometimes when we were cooking or shopping together, I would forget who I was talking to and say too much, even things Maggie shouldn't hear. This time I was careful. I described the hassle of getting to our destination, and the dreary French weather, but I assured her that the lovely food and sights were well worth the trouble.

"So you had a nice time, and you came home in one piece." Her smile flattened, and she touched my arm. "I didn't want to say so before you left, but I've been worried sick about you two. Nico's had a hard time starting over."

She was right. Nico only treated problems on the surface. He spent his days handing out topical treatments guaranteed to cool down stubborn rashes or iron out laugh lines. Sometimes, of course, he would see serious skin conditions—severe eczema, third-degree burns, discolored moles. He could freeze off a wart or lance a boil without flinching, but he never had to watch patients die.

That night he came home late and slept on the couch. I crawled into Maggie's bed. She was still wearing her Pocahontas costume, the one she had insisted on wearing every day since Halloween, even to bed. We always gave in. I touched the fake suede headband and kissed her hair. She took my hand. I was off to work before she woke. By that evening her room was empty, all traces of the girl vanished.

In between songs, a breeze moved through Eric's hair. The fan had started working. He doubled over. "Boxing is great large muscle exercise, ma'am. I'll give you that." He grabbed his water bottle and chugged it down.

"Ma'am?" Raphael said. "All this punching makes you feel better, but not us."

Before I could defend myself, Eric moved toward the stereo. Again, he turned my CD off and switched on the radio. A song by Miami Sound Machine blared out of the speakers. He whipped off his shirt and tied it around his head. Soon, he was leading Tony and Raphael in a conga line. All of them were smiling, and color showed on Tony's ears.

I turned down the volume. "No, no," I said. "One horizontal row."

Eric ditched the others. He cranked up the volume and waltzed me away from the stereo. I tried to break free, but he had me in his grip, leading me into a salsa dance. The smell of his sweat was like nothing I'd ever smelled at Curves.

"Step two three," he whispered, placing my hand on his bare shoulder. "Back two three. Back, back."

The percussion sped up, brought us closer to the mirror. Laced between my fingers, his fingertips glowed pink. He caught my eye in our reflection, our red faces.

Eric led, so I had to dance backwards most of the time. It was hard to keep up, and when he moved too fast, I stumbled. He shoved me into the mirror.

"This song is bad for my temper," he said, his nostrils red and open now. "You should've thought about that before you got here. Think about what music can do."

We were close to the stereo. *Stand up and take some action,* Gloria Estefan sang, but it was the lounge singer—Jenna Marie Bonet—that I heard, and it was her face that looked back at me in the mirror, the same way she looked at me in my nightmares, saying, "You could have saved me." Eric reached over and punched her off.

I had my back to the mirror now, and I was sliding sideways along it, away from him. "You're showing color," I said.

"You're not good for my temper either." He lunged at me, the Bengal tiger's eyes and teeth stretched over the top of his head. "You all think you're so much help."

"No, I don't. Mark said—"

He grabbed me by the collar and slipped his fingers inside my sweatshirt, under my bra straps. "Only help you'll be is when you're out of my way!" He pulled me away from the mirror, turned me ninety degrees, and swept his foot under my legs until I was tipping back and hanging by his fingers. If he let go, I'd fall and hit my head on the wood floor.

He let go. My elbow hit first, then my head.

When I came to, Jenna Marie Bonet was standing over me, all dressed up, smiling. I blinked, and then it was Nico's wife standing there. Another blink. My mother.

"It isn't your fault," she said, reaching down to help me up. Her long, black braid swung over her shoulder. "None of this is your responsibility to fix, honey."

I held my arms up and closed my eyes to let the tears out, because what did it matter now?

No one lifted me. Eric's voice was right in my face, apologizing. The fans squealed.

Another set of feet ran up to us. I opened my eyes. Raphael was behind Eric now, pulling him up and into a headlock.

"Not sorry enough!" he said. "You know better, Eric. Stay away from her. You know you have to be alone when you get like that."

He led Eric to the equipment room, and Tony followed. Raphael shut the door, and they didn't fight or question him. They were already punishing themselves.

Raphael picked up a towel from the stack and walked back to me, so softly that I didn't hear his feet. He opened the towel and held it out as he moved closer. He sat me up, wrapped the towel around me, and lifted me.

Everything hurt. Whatever conditions I'd have now—broken funny bone, fractured spine, concussion—didn't make any difference. It would take a long time to heal. I wouldn't be able to come back here to help Mark. These guys would have to start over with him or someone else who could promise a new method of healing. Another new guide.

And I wouldn't be able to work at full throttle for the rest of tax season. Driving would be hard. I wouldn't be able to cruise through neighborhoods on the other side of Pleasant Ridge, looking for Maggie's curls in a lit-up window, or Nico's silhouette in a chair, pointing his remote control at the source of light that carved his shape. Who was doing his taxes now, and did they know how to get him the refund he deserved?

Raphael carried me past the equipment room. Tony's face was up at the glass again, but Eric was hunched over on the floor in there, with his shirt back on and his head in his hands.

It was a quiet rescue. Raphael didn't lie and tell me I was going to be fine. He didn't say anything at all as he moved me down that bright hallway, past Cincinnatus, into the waiting area, where I joined the injured women.

THE CLIFFS OF DOVER

Mr. Trottier is the last of the grown-ups to sign the marriage license form. I can't watch, so I look out the window to Lyle, who's asleep in the car. He deserves a better wife than me. I'd just burn dinner and wash reds with whites. Not how he wants to spend his final days, I'm sure.

After Mr. Trottier signs, it'll be my turn, and then we'll all walk out to Lyle and watch him sign. Mr. Trottier's long nails scratch against the pen as he fills in his signature line. Before he dots the last *i* in his name, I reach under his arm, snatch the form, and run—out of the judge's office, down the front steps of the courthouse, past Lyle, past St. Anne's Cathedral and Marie's for Hair and Dover High, until I'm cruising along empty pastures.

It's a good four miles home, and there's only one road to get me there. When I'm halfway, I reach KFC and lock myself into a bathroom stall. In my hand, the form is wrinkled from the wind. I imagine what everybody in the judge's office—Lyle's sister, my grandma, Mr. Trottier, and the judge who will marry me and Lyle next Friday—will do now without this. Lyle's sister is the only one who could possibly see things my way, but she's Lyle's guardian, and even though she's only a fifth cousin to Mr. Trottier, she has to follow his orders.

I fold the form into smaller and smaller squares and squeeze it hard. I stuff it into the bottom of my backpack, where I keep my copy of Mr. Trottier's will and the other papers he wants me to sign, saying what his family will do for me if I promise to give them a male child.

When I reach my street, the elms by the corner are dropping golden leaves, but down the block, the tree across from my grandma's house is bald, rotting, and dotted with vultures. Vultures are all they got in Dover. No deer, no butterflies, no dolphins popping up for air. In the six months since I left Hawaii for this place, I haven't seen a single pig or cow munching away behind a fence. I don't know what the vultures eat for supper, but it's got to be living and dying close by, because the big males are making a lot of noise.

In our driveway, Mr. Trottier's driver waits. Other Trottiers have been to our house before, but never *the* Eugene Trottier or anyone in his immediate family. I hug myself and fixate on the vultures, try to guess the circumference of their heads.

When I can't take the cold anymore, I gather up my breath and go inside. I open the door to a strange silence. No soap operas or *Lifestyles* blare out of the TV. No *Wild Kingdom*.

Inside, Eugene Trottier is sitting in Grandpa's chair at the head of the dinner table. No one has sat in it since Grandpa died. He wears a scarf and sips from one of Grandma's best china cups.

"Lyle doesn't have much time, Cora," he says. "Neither do I. You've stalled enough."

The first part of what Mr. Trottier says is no joke, but I don't buy the rest, because everybody knows Mr. Trottier's still healthy enough to hunt. For what, I have no idea. Last year, he hunted with Lyle. Now he hunts with his lawyer brother, the silent partner of Trottier Menswear.

Instead of a cup and saucer, my grandma has set a place in front of my chair with a dinner plate and a new marriage license form on it. There's only one blank signature line. Instead of a knife and fork, Gram has set out her nicest pen. The judge and the guardians of the bride and groom are all supposed to watch me sign, but Mr. Trottier must've worked out a deal with the judge.

"With respect, Mr. Trottier," I say, "I need more time to think it over."

He massages the arm of Grandpa's chair. All of the chair arms and legs are fashioned as lion limbs. Mr. Trottier's fingertips line up over each claw.

"Think *what* over?" he says. "You're the future of my business."

Gram pushes me down into my chair.

"Line 'em up, kid," Gram says. She gives me a pursed look that tells me to put that expensive ink to work and line my letters up straight, because we need this marriage. "No tricks."

I don't touch the pen. Dad warned me not to fall prey to the Trottiers, and I won't.

Mr. Trottier tugs at his scarf. He's all in knots over this. He'd hoped his daughters would marry well, so he sent them to quaint colleges, expecting they'd find husbands of good stock who'd manage Trottier Menswear and produce fine, broad-shouldered grandsons. Both daughters failed out, returned to Dover unaccompanied, and married locals: some guy in charge of ordering supplies for the company and Rudy, the supervisor who orders me around in the factory. So Mr. Trottier chose a distant cousin, Lyle Trottier, a commoner with uncommon intelligence and talent, to be his heir.

Mr. Trottier gives me two more days—until Thursday night—to sign over my future as Lyle's wife. He makes a theater out of coughing as he excuses himself and returns to his car. I watch through the window as his driver helps him into the backseat and then scowls at me before he gets behind the wheel.

Just as I fall asleep, Gram barges into my room and kneels beside my bed. "You don't have to die at those sewing machines," she says. "You can have your whole life to yourself."

A slice of moonlight shines up her gnarled hands as they take mine. King Genie's wife has her housekeeper bring the family's alterations to Gram. Gram is that good. It's a few bucks here and there, but it's not enough. I hate that she hasn't been able to buy basic stuff like arthritis medication, and if I do as the Trottiers ask of me, I will be able to buy her all the medicine she wants.

She and I both want me to provide for her, but the part that only she wants is for me to lead a life even lonelier than hers: steady work, a child, a husband to die young and leave me be.

While Gram carries on about the golden road before me if only I make the right choice—and besides, she knows how I feel about Lyle, so why not choose him?—I picture vultures at the end of that road, waiting for the next mound of flesh.

"No, Gram," I say. "My life will belong to the Trottiers."

"That's what they think. Let them. Play their game a few years, until old King Genie croaks." She squeezes my fingers too hard. "Just hold on. They'll belong to *you*."

When I wake up on Wednesday, I think about what Gram said. I keep the blinds closed, because my room faces the vultures' roost, and I shouldn't watch anyone brood and wait for the smell of death at a time like this. I should focus on creating life, a male life that I will groom to be the next king of Trottier Menswear. The first king, Eugene Trottier's grandfather, started in 1898 as an ant in an army of French laborers and soon rose to supervisor. His charisma and his vision, people say, are what lifted him above his Catholic name, to floor manager, salesman, director. Eventually, after much deliberation and prayer, the founder, whose sons had all fallen to consumption or Spanish bullets, chose Trottier as his heir and renamed the company after him. That first Trottier showed them that things can change, even in a town like this.

I turned sixteen at the end of the last school year, and the next day I started working in trousers at the factory. Inseams and waistbands and zippers at the fly. It wasn't bad. At first I was a cutter and then a ripper for the mistakes, and then we were short staffed, so I got to sit at a machine by myself and be a piecer, sewing the front and back panels of trousers together. After six weeks, I'd created enough suit pants for an army of town men, and the supervisor, Rudy, needed me to help out with jackets. Those were the challenge, he said, and he put me on assist for Lyle's sister, Annette. She'd already started driving me to and from work, so I had earned her trust and her cautious brand of friendship. It wasn't long before I started getting the phone calls from Eugene Trottier's lawyer brother, proposing marriage.

The school bus drops me off near the factory every afternoon. Today when I get there, Annette whisks me into the bathroom. She sticks one end of a mop handle under the doorknob and the other end into a divot in the tile so that no one can enter. I wonder what she's going to do to me for not signing the forms, the ones that will make us sisters. She reaches under her smock and pulls out a suit jacket. It's the model we are cranking out by the hundreds this week. She tries it on over her clothes. It is a size 48, in navy blue, which slims her figure.

Last summer, Annette turned eighteen and went full-time at the factory. When I started working there in June, she asked me to lie for her while she had to take sick days, so I told everyone it was her down with the flu instead of Lyle down with something much worse. I never had a friend before, and I needed one now that Mom was dead and Dad had sent me to Dover.

She turns this way and that in the mirror, and her steel-toe boots smash her shoelaces on the tile. For a big girl, she has fit arms, and when she lifts them out wide and flaps them, the sleeves' extra material hangs below.

My face burns. She's going to drill me about the forms any minute.

"Be honest," she says. We catch each other's reflections in the cloudy mirror. "Is it me?"

I circle her to inspect the fit of the garment, thinking of how dead I'd be if I stole something from this place and wonder if the same rules apply to somebody like Annette, who carries the Trottier name.

"You're going to get in trouble," I say. I have to raise my voice over the running toilets.

"It's not like I took a camel-hair jacket." She pinches my cheek. "A girl's got to live."

I squirm away. "Still. You shouldn't."

She shows me the irregular stitching of the hem. "It'll just sit in the reject room anyway."

Annette would know. She and Rudy count inventory in there three nights a week. I wait for them to finish so Annette can drive me home. Rudy won't let me in there, but Annette says the mistakes—all the irregular stitching, snags, rips, uneven sleeves, even a perfectly good trouser leg that got sneezed on—just pile up until Rudy hauls them away to Goodwill. If we make one wrong move with a garment, we have to pay for it, and it goes up to that room.

I breathe deep. A mildew-bleach-piss odor burns my nose. "Honestly? You look great."

Annette smiles. She takes a pin out of her hair and puts it in her mouth, pulls my hair back out of my face and pins it. "There," she says. "So do you. A real beauty." She moves in for a hug, and those big, dark sleeves close around me.

I'm too small for beauty, but I hug back anyway, to let her know I won't rat her out. I will keep quiet about anything she does.

After break, there is a team meeting. Rudy's chicken legs

stand on a landing halfway up to the reject room while we workers gather on the factory floor. Today's pep talk is all about the Trottier brand being back on block, "because shoppers want to see that 'Made in the USA' label," Rudy says.

All of the adults who work here are married or widowed, and almost every one of them is a distant Trottier relative. Cousins many times removed, claiming either the blood or the name, and sometimes both. A few of the older women clap for Rudy, and one of them amens. Annette lets out a dog whistle.

Rudy holds his arms out wide and leans forward. A lot of the women here call him a gold digger, but I've seen his nails: short and wide, useless for digging. He reminds us that by the end of October, we have to finish hundreds more of these jackets so he can ship them to the department stores, where the town women will buy them as Christmas gifts. "This holiday," he says, "our line is different. We're making more than suits. We're making a name for ourselves."

Finally, Rudy finishes, with his finger pointing in the air, sweat shining up his hairline. "This Christmas, they want Trottier!"

At my work station, the camel hair feels soft in my hands. I hold a sleeve up to my face, just for a second, and then I set to work on the cuff. Rudy just promoted me to special fabrics, and I don't want to blow my chance, so I am extra careful with every step. I lower the machine's foot down onto the seam, push the pedal, and watch the needle pierce the fabric.

Next to me, Annette is working on a sleeve. She leans deeper into her machine's pedal until she starts to vibrate, cheeks and chins wiggling. She stops and bites off a tail of thread.

"We'd marry Lyle to a cousin," she says, "but you can't get away with that these days."

Here we go. I hand her my ripper tool. She takes it and hacks away at her seam.

"You're smart, and you're an out-of-towner," she says. "We

know what we're in for with the homegrown girls." She hands the ripper back to me, but she won't let it go. "I asked old Trottier to give you only one day instead of two, so you have him to thank when you turn in the forms tomorrow."

I recall the women I used to see in Honolulu, young and old, all on their own. "I'm still thinking on it."

She catches me staring absently at her gut. "All right, so I missed a few periods. Stop staring."

Annette is so fat I didn't notice. Now I see that her belly is hardening. "You and Rudy?"

"Since last winter. To stay warm." She laughs. "Soon enough, you'll be in my place."

I go cold all over.

Rudy's voice cuts in. "Nice stitching." He's standing behind me, reeking of pork rinds.

I try to focus on the work in front of me, but I can't. It doesn't make sense, Rudy and Annette. If anyone finds out her kid is his, Rudy is toast. Since he married Mr. Trottier's daughter, he's gotten in good with Mr. Trottier's brother, Victor, the silent partner. Rudy even visits him in Pittsburgh, where he lives with his wife and the daughter they adopted from China.

"Let's see you in action, Cora," Rudy says. He hands me a collar and lapel piece.

I pick up the jacket-in-progress, which is just the fronts, back, and sleeves, in a size 38. The next step is attaching the collar and lapel. I push the pedal, and soon the machine hits a high note. The camel hair's texture is like feathers under my hands. This is what a town woman will think when she pets this jacket in a department store. This sleeve will feel soft when she loops her arm through her husband's or when she helps her son into it before church.

The machine stops, and its silence pulls me out of my daydream. Rudy has turned off its power switch. I've swerved across the front of the jacket.

"Keep your head in the game, Cora!" Rudy says. He releases the jacket from the machine and pulls it away. "That's it. You're off special fabrics."

Up he walks, to the reject room, with another mistake to add to the pile.

At school, my locker partner is a distant Trottier relative. So is Jimmy Hawkins, the guy she sucks face with in front of our locker when all I want is to reach in there and hang up my jacket. When I get there on Thursday, Jimmy has shaved his head for some wrestling team ritual. His shirt says "Be All You Can Be."

He hands me a folded piece of paper. "Telegram from Fat Boy. He's back in school."

My locker partner shoves him. "Don't call Lyle fat. He got skinny this summer, and *hot*."

They have no idea why.

A half hour before the school day ends, I tell my French teacher, Madame Beauchamp, that I have to leave class right now, *s'il vous plaît*. She looks at me with one eye closed.

"*Problèmes de femmes*," I say.

I hurry to the music room with the note from Lyle in my bra and the signed forms tucked into my pants. I pass the home ec room, where my locker partner is dipping chunks of dead animal into a deep fryer.

We didn't have that machine when I started at Dover High last March. Everybody had partnered up in January, so I had to cook and sew alone, near the door. Lyle had biology that period, and he was always off to the bathroom. When he passed by one day, he stopped and pointed at my cross stitch. "What you got there?" he said. Instead of "Welcome Friends," I was sewing "Die, Fat Cow." I thought it would offend him, but he said, "A gift for the teacher?"

"For all of them." I thumbed behind me, to where she was gossiping with the other girls.

He laughed. "Thanks. I needed that today. Same time tomorrow?"

Each day after that, I gave him ranger cookies or soft-boiled eggs or googly-eyed sock puppets—whatever I'd made. I didn't know then why Lyle was always in the bathroom, but I could tell something was empty in him, just like I was empty in the place where Mom used to be.

Over the summer, I told Annette I liked her brother, that I wanted to see him, and where was he? Why wasn't he working at the warehouse like the other boys? She pretended she didn't hear me, so I kept asking. After a month, when Annette and I had gotten close enough, she finally filled me in on the secret. On school tests, Lyle had always outperformed most of the inner-circle Trottier kids whose dads worked in the factory's front office and got invited to golf outings with Eugene Trottier and his customers. And every Christmas, Lyle was asked to play piano for the city tree-lighting concert. But once he won that piano competition in Philadelphia last January, he proved to hold a higher grade of intelligence and talent than was expected of his position in the Trottier gene pool. The next week, old Eugene publicly announced Lyle as his heir.

When Lyle got his prognosis a few months later, Mr. Trottier visited him in the hospital. He brought his lawyer brother, Victor, and they kicked the nurses out of the room. Together with Lyle and Annette, the Trottier brothers made a pact not to breathe a word about Lyle's illness to anyone. Lyle would quietly soldier through the home stretch of last school year and maybe half of this one, counting on the leniency of star-struck teachers who were sure to excuse him of anything now that he had been chosen to move from the outermost rings of the extended Trottier family system into the inner circle, with King Genie and his women, crowned and cloaked.

Annette told me she did her part to stay quiet, too. She

spent her final days at Dover High hunting for a suitable wife for Lyle, never saying a word to anyone about his numbered days. She was careful to treat him with the same amount of disdain that an older sister is expected to show toward her younger brother in the halls, where kids like Jimmy Hawkins don't tolerate kindness in any form. Kill or get roasted. That was the way.

In the home ec room now, my locker partner looks up and sees me through the open door. She elbows the girl next to her, a girl with a high forehead and a long, bare neck. They stare me down. I walk faster.

When I reach the music room, I nudge the door open. It's a big room with a high ceiling and a stairway up to an office nobody uses anymore. There's a piano by the window. Kettle-drums stand along the back wall, with black dust covers hanging down over their skinny legs. In the corner, there's a stack of trumpets. When the school had band and orchestra, they practiced in here. Now it's an instrument graveyard.

Lyle will be here any minute, but I'm not ready for him to see me, so I walk over to the closet and duck behind its curtain. Inside, the concert uniform jackets and skirts are hung up small to large. They're royal blue polyester, and the tags on them say, "Trottier Menswear, Made in the USA."

Someone starts playing the piano. I peek around the edge of the curtain. It's Lyle. All of a sudden, he's forty pounds lighter, like that one day in November when all the leaves are gone, but for three months you didn't notice a single one of them falling.

Sunlight touches him through the windows. He's so thin now that his nose looks bigger and his neck longer. There's plenty of hair on his head despite the cancer treatments.

The song he plays sounds violent and familiar. I imagine these uniforms walking out to their chairs and music stands. When the piano speeds up, the uniforms kick the chairs and stands over. When the piano slows down, I search the tags on the jacket collars until I find Lyle's initials, in Annette's expert stitching, on a size 46 tag. I slip my left arm into Lyle's sleeve. It smells like Ban deodorant.

I peek at him again. Sunlight glows brighter now along the curve of his back, and along his hands as they stream over the keys. I rub the cuff of old, fat Lyle's jacket until it slips out of my hands, and its hanger clangs on the floor. The new, skinny Lyle stops playing. I pick up the jacket and step out from the curtain. He stands and walks toward me. I expect a sick, mediciney scent, but all I smell on him is Ban and Listerine.

"You're late," he says. He wears ironed khakis and a starched white shirt. He looks brand new. "I stepped out into the hall to look for you. You must've slipped in the other door then."

I walk closer to him. "Sorry. That was nice. The song."

"Just killing time."

I pull the forms from under my belt. Lyle reaches out real slow, takes them, and stuffs them in his pocket. Tonight he'll deliver them to Eugene Trottier, and my surrender will be official.

He reaches into his other pocket and pulls out a comb. It's a girl's comb, the kind that stays in your hair when you go someplace fancy. "Here," he says. I hold out my hands and he drops it in. "Belonged to one of my dead aunts. Least that's what Annette claims."

I move my hand to let its rhinestones catch more light. "You sure? I mean, it's pretty—"

"Wear it next Friday." He sets it in my hair. "Cora Leary, I'm proud to call you my wife."

"Why? I'm nobody special."

"Your dad's a hotshot pilot, for starters. My dad doesn't remember much and doesn't talk much, but the other day he mumbled something about your grandpa, too, the supervisor."

Annette has been mothering Lyle for so long that I forget about their parents. The only time I saw them was last summer, when Annette brought me to their house but wouldn't let me see Lyle. They were the stillest of all Trottiers. When I recall them now, I don't see them as themselves in their own living room, but as two mannequins in a sad kind of department store window display, their stony eyes aimed at the TV, and their laps balancing Swanson dinners, each fork raising a chunk of dead animal up to a mouth. The mom's oxygen tank rests against the couch, and the dad holds a paper pad in one hand. It shows a list of names. He has brain damage from an accident on the factory loading dock, so he can't remember his own kids' names, but he remembers my relatives and their posts at the factory.

"And your grandma," Lyle says. "She ran that floor. Not bad for an Amish runaway."

"Defect," I say. We both glance down at his old jacket, still in my hand. "She defected."

"Still," he says, "she's a legend. Your family's pretty upstanding. You got a name to be proud of."

"I'm not so sure about that."

He looks at me dead-on now. His eyes are so big, so minty green, now that they're not surrounded by chub. "I have one job to do before I go. I wanted to play piano for people. Whatever good or bad I might do elsewise, at least I'd have that to offer." He places his bony hands on my shoulders, and I start to melt. "But there's no time for that now. I can contribute one thing to this town. You and me. We got to make our offering. Soon."

I drop the jacket and take off my belt. I slide my belt around him, at the armpits. He holds his arms out to the sides so I can measure the circumference of his chest with it, but then his arms close around me.

"I'm a size 38 now," he says. That's a bit beyond the length of my belt.

Squeaking shoes enter the room. The drums shudder. Me and Lyle step apart and turn.

It's Jimmy Hawkins, entering from above. He has been hiding in the upstairs office the whole time.

He jumps down from the railing, holding his arms out wide. When he lands, I expect him to tackle and maul us, like he does to my locker partner and his wrestling buddies, but he pounds on the kettledrum instead.

"Hands off, Cordelia Leary," he says. "Lyle's ours."

My parents never talked about family bloodlines, at least not anything you'd call upstanding. Mom told me her father was a farrier who moved the family around to follow the work. He and her mother both died young. And then Mom married Dad, had me, and hopped from base to base until we settled on Oahu in the middle of my fourth-grade year. End of story.

When Mom died, I lost Dad, too. He didn't move a muscle after she went stiff. At her wake, he didn't hold my hand and walk me up to her. He hasn't even lifted one finger to mail Gram a check or dial our number.

Tonight, the phone rings.

"I sure do miss you, puppy dog," Dad says. "I've been thinking—I'm on day shifts now and shouldn't see another deployment for a good eight months." He goes on about how they've got him behind a desk instead of flying planes now that his eyesight is going. He gets real sick of all the papers, so he folds them into little cranes—a trick we all learned in Hawaii. "So why don't you come back and finish the school year here? See your pals at the bird hospital, huh?"

My only friends in Hawaii were the old ladies Mom worked with at a bird sanctuary.

"I have a job now, Dad. I have responsibilities. Didn't Gram tell you?"

He knows which responsibility I mean. "I just don't want to believe it, pup," he says.

"But it'll make us Trottiers."

He sucks in a sharp breath. He is not impressed. "Your

grandma *is* your guardian now, so she's got a right to sign that permission slip." Permission slip. Like I'm going on a school field trip to the courthouse. "But dammit, Cora, I'm still your dad, and I ain't ready to give you away."

"You already gave me away," I say.

We stay quiet for a while after that, as trucks roar past, and vultures pull up to roost. I've stung Dad, and now we're both making the throat-clearing noises you make when you try to stand taller, stiffer, like you and the person on the other end of the line can see each other falling apart.

"Look," he says. "I tried to accept it, but I can't. I'm coming up there to bring you back."

I wipe the sweat off my palms, onto my jeans. "But the forms. I already—"

"To hell with the forms. I won't let you fall for another Trottier scheme."

An hour later, when I'm staring out the window at the rotting tree, Gram emerges from her sewing room and yanks the drapes shut.

"Let the buzzard hawks alone," she says.

"They're vultures, Gram. Turkey vultures got red on the neck. Hawks don't."

"Oh, you and your aviation sanatorium." She pulls me up by my arm and leads me into the sewing room.

"Avian sanctuary," I say, but she doesn't listen.

In the room, she's got my First Communion dress altered and ready for matrimony.

"Your father's all bark," she says, zipping me into the dress. "He won't show his face."

She places her hands on my shoulders and turns me around in front of the mirror. Even though Gram enlarged the dress, I still look ten years old, standing on that cliff, with Mom's hands on my shoulders. After I'd made my First Communion, all the other families took their pictures in front of the church, but Dad drove me and Mom up to our favorite overlook. It was a busy Sunday, with lots of tourists lined up to walk out as far as they could over the sea, drink in the view and the breeze and the fresh smells, and then snap their photo on the cliff. You had to stand back and wait your turn. Then you clasped hands and stepped carefully up to the edge.

"Unzip me, Gram," I say. "I'm not wearing this dress. It's still too tight."

Gram gives me a squeeze. "Finally putting on some weight. Have you started eating meat when I'm not around to see it?" After work on Friday, I study alone in the break room for a long time while Annette counts inventory with Rudy. A big shipment of rejects is headed to Pittsburgh next week with the suits, but I'm not dumb enough to believe that the camel-hair jacket I messed up will ever reach Goodwill. Rudy will sell it. He'd like to keep it for himself, I'm sure, but it's too small. It will only fit Lyle.

While I rehearse my recitation project for French class, I imagine the other employees sitting here, listening to me. It calms my nerves. Once I finish all my homework, I'm starving. I kill more time by looking at the photos lining the hallways. There's a series of nicely framed pictures showing Eugene Trottier around town: lighting the huge outdoor Christmas tree, accepting his Man of the Year Award, holding the key to the city. His daughters and past generations of inner-circle Trottier daughters are shown in the parades, crowned as prom queens or Miss Dover. Next are the portraits of Trottier mothers, with heads held high and hands clasped in front of fine wool coats made from sheep willing to stand still and let the clippers dig into them, take everything they've got.

Then there are photos of laborers in action, and here Gram is, not wasting time to look up at the camera. She's got sewing pins poking out of her mouth and a loose sleeve piece tucked under her arm. She is hand-stitching a seam that connects the collar and lapel to the rest of the coat. The caption says, "Betta Leary, The Fixer."

When my stomach roars and I can't wait any longer, I run up to the reject room. If I catch Rudy and Annette in the act, I'll just grab the jacket and Annette's keys, drive myself home without a license. That's how hungry I am.

I use Annette's hairpin to pick the lock. Inside, I don't see Rudy or Annette. In the middle of the floor is a huge pile of misstitched and ripped and discolored garments, like Rudy is preparing a bonfire of all the mistakes. Beyond the pile of rejects is a door.

I can't help but notice that Annette's stolen jacket is not in the piles. Maybe Rudy's forgiven me just like he forgave Annette's theft, and he's saving the camel-hair jacket in a special place for me. But then, in the corner of the room, on top of a smaller heap, I spot the camel-hair jacket. I reach under its plastic cover, pet the sleeve, close my eyes, and see the judge in his robe, saying, "Do you Cordelia take Carlyle . . . ?"

Voices rise and fall behind the door. They're either laughing or crying. I ease the door open. Rudy and Annette are too busy to notice me, but they aren't counting inventory. They aren't digging their nails into each other's backs. I know from the look on Annette's face and the way Rudy brushes her hair away from her forehead that she has lost something big.

In the parking lot, the camel-hair jacket keeps me warm. I search through the clouds for a star, but all I can see is Annette's sad face. Losing a baby might be a blessing in the long run for her, but it would be a curse for me. If I lose Lyle's baby after a few months, I'm out of chances.

The door groans open behind me. Rudy walks out. He doesn't mention the jacket.

"I'm driving you," he says. "Annette'll lock up. She needs time alone before she leaves."

As I follow Rudy to his car, I imagine I'm walking on a cliff. I breathe deep, pretend there's fresh smells in the wind and a nice view ahead, where dolphins break the surface of a calm sea.

Rudy's Cutlass is souped up with sparkly trim and white wall tires. There's no way his wife allows him to drive this vehicle anywhere near her parents. He and Regina must have another real nice car. Maybe they have their own driver, too. Inside this one, there's Vanillaroma trees and a St. Christopher statue on the dash. The car is spotless. Rudy taps his left foot against the rubber floor mat while he checks the mirrors. He punches the radio buttons with his block-shaped fingertips. I turn toward the window and ignore him. When we pass by the first mile of open fields, I wonder what's rotting in the grass and how soon a vulture will gobble it up.

He slows onto a dirt road. Lyle's road. An Amish horse carriage taps along in front of us.

Rudy stops the car. "You and me, Cora. We're—"

"No. You're just my boss," I say, because I trusted him to drive me home.

But he doesn't try to touch me or talk me into becoming his next Annette. He pants for a minute and then he blurts it out: "Kin, Cora. We're kin." He turns to face me. Veins bulge and zigzag over his temples. "You know who my real dad is, right?"

I pull the jacket closer around me and say nothing. I don't care.

"Your mother and him . . . before she married your dad." He faces straight ahead again, flattens his hands on the wheel. The dashboard lights shine up his short, wide nails. Mom's nails.

"When I was one day old, some nice people adopted me, and my dad moved to Pittsburgh."

I realize what he's telling me, but it's so much easier to play dumb. "With your mother?"

"No. She moved south. My mother is your mother."

Dad was right. This town is full of schemers and liars. I burst out of the passenger door and run toward the paved road, but Rudy catches me by the shoulders, pulling the jacket off.

"Please believe me," he says. "I got Trottier blood, but I can't get the name no way."

My mother was a non-Trottier, but I don't care what kind of Trottier Rudy's father is.

I peel Rudy's hands off of me. "Good for you. You got the blood."

"I know you don't have the blood, but you'll carry it in the seed, once you have the name." He holds my fingers real gentle, like he's a priest about to bless me. "Do your part, sis."

I pull my hands away from him. "What do you care if I carry the Trottier seed?"

He smiles and points at me, like I'm caught. "You *did* sign the forms, didn't you?"

Blood pulses behind my ears, and I know I'm blushing. "Yesterday afternoon."

"That Annette. It would be just like her to not tell me. She keeps so much under wraps." He swings an arm around my shoulder and walks me back to the car. "So anyway, Victor Trottier showed up at my door the night before my wedding. Takes me out to celebrate, gets me drunk, and then the guy tells me he's my father. Can you believe that?"

We get to the car, and he sets the camel-hair jacket in the backseat. He starts driving.

"The wedding was the next day," he says, "and here's this muckety-muck silent partner telling me my parents adopted me, and I've got to back out of this marriage because I'm a Trottier, for God's sake, about to marry my first cousin." I don't want to know Rudy's secrets, certainly not this one. "So here I am, husband to Regina Trottier herself, and I can't touch her."

"You mean you and Regina have never—"

"We been married a year next month. I just can't."

The dirt roads don't have streetlights, and there's no moon to speak of behind the cloud cover. Just Rudy's high beams and whatever they show in our path.

"What about Annette?" I say.

"Annette's like my fourth cousin twice removed or something. Our kid will only have two heads." So they didn't lose the baby. Annette was crying over something else. "Three heads, tops," Rudy says. "No law against that."

We laugh. We have to. I know now that Rudy would be the kind of brother I could call on to make things lighter for me, to walk me up to Mom's casket, if he'd been at her wake. When I reached her, I put my hand on her head and held it there, just like I'd done before taking her temperature in the final months. It would've been nice if Rudy'd been there to help me open my locket, take out the extra Communion host, and place it in her hands.

I turn toward Rudy, but what can I say? So our mom was no better than Annette when she was a girl at the factory. Who could blame her in a place like that, in a town like Dover?

When we finally get to Gram's house, I open the passenger door before the car even stops. I have to get out and call Dad, tell him to send for me. To hell with the forms.

"Thanks for the ride, Rudy," I say.

Rudy holds a finger to his lips. "No one knows except me and my real dad," he says. "He had me promoted and all that. Vic's the one who calls the shots, you know, not old King Genie." Rudy starts talking faster and smiling, like he's proud of his father, Victor, this man who shamed our mother. "We agreed not to tell anybody this secret, but when your mother—our mother—passed and then you showed up in Dover, well, I felt like I had to tell you." He pulls me into a hug. My mouth hits his collarbone. "You're not alone out here," he says. "You got me."

I can't swear my secrecy yet. "You would have been born in Georgia. It doesn't add up."

"I was, but he paid St. Anne's to say I came from some adoption agency."

I decide to believe that, but I still look at him with one eye closed. "How old are you?"

"Twenty."

I do the math. No. Victor Trottier can't be my dad. I'm not a Trottier. Not yet.

It makes a little more sense now, why Mom was always gazing out the window toward Mamala Bay, like she was watching for some particular ship or plane to arrive, even when Dad was right there with us, his eyes glued to *Wheel of Fortune*. Other kids on the base had sisters or brothers to play and fight with, but I just had Mom and Dad, staring into their separate plates of glass. Older siblings would leave eventually, gone to boot camp or officer training or college, or just plain gone, to places their parents couldn't brag about. But near or far, a sibling was someone to call on when you needed backup. It never dawned on me that I might have one out beyond the sea, waiting for me to come home.

Rudy wants to make up for lost time, and I figure I owe him a story in return, a piece of Mom, so I close the car door and give him my best one. "Mom's father was one of those guys that put shoes on horses," I say, grabbing the top of the dashboard. "She used to go with him." Rudy plays with his dangling keys as he listens. "He hated bringing pain on the horses," I say, "but he was real good at what he did." I tell Rudy about a cleanup job they did after some hack farrier had pounded the shoes into the horse's leg bones instead of his hooves and left him there to bleed. My voice wavers. I haven't thought about this since Mom told it to me as a bedtime story. "By the time they got there, it was too late. The horse's body was bloated and rotting."

Rudy scratches his ear. "No wonder she died early."

I've given him too much of Mom. I get out of the car and hold the door open.

"Call your real dad," I say. "Tell him this town needs him."

I go inside then, expecting my own dad to be there, sitting in Grandpa's seat and asking who was that outside. But the chairs are empty, and Gram is asleep.

The next week, Annette only shows up to work on Tuesday. She barely talks to me. Too much inventory. She looks like shit—greasy hair, pale skin, bloodshot eyes.

I stare at her until she finally meets my gaze. "What's going on?" I say. "Just tell me."

"Lyle will be out sick a while. The doctors want to run more tests."

At school, a haze covers everything. I pass by the music room. So quiet. The house Lyle and I will move into this weekend will be quiet, too. The Trottiers bought us TVs and stereos and appliances that chop and puree, but I won't hit a single power button. There'll be enough noise from nurses' and housekeepers' visits. And Eugene Trottier's daughters might come over to mother me, their fake nails digging into my back with every hug. Lyle and I won't have any time alone.

On Friday afternoon, two hours before my wedding, I have to give my French recitation in front of the class. I thank Madame Beauchamp before I begin, because she let us memorize and recite whatever we wanted as long as we could keep talking in French for three minutes. From the back row, Jimmy Hawkins puckers his lips at me, but I don't care. I'm not a kiss-up.

I pull in a deep breath and take my time letting it out. I recite three poems by somebody named Mallarmé—"The Afternoon of a Faun," "A Funeral Toast," something about a throw of the dice—and I end with the Apostles' Creed. Most of the class sleeps right through it.

As soon as I reach the last line of the Creed, where I give thanks to the living and the dead, Madame Beauchamp claps.

She's weeping. "*Merci*, Cora," she says. "*Très, très bien.*"

The bell rings to mark the end of last period. Hollers and whoops erupt in the classroom—the weekend is here. Madame Beauchamp makes me stay late. She gives me the same look the ladies at the bird sanctuary always did, like I'd better start flapping my wings.

"I see a future for you," she says, "and getting more involved with your studies is the way forward." She invites me to join the afterschool French Club. "We'd like to give you a chance."

The home ec girls are in French Club. Some of the smart kids are, too, the kids that will leave Dover and then come back to make their contribution to it. Madame Beauchamp doesn't know anything about the future that waits down the road I've chosen.

"No, thank you," I say, turning to leave. "Nothing after school for me, ma'am."

If I had a chance, I'd spin around and hurry back to the past, where I spent my afternoons with Mom at the avian sanctuary. But I'd run into a turkey vulture on that road, too, standing with wings outstretched in the middle of my seventh-grade year. He got to the island from who knew where and picked up some rare disease. Mom made sure to feed him when I wasn't around. She had to set the carcasses right in his cage—of mice or rats or other birds we couldn't save.

When they'd run out of dead bodies to give him, the only carcass available was of my favorite parrot, who'd just gone cold, so Mom had to serve him up. That was a quiet day. No more replaying of sounds the parrot must have learned when he was somebody's pet: oven timers and flushing toilets, ringing phones and voices asking who's calling. No more of his singing either. Mom had made up little songs to teach him while I was at school. *Cora Lora Lie, Cora Lora Loo. I. Love. You.* She would join in with him, too, her strawberry blonde hair swinging as she sang.

A half hour before my wedding, I put on one of Mom's blue pantsuits and drive to the courthouse in Grandpa's truck. Neither me nor Gram has a license, but I've been driving the truck around the block once a week. I can get us into town today.

The courthouse has animals carved into it. As me and Gram climb the steps, hawk statues leer at us from the tops of the pillars. Lions wait by the doors, staring out through blank eyes. I look behind us, to St. Anne's across the street. Each archangel reaches down to entering worshippers with one hand and reaches up with the other. Their eyes are blank, too.

We wait in a lobby with the judge. When Lyle and Annette are fifteen minutes late, the judge cracks a joke about cold feet. I don't laugh. Gram braids and rebraids my hair, placing Lyle's aunt's comb in a different spot every time. When Lyle is forty-five minutes late, the judge goes outside to smoke. The sleeves of his robe fan out as he walks down the hall.

Gram finally lands on a hairdo she can live with. She hands me her compact. I take a look and see that she's braided my hair the way Mom always did her own hair.

I start pacing. "How did Mom meet Dad?"

Gram sits on a bench. "He worked with her at the factory before he went into the service." She pats the seat next to her, so I sit. "He was just a boy with a crush. Harmless puppy." She pets my hand. "After they each left this place, they wrote letters. A few years go by, he's stationed in Georgia, they meet up, and boom—we get a phone call about a wedding."

"She never saw Victor Trottier again?"

Gram picks at her teeth with her thumbnail. "She knew when to cut loose thread."

The sound of boot heels and clanging metal approaches. From around the corner comes Rudy, the judge, and then Annette, pushing Lyle in a wheelchair. When I see Lyle, I know he's what Annette was crying over. His skin is gray and sweaty. He is impossibly thin now, and shivering, with a blanket over his shoulders. Under it, I see a white collar, necktie, and thick sweater. He glows when he smiles at me, like he's so proud of what I'm about to accomplish.

Gram hugs Annette and even Rudy. She whispers hello to them more tenderly than she has ever greeted me, as if the marriage has already happened, and she's already entered safely into the Trottier circle.

Rudy walks over to me and whispers, "I know you didn't exactly invite me, but I didn't want to miss it." He gives my arm a squeeze. "You'll do great."

I stammer and shake the whole time. Lyle's the one who does great, through all the vows and signatures.

Gram and Annette and Rudy embrace again, and they invite me and Lyle to join. We all kneel to get to Lyle's eye level and lean forward into a five-person huddle. Me and Annette on either side of Lyle, Gram on my right side, and Rudy between her and Annette.

Behind us, the judge's heels click down the hall.

While Gram blesses us with a round of prayers, Rudy rests his hand on the crown of my head. His fingers settle on the comb.

I take Lyle's hand, and it's ice cold. He wraps his fingers around mine. I want to jump in his lap and kiss him, but even though I'm only ninety-one pounds on a rainy day, he is a sliver of his usual size—my weight might crush him. I want to warm him, feed him, fatten him up, but I know it is too late. All I can do as a wife is take his offering and pass it on.

Lyle grabs at Annette's shirt cuff. His face is green now, his hands bone white.

"You got it, buddy," she says. "Off we go." She is blinking and sniffling and throat clearing now, trying to play it cool as she rushes him out.

Rudy hugs me, and this time I hug back. He says he'll be over tomorrow with Annette to help move me into the new house. We can't move in tonight because the painters just finished the bathrooms, and the fumes would be too much for Lyle.

I am a married woman now. On the drive home I think about other lives, like the one Madame Beauchamp promised if I'd only spend more time at school. Maybe down that road, I'd end up like her—a childless wife, always whining in some language nobody wants to speak with her.

Gram wants to use the extra evening at home together to cook. I'll have to feed Lyle special foods Gram has never heard of, foods that will squeeze extra minutes, extra life out of him. So we give it a try, chopping and pureeing more vegetables than I've ever seen in Gram's kitchen all at once. It smells like Hawaii after a rain. I beat egg whites and think of my life there, a life where I'm twelve forever, and my parrot never gets sick, and Mom's still singing. If I could go back now, as a sixteen-year-old, would I still want to be at her side, helping her save the birds, or would I want to be gone?

Dover's only funeral home is booked up, so Lyle's wake happens at St. Anne's Cathedral. I dress in black and carry my suitcase out to the truck. After I start the engine, I get out and walk across the street, right up to the dead tree. I hold out my arm to one of the big male vultures on the lowest branch, until my hand is inches from his beak.

"Go on," I say. "Take a bite!"

He leans down until his beak almost touches my thumb. His bald neck wrinkles with the movement. He doesn't start pecking away or calling his buddies to join in the feast. Vultures are too lazy to eat anybody alive, so they just wait till you die. Then they take you for everything.

When me and Gram are halfway to St. Anne's, a shadow passes over the road in front of us. It belongs to a large, low flying bird. I turn into the KFC parking lot, cut the engine, and grab my suitcase from the middle seat.

I hand Gram the keys. "You're driving the rest of the way," I say, "by yourself."

She pulls my hand off of the suitcase, pries my fingers open, and presses the keys into my palm. I stick the keys in the ignition, pick up my bag, and run inside.

Gram yells to me out the window, "Stubborn mother, stubborn kid!" and drives away.

Blood pulses behind my ears. She's never said a bad word about Mom before. I speed up, only stopping to kiss the colonel's cheek. In the bathroom, I let out all my breath real slow.

When I zip into the white dress, it puckers at my waist and hugs my shoulders, but Gram has made it fit. In the mirror above the sink, I see my ten-year-old self in my First Communion photo with Mom and Dad, but Rudy is with us on that cliff, next to me. He's fourteen, and wearing a tan suit.

I walk out of KFC and there's Dad, pinching a cigarette. Why would he fly all the way here now? He's wearing glasses and his air force uniform, resting his elbow on Colonel Sanders's shoulder. Blue suit, white suit. Red lettering shouts behind them, on the brightest building in all of Dover, home of the most delicious dead birds, fried to perfection and guaranteed to fatten us all up, kill us by the bucket. But I don't say that. Dad never listens to any talk about disease or what caused it. It's all sour grapes to him.

I don't say anything at all, not a word about him arriving too late or looking funny in his new glasses. I just walk past him, with goose bumps on my arms.

He catches up with me quick. We walk along the shoulder of the road, past the empty pastures. I listen to the tap of our heels, the swish of his trousers and sleeves. I start to wheeze.

"Don't cry," he says. "You pay your respects today, and then you steer your way out."

Anger is a good way to stop the tears. I decide it's best if I yell. "Steer my way out?" I spot a dead deer up ahead—where had it come from?—so I stop walking. "You sent me here!" I say. "You sent me to *this place*." But the tears beat the anger. Big, heavy tears, and a rock in my throat. "The Trottiers chose me for this, and I didn't act on it fast enough."

I can't breathe, so I move away from the road, down a dirt path that divides the field. I walk in circles, with my head down, counting dead worms, dead bugs, empty anthills, until screeching and clicking sounds make me lose count of the critters.

"Feeding time," Dad says.

Down the road, the vultures close in on the deer carcass. They slurp and suck and dig.

I look away, start counting anthills again. I'd planned to show off my big, fat belly on this day, maybe even a wailing infant in my arms. I would sit with Annette and let all the Trottiers see that I was one of them now. I was a worthy vessel. But today came too soon.

"Head up," Dad says. "This town may be your new world, but it ain't the whole world."

I sit down on the anthills. "I killed him, Daddy."

He sits, picks a blade of grass, and chews it. "How do you figure that? The boy was sick."

"I waited too long, and that kept him from having a son." I rip some grass out of the ground, too. "That would've let the Trottier line carry on." I drop the grass. "I blew it."

"Suppose you'd hurried up and did what they asked but had a baby girl? What then?"

He takes off the glasses, and I see it in his face now, in the way he chews, in his hollow eyes: Dad doesn't have a son.

"Look," he says. "You can stay here in Dover if that's what you want. The Trottiers will forgive you. They'll realize how dumb this plan was and give you a high post in the company as soon as you graduate." He spits the grass out. "They love you, puppy dog. Family or not."

"I'm not sure. They wouldn't let a Leary rise too high any-way. Maybe it was all a trick."

Dad hangs his head. I stung him again. I didn't mean to put down his name, but it's true: there's only one name allowed in this town. But then I remember Gram's photo, placed so close to the pictures of high-ranking Trottiers. When I try to hug Dad, he stands and pulls me up. He brushes dirt off of my dress and hands. Behind us, the vultures get real loud.

"Things can change," Dad says. "You'll show them that much."

I walk in one more wide circle, head up this time, watching the tops of the trees.

"I got here too late to put my hands on your marriage li-cense forms," Dad says, "but I read Eugene Trottier's damn will. There's only one line they gotta change to clean up this mess."

When we enter St. Anne's, I don't stop at the holy water foun-tain or let the usher seat me. Up front, Eugene Trottier's im-mediate family sits in the same pew as Annette and her par-ents. And Gram. Annette is crying into Gram's shoulder and wearing the blue blazer she stole from work. It blends in with Gram's black shawl and the rest of the front-row Trottiers' black suits. I stop and genuflect next to a middle pew, but Dad pulls me up and back to the row behind Rudy, where a nicely dressed couple kneels with a Chinese girl about my age. Victor Trottier's daughter. Instead of puffing out his chest in the front row, Victor hangs his bald head back here, as close as he can get to his son without anyone noticing.

Dad pushes me into the pew. I whisper to Victor Trottier that I need to speak with him. He flips the kneeler up and lets me and Dad lead him outside. On the sidewalk, we stand in a triangle so that I face the street and the courthouse, the silent partner faces the church, and Dad faces whatever is down the road. The men keep their heads bowed, but I lift mine and stand tall, face the silent partner, Victor. Finally, he looks at me. Here I am, with my mother's freckles and teeth, wearing a white dress she made.

"Do you know who I am?" I say.

He folds his hands, like a priest would do when listening to a child. "Of course."

"Annette will be my business partner. Fifty-fifty. You'll put that on record tomorrow."

Sun lights up beads of sweat on Victor's head. Behind and above him, a bronzed eagle stands tall on top of the courthouse, wings outstretched, waiting for thermal currents to lift him.

"Tomorrow's the funeral," Victor says.

Dad doesn't chew on grass or reach for his cigarettes. He stays cool as he gives orders. "You'll do it first thing in the morning," he says, "and you'll change the clause about heirs to say, 'all children of Mr. and Mrs. Carlyle Trottier *and* all children of Miss Annette Trottier.'"

Behind me, a hymn pours out of the church, and over it, a woman cries. The noise gets louder, closer. I turn around, and Madame Beauchamp is coming right at me.

"It's a beautiful jacket, Cora," she says. "Camel hair really suits Lyle."

"*Merci*," I say, and I mean it, even though it wasn't me who did the handiwork to correct my mistake. Rudy must have given the jacket to Annette to fix up. Or maybe Gram made it right.

She touches my eyebrow with her thumb, to let me know she's okay with what I do after school, lets it linger there a while over the organ and the voices—*where there is darkness, only light*—and then she's off, toward the parking lot.

Dad tips his cap to Victor Trottier. "Sir."

He puts his arm around me and walks me back in. We kneel next to Rudy, another new silent partner.

Mourners can go up and view Lyle any time, but most of us wait until the priest's cue. He tells us that those seated in the front row will be the first to see the dead. The front-row Trottiers stand when Father tells them to, and when he waves them forward, they become one black curtain, closing in on the body. Dad and Rudy each take one of my hands, and we wait for our turn.

ACKNOWLEDGMENTS

Many people brought this book to life. I am grateful to the following organizations, families, and individuals for their generous support during the creation of this book: The Jentel Artist Residency Program, for giving these stories wide-open space; the Coombe family and everyone in and near the Seven Hills School, for choosing me as their first writer-in-residence and welcoming me to Cincinnati, especially Sandra Smythe, Nick Francis, Tricia Hoar, Susan Marrs, Wynne Curry, Diane Kruer, Jen Faber, and Mica Darley-Emerson, as well as the Sittenfeld, Schiff, and Cefalu families; the Lojo Foundation, Jodie Ireland, and the Squaw Valley Community of Writers; the California State University Fresno Division of Graduate Studies, the CSU Fresno Foundation, and the King family; and DePaul University.

I am also very grateful to everyone at West Virginia University Press: Than Saffel, Will Tyler, Jason Gosnell, Derek Krissoff, Meagan Szekely, Floann Downey, Heather Lundine, Laura Long, the Board, and especially Abby Freeland.

Thank you to my husband, Marlin, who patiently watched me work on this book for years and believed in me when I didn't believe in myself. Thank you to my family, especially my parents, who filled our home with books, music, film, art, and faith, and let us pursue them all. To my mom and stepdad, Joanne and Denny, for their unwavering optimism and support, for helping out with research, and for so much more. Thanks, Mom, for all the books that helped me write this one and for showing me how you sew. To my sister and brother-in-law, Julie and Scott, for their encouragement and their help with research. Thank you, Big Sister, for letting Little Sister tag along through the forest, for showing the way to the best paths, and sharing stories only a camera can tell. To my brother, Dan, for teaching me about lyrics and tone and harmony, and for guiding me toward better music. To my grandmother, for her poems and her vision. To my dad, a reader and believer and guide—and dog lover—like no other. To Aileen, Kathy, Pat, Cathy, Bill, Edee, Tom, Peter, George, Mary, Tommy, Katie, and all of the relatives and friends in whom my dad keeps living: Thank you always.

To my teachers, from aerobics to English, film to foreign language: for waking me up, training my eyes and ears, and putting a pen in my hand. *Merci*. To the authors who taught me to write, especially Michele Morano and the late Christopher T. Leland. Very special thanks go to Steve Yarbrough, for coaching me and for investing so much time and faith in my writing.

To all in and near the CSU English departments in Channel Islands and especially in Fresno, past and present: Ewa Hryniewicz-Yarbrough, David Anthony Durham, Alex Espinoza, Steven Church, John Hales, Liza Wieland, Daniel Chacón, Toni Wein, Dr. Lyn Johnson, Samina Najmi, Tim Skeen, Linnea Alexander, Tanya Nichols, Rachel Jackson, Dr. Vida Samiian, Dr. James Walton, Akiko Peterson, Liz Scheid-Blau, Ginny Crisco, Jefferson Beavers, and Lisa Lieberman. Thank you to Connie Hales, Sasha Pimentel, Burlee Vang, and to all of the other poets who have made Fresno a wonderful place to write. I am also deeply grateful for the chance to have known the kindness of Franny and Philip Levine, in whose home several of these stories were written. Phil's life and work will always be celebrated— from Fresno to Detroit and far beyond. Thank you so much.

To the writers who read early drafts: Jennifer Haigh, Elise Blackwell, Randall Kenan, Margot Livesey, Vikram Chandra, Jim Krusoe, Tony Bonds, Kristofer Whited, Erin Lynn Cook, Neal Blaikie, Tabitha Villalba, Steven Howland, Nora Boxer, Kelly Luce, Caitlin Myer, Shanda Connolly, Kaitlin Solimine, and big thanks to Elizabeth Schulte Martin, Carol Vitali, Candace Duerksen, and Bridget Boland.

To those who brought these stories to the pages of magazines: Daniel Degnan, Martin Clark and the North Carolina Writers Network, Robert L. Giron, Anne R. Zahlan, Stephanie G'Schwind, Odette Heideman, Willard Cook, Martin Rock, Brenda Peynado, Steve Himmer, Kristin vanNamen, and Matthew Limpede. To those who brought these stories to live audiences: Sally Shore, Pasadena Arts Council, Valerie Fioravanti, Victoria Goldblatt, and Sue Staats. Thanks also to James Warner, Lauren Becker, Sean Carswell, Brad Monsma, and Mary Adler.

To the other friends who helped me keep going toward the end: Monica Zarazua, Lysley Tenorio, Martha Schermerhorn, Leslie Jamison, Tracy Lynn Pristas, Denise Iris, Ben Gibson, Megan McKnight, and especially Rawna Romero.

To the kind people who answered my research questions: Sergeant Larry Snelling, Steven Church, Mary Kate Monahan, Steve Almond, Sarah Dunn, librarians, and beautiful strangers at *The Daily Southtown*, the Chicago History Museum, and elsewhere along the way.

Works by many authors were invaluable during the creation of this book, especially Joan Acocella, Steven Church, Stuart Dybek, Gina Gallo, Marion E. Gold, William Kalush, Jhumpa Lahiri, Ellen Litman, Joe Meno, Haruki Murakami, Azar Nafisi, Vaslav Nijinsky, Dominic A. Pacyga, William Shakespeare, Larry Sloman, Robert L. Snow, Mary Yukari Waters, and David Wroblewski.

READING AND DISCUSSION QUESTIONS

1. In "Queen City Playhouse," Tess decides to give Mr. Duesler his medications all at once because she fears that Joe might disgrace the Duesler family by stealing the pills and selling them. What are some other reasons why Tess decides to give Mr. D an overdose?

2. Rosie from "Canis Major" has a crush on Officer Ryan, while her cousin, Vivvi, can't stand him. Do they each respond to him in the way you expect? Explain.

3. Richard, in "A New Kukla," cannot let his daughter visit him because he cannot let his wife's family or church know that he is a divorced man with a child. What does this lie, as well as his other lies, reveal about his adjustment to the social climate of the United States in the 1960s and 70s, and particularly the social world of his Catholic wife?

4. In "White Rabbit," we catch up with Richard and Bobby ten years later, when Ollie is in the fourth grade and acting out the family's problems at school. What do Ollie's observations of the adults around him reveal about the lies and secrets with which they live, as well as the lies and secrets of the time period?

5. Andrea, in "The Lost Bureau," is torn between her desire to prove herself both in the masculine world of policing and in the feminine world of home, where she is mothering her younger sister. In what ways do these desires get in the way of each other? In what ways do they help her as she tries to navigate through each world?

6. As her future dance career slips away in "Representing the Beast," Keiko becomes more and more enthralled by Vaslav Nijinsky's diaries. What parallels can you find among the experiences of Nijinsky, Keiko, and Aunt Yumi? How are their emotional or psychological experiences revealed in their bodies?

7. In "The Music She Will Never Hear," Jace remarks that Phish followers like Brad have flown off to "some aquamarine planet where everyone let(s) the job of being a music fan distract them from making their own music." Together with Keiko, they are musicians and dancers who no longer practice their art. What does the historian suggest to Jace about "hiding behind your instrument" and the need to hold on to Keiko? How do the phone calls with Ollie affect Jace and his perception of Brad, Keiko, Jace's parents, the historian, and his own life?

8. Delia, in "Center of Population," is trying to use exercise to help heal a circulation problem caused by frostbite. What other, less visible conditions is she being asked to confront during the class? What's at stake once her own conditions surface? How does the body contain or release psychological and emotional pain in this story?

9. Cora, in "The Cliffs of Dover," is chosen to bear the male heir to the business empire that the Trottier family owns, but why does she wait so long to agree to the deal? How do Cora and other residents of Dover accept or challenge their positions in the town's social class system? As a newcomer to the town, what harm and help does Cora bring?

What does it mean that she goes through with the marriage but does not produce the child she agreed to give them?

10. Throughout all nine stories, characters look to animals, angels, saints, and mythological figures to guide, forgive, praise, console, or incriminate them. What do their perceptions of these nonhuman entities reveal that the human characters cannot? How does their presence in the characters' lives terrify, strengthen, or mobilize the characters?

ABOUT THE AUTHOR

Born in suburban Detroit, Kristin FitzPatrick grew up surrounded by music and books. She fell in love with old movies, photography, endurance running, and poetry before she started writing seriously. Her inspiration has come from music and from the people she met while working as a stagehand, nanny, waitress, editorial assistant, and English conversation teacher.

Kristin earned degrees from Michigan State, DePaul University, and Cal State Fresno, where she began writing and publishing some of the stories in this collection.

A semifinalist for the 2014 Mary McCarthy Prize in Short Fiction, Kristin is the recipient of residencies from Jentel and the Seven Hills School in Cincinnati, where she held a creative writing teaching fellowship. Her work has been chosen for the Thomas Wolfe Fiction Prize and has appeared in publications such as *Colorado Review*, *Southeast Review*, *Epiphany*, and *The Best of Gival Press Short Stories*, as well as on stage in Sacramento and Los Angeles.

Kristin and her husband live in Southern California, among rows of vinyl records and books. She's working on a novel and teaching writing to students whose stories inspire her to wake early, turn the volume up, and listen for more. www.kristinfitzpatrick.com